I stepped into my sister and took over her body for the time being. People called it possession, but I didn't like to use that term in regards to Lark. Thankfully, she was just asleep. I opened my eyes—Lark's eyes.

Mason looked down at me. He frowned. "You're not her," he whispered.

I managed a small smile, impressed that he could tell the difference between us—most people couldn't. "You can let her...me, go now. Thanks."

He dropped his arms like I was on fire. I stumbled, but managed to catch myself. Wearing Lark was fairly comfortable, but I wasn't used to having substance in this realm. Limbs were heavy, clumsy. I braced my hand against the roof of Nan's car.

This was different from when Lark was awake and I shared her body. Despite the heavy limbs and awkwardness of them, they felt like mine. I was in control, not my sister, and it...it was *wonderful*. And strange. So strange.

Praise for *The Girl with the Iron Touch*:

"A well-calculated blend of paranormal romance and genuinely innovative story."

—*Kirkus Reviews*

Praise for *The Girl in the Clockwork Collar*:

"Surprising, vivid and cohesive—the work of a pro."

—*Kirkus Reviews* (starred review)

"Teens will enjoy the fast-paced action."

—*VOYA*

Praise for *The Girl in the Steel Corset*:

"A steampunk mystery with a delicious love triangle and entertaining Jekyll and Hyde element."

—*RT Book Reviews*

KADY CROSS

sisters

of

blood

and

spirit

HARLEQUIN®TEEN

ISBN-13: 978-0-373-21148-7

Sisters of Blood and Spirit

HARLEQUIN®TEEN
™ www.HarlequinTEEN.com

ted in U.S.A.

This book is for Mom, who instilled in me
a love of things that go bump in the night. Thanks, and I miss you.

It's also for my sisters—I'd fight a ghost for each of you!

And last, but not least, this book is for Steve, who supported me
from the very beginning. I couldn't do it without you.

chapter one

"Abandon all hope, ye who enter here."
—*Dante*

LARK

The scars on my wrists itched. I curled my fingers and tugged on my cuffs as I rubbed my arms against my jeans. Everyone stared at me as I walked down the hall. Maybe not *everyone*, but enough to make me lift my chin and straighten my shoulders. I glared back. Most of them looked away. Don't provoke the crazy girl. At Bell Hill, no one had looked at me.

I'd thought my second day of high school would be easier than the first, but it was worse. Gossip had spread, and now everyone knew who I was and what I'd done.

I scared them—it was obvious. Even the ones who smirked at me or made remarks were afraid. They wanted to look tough to their friends. Hey, if making fun of me made them feel strong, then they obviously had their own problems.

I'd known some of them for most of my life. New Devon wasn't a very big town, and at one time I'd been a popular kid. In day care and elementary school everyone had wanted to play with me and my sister the ghost. I wish I could have seen my own face the first time someone told me I was too old to have an imaginary friend anymore.

Imaginary? The word echoed in my head. People applied terms like *overly imaginative* when I was still young. Eventually they began to say things like, "dissociative," "delusional" and my personal favorite, "troubled." No shit. There had never been a teenager in the history of the world that wasn't troubled by something. It was kind of our thing.

I walked past a small group of girls clustered in front of a section of lockers painted in the school colors of purple and gray. They drew back, as though I was contagious. They didn't say anything—didn't even giggle. If they'd been mean I would have been more comfortable.

I didn't hang my head. I had nothing to be ashamed of. Maybe I'd made a couple of bad choices, but they had been mine.

I wasn't crazy. I might be a freak, but I wasn't crazy, and I never had been. I had proof of that, and other people knew it, too—not many, but enough.

As luck would have it, my locker was just a few down from where the girls stood watching me warily. I stopped and opened it, placing my bag inside so I could take out what I needed for my first class.

"Why are we here?" my twin sister, Wren, asked. She stood by the locker next to mine, arms crossed over her chest. Her vivid red hair fell over her shoulders in a straight curtain that required absolutely no work—no style she wanted ever did, because it was of her making. There weren't any hair styling tools in the Shadow Lands.

I didn't respond. Talking out loud to someone no one else could see would make them all think they were right, that I was still crazy. I was supposed to be cured. That was the only way the school would take me back. Although, at that moment, I had to wonder as well what the hell I was doing there.

Oh, *right*. My parents didn't want me, so I'd had no choice but to move in with my grandmother in my old hometown while Mom and Dad had a fresh and shiny new life in Massachusetts. My mother just couldn't deal with the fact that I could see and interact with Wren. Not because she thought I was lying, but because she was mad Wren didn't talk to her.

I wasn't cured. I wasn't crazy, either. But there was just no easy way to explain why Wren was there with me—she'd been dead since the day we were born. I came out breathing and she...didn't. I think someone made a mistake somewhere along the way, because my hair was stark white and hers was deep, vivid red. I should be the ghost, not her. God—if there was one who even cared—knew I liked the dead a lot more than the living most days. Other than our hair and style, we were identical, to the point that if I dyed my hair her color even we'd get confused over who was who.

For years my relationship with Wren was seen as cute if not sad—a little girl playing with her "imaginary" dead twin. As I got older, my knowing things about how people died because "Wren told me" made me look weird, guilty even. People would ask me to communicate with their dead relatives, but it was Wren who did all the legwork.

People called me a liar. Called me crazy. Called me a freak. Eventually, I began to believe them. That was when I got desperate and made the scars on my wrists.

I closed my locker and walked down the hall, pushing my way through the crowd of teeming hormones. People stared. Some said things. I ignored them, staring straight ahead. I just wanted to get this day over with. These people didn't matter; I knew who and what I was.

I just didn't know *why*.

"I suppose you have to ignore me while you're here, don't you?" My sister sighed—rather dramatically I thought. She knew the drill. The time I'd spent locked up made her a little…needy. Other than me she didn't have anyone to talk to except an old woman who stuck around to watch over her family and a crazy man from the 1700s who liked to haunt his old house just for the hell of it. Although, I think she'd have more friends if she wasn't with me all the time. Unfortunately, the few other "nice" ghosts we'd had contact with had moved on once we did what they asked of us, and hanging out with the scary ones wasn't an option.

"Mmm." It was the only response I could make without anyone noticing.

"Fine. I'm going to the library. I'll find you later." With that, she walked through a wall and was gone. I hated when she did that—mostly because I couldn't.

I followed the swarm, rounding a corner toward what would be my homeroom for the rest of this year. A small group of kids were gathered against the wall just a few feet away. A few guys—mostly girls. Seniors. I could tell just by looking at them—they had that faint smug superiority of knowing they had to make it only until June and then they were free, done with the insane asylum that was high school.

I might have sneered at them as I walked by if one of the guys hadn't raised his head and looked right at me.

I froze. It was just a second, but I froze like he was a speeding car and I was a raccoon out for an evening stroll on the center line. Mason Ryan was even more gorgeous than he had been the last time I'd seen him, a fact for which I resolved then and there to despise him. Gold-streaked brown hair, hazel eyes—and lips no guy deserved to have. Black button-down and jeans. He was one of those guys who was so beautiful it hurt to look at him.

But it hurt for other reasons. I needed to avoid him if I could—and not just because his father was chief of police. Mace and I had a secret. Well, not really a secret. A few people in town knew that he had been the one to find me bleeding out on the floor, but knowing and understanding were two different things. Nobody but he and I knew exactly what we'd shared, and it would always be there, lingering between us like a breath.

One of the girls with him turned to look at me, as well. She had a nasty-looking scratch on the side of her face that kept her from being model-gorgeous. I barely glanced at her; my attention was solely on Mace. The sight of him made me want to puke, tied my gut up in knots and shoved bile into the back of my throat.

Funny how much sick tasted like shame.

Mace didn't look as though he felt much better. I didn't want to think of the state I'd been in that day when he'd held me in his arms and begged me not to die on him because he'd have to live with that. He straightened away from the wall he'd been leaning against, and took a step forward—toward me. *Ohhh, no.* Not today. Not ever, if I could help it.

I broke into a sprint, straight into the classroom where I found a seat at the back of the room and dropped into it, trying to keep my heart in my chest. A few heads turned to look at me. Whispers and coy glances exchanged. Let them talk. I didn't care. My heart hammered and my stomach twitched, but I was safe for the time being. As safe as I could be in a small Connecticut town where everyone knew practically everyone else, and even if they didn't they still talked about them.

"Lark?"

Now what? I looked up, turned my head. Sitting right across from me was a familiar face—tanned skin, dark eyes and even darker hair. She smiled at me. I almost smiled back. Almost. "Rox."

Roxi Taylor was a month or two younger than me and was always very friendly—like crazy-ass friendly. It would be easy to dismiss her as fake, but she really was just a good, sweet person.

I didn't get it.

People like me, who could see things other people couldn't, didn't get to be ignorant of human nature for long—not when people either wanted to use you or hurt you. I'd tried to hate Roxi for years, but it just wouldn't take, and that part of me that distrusted everyone wanted very badly to distrust her, but could never quite manage it, even though I was sure that no one could be *that* nice all the time. But Roxi had never asked me for anything—ever. Never made me feel like there was something wrong with me. I always wondered what was wrong with her that she wanted to be my friend.

She grinned—she'd gotten her braces off since the last time I'd seen her—and threw her arms around me. "It's so good to see you!"

Shit. I did not want this attention, but it would be a lie if I said it wasn't nice to find someone who was happy to see me, that part of me didn't want to hug her back. It didn't matter that a little voice inside screamed for me not to trust her. I let myself have that moment.

"Dykes," someone muttered.

A few laughs followed. Then someone else said, "Don't, man. She's like, the angel of death or something."

I pulled away from Roxi and turned to face our audience. What annoyed me more than the smirks were the few expressions of genuine fear. I mean, sometimes being thought of as scary was a good thing, but having people be scared *of* you was different, especially when I hadn't given them any reason to be afraid.

Yet.

"If I was the angel of death, you think I'd be here?"

They seemed to consider this, their shared brain struggling to make the connection.

"Why *are* you here?" A blond guy with a big zit on his chin asked. From his voice I knew he was the same one who'd made the "dyke" remark. His name was Aaron or Albert or something. I remembered him from last year. "Shouldn't you be locked up with the rest of the retards?"

Heat rushed to my cheeks as people laughed, but I didn't look away. Homeschooling was the only way I'd been able to return to my correct year. I'd busted my ass to not get left behind. Wren had been right there with me.

"They kicked me out because they needed room for your mother." Lame, but it was the first thing that came to mind. "And I'm not retarded, asshole. I'm crazy—there's a difference. Which you'd know if your parents weren't brother and sister." More laughter, but this time it was *for* me, not against me.

Andrew—that was his name—turned red, which only made that ugly zit stand out more. I wanted to smack it with the heel of my shoe while my foot was still inside, bust it wide-open. Gross, right? "Bitch."

I raised a brow. "Seriously? That's the best you can do?"

A hand settled on my arm. I looked down, expecting it to be Roxi. It wasn't. It was Wren. Damn.

"Who are you looking at?" Andrew demanded. Then his expression turned mean—happily mean. "Is your sister here? Your *dead* sister?"

In books, the hero's blood sometimes "turns to ice" in his or her veins, but that's not right. It's not the blood that freezes, it's everything around it, so that your blood actually feels like hot razor blades ripping through your entire body. I lifted my head. What laughter there was gave way to uneasy, half-assed giggles. "Don't talk about my sister."

I shouldn't have said anything.

"How did she die anyway?" Andrew asked with a mocking grin. "I bet your mother saw that there was two of you and lost her shit. Did she know that she killed the wrong one? It should have been you she killed."

No one had killed Wren, she had been stillborn, and our

mother had never gotten over her loss. And yeah, I wondered if the wrong one had died all the damn time.

Beside me Wren's shape shimmered, like the edges of her were fraying. It was what happened when she got mad. Really mad. She picked up on my emotions like I'd dropped them on the floor in front of her. It meant I had to be really careful when I lied to her.

Her anger picked up my hair like a breeze.

"Don't," I whispered.

"Oh, are you going to cry?" Andrew pressed in a whiny voice. "Did I upset you?"

I met his gaze with a hard glare as warmth spread through me—a dry summer breeze on a hot beach. Oh, hell. I'd promised myself this wouldn't happen. It was only the second freaking day! Wren settled in, her spirit fitting me perfectly, like a glove tailor-made for a hand. She smiled, using my lips. "She wasn't talking to you." It wasn't my voice—it was lower, softer.

Andrew frowned. "What...?"

I hated when Wren possessed me without asking, but she was so powerful—like nothing I'd ever felt before. I felt strong—invincible—when we were joined together like this.

The lights flickered. Concerned murmurs rose up. People glanced at me. I shrugged—crazy didn't affect the electricity. The lights flickered again—then the fire alarm went off, shrieking like a banshee. Hoots and cheers filled the air. Fire alarm on the second day—a lovely way to start the year. Everyone tore from the room, and Roxi didn't wait for me— smart girl. Andrew rose from his seat, but I stopped him by grabbing his wrist.

My sister was strong. *Inhumanly* strong. Under my fingers, Andrew's wrist felt as fragile as dry twigs. He tried to tug free. "Let me go, freak!"

"Sit down," Wren commanded through my mouth. He wasn't as stupid as he looked, because he did what he was told.

"Good boy," I said, rising to my feet. Wren slipped out of me as easily as she'd entered. I felt her loss like someone had taken my eye or a limb. It never got any easier. She had physical contact now, sorta, and it was better if I didn't stick around. "You just sit there a minute. There's someone who wants to meet you."

Andrew lifted his gaze to mine as I gathered my things. He didn't look so smug now. "Wh-who?"

"My sister," I told him, smiling just a little when he looked down at his wrist, still in Wren's ghostly grip. He had to feel the cold fingers biting into his skin even though he couldn't see them. "You know—my *dead* sister?"

I walked to the door, Wren's low voice following my every step as she whispered words I couldn't make out. I hesitated when I heard Andrew whimper.

"Go," my sister told me.

I didn't look, I just kept walking.

A few minutes before the end of first class I got summoned to the principal's office. I was surprised they waited that long. Andrew was absent, and people had been looking from his empty seat to me since we were let back into the school after the alarm.

Not like they could blame me for anything. After all, I'd been outside with everyone else. If not for Roxi I would have been standing alone, with an invisible boundary around me that no one dared cross. Seriously, no one had come closer than two or three feet. It was like I had pink eye or something.

With a sigh, I packed up my books and left the classroom. Even though I'd been gone since almost the beginning of the previous year, I knew exactly how to get to the office. I'd spent a lot of time there before what my mother called the "incident."

Incident. Somehow it didn't have the same punch as "attempted suicide."

I was one of those teenagers categorized as a problem or "troubled." I got it. Last year I was troubled, and I had lots of problems. The biggest one of which was that I let myself believe the people who called me crazy, and I stopped believing in Wren..

So, yeah. I was messed up and I did some things that I really regret doing. Things that I refused to think about as I made my way down the hallway to the main staircase near the office.

I had to check in with the guy at the desk and tell him who I was. I could tell from the way he looked at me that he already knew. He pointed at the waiting area and told me to have a seat. Principal Grant would be with me in a minute.

A few seconds later a guy sat down in an empty chair across from mine. He was tall and lean, wearing jeans and a gray shirt. He had a young Keanu/Ezra Miller thing going on. Very cute, despite having a bit of a black eye.

"Rough morning?" I asked.

He grinned as he slouched in his chair. Yeah, he was really cute, even though he seemed surprised that I had spoken to him. "This?" He pointed to his eye. "This was yesterday. You should see the other guy."

Corny, too. I smiled back. "If it happened yesterday why are you here?"

He lifted his chin toward Principal Grant's office. "Waiting."

I was saved from trying to figure out something witty to say by the opening of the principal's door. A girl a year or so younger than me walked out. She took one look at Keanu and her brown eyes narrowed. The resemblance was obvious. She tossed her long, straight hair. "What are you doing here?"

He stood up, shoving his hands in his pockets. "I'm supposed to take you home."

The girl glanced at me, and for a second her eyes widened. Then she smirked at her brother. "I can go back in if you want to wait a little longer."

What was that supposed to mean? Keanu's cheeks flushed, but he didn't look away from her. And he didn't look impressed. "Let's go."

She flashed that smirk at me before flouncing past. Her brother gave me an apologetic look. "Sorry you have to follow that."

I laughed. "And here I was feeling bad for you."

He smiled. "See you around, I guess."

I nodded, and he was gone.

The door to the principal's office opened again. "Miss Noble, please come in."

Principal Grant was about six feet tall and imposing. I wouldn't call her pretty, but she had an interesting face and curly dark hair. I was nervous as I crossed the threshold into her office.

"It's only your second day back, Miss Noble," she said as she closed the door behind me. "It's not good that you're in my office already."

"I didn't do anything," I told her.

She gestured to a stiff-backed chair in front of her desk. "Sit, please."

I did.

She sat down behind the desk and folded her hands on the top. She looked like a judge with her black suit and severe expression. I tried to keep my attention focused solely on her. "You were allowed to return to this school because of your grandmother's ties to the community and her promise that you wouldn't be any trouble. Are you going to make her break that promise?"

The mention of Nan yanked on my temper. "I didn't do anything."

"Then why did a young man have to leave school after an altercation with you?"

My eyebrows shot up. "What?"

She wasn't buying it. "Do not play coy with me, young lady. What did you say to Andrew?"

"He was the one doing all the talking," I replied hotly. "He insinuated that I was a lesbian, and then he made every joke he could at my expense. I told him to shut up. Then the fire alarm went off and we all left the room. Ask Roxi Taylor. I was with her the whole time." Except for those few minutes with Wren...

"I will," Principal Grant promised. And then she surprised me. "He called you lesbian?"

I shrugged. Again, I tried to keep my gaze focused on her, and not what was behind her. "A dyke. He was just being a jerk."

"I take that sort of harassment very seriously, Miss Noble. This school has zero tolerance for bullying."

"When did that happen?" I asked before I could stop myself. "Because it certainly didn't the last time I was here."

She looked embarrassed. "That was before I took over as principal." Yeah, she'd been the vice principal then. "Things are different now, I promise you. If Andrew returns to school, he won't speak to you in that manner again."

If? Huh. "You kicking him out for picking on me won't make my life any easier. I don't care if he comes back, so long as he leaves me alone."

Ms. Grant stared at me for a few seconds—enough to make me nervous. "I'll take that under advisement. You'd better get back to class."

That was it? "Okay." I stood up and made for the door.

"Oh, Miss Noble?"

I stopped, hand on the doorknob, and turned. "Yeah?" *Don't look. Don't look.*

"Victim or instigator, I don't want to see you in my office again. Am I understood?"

I nodded. "No offense, Principal Grant, but I don't want to see you again, either."

Or the ghost of the former principal standing behind her, his brains blown all over the wall.

★ ★ ★

"What did you do to Andrew?"

I glanced up as Roxi fell into step beside me on the walk home that day. My heart gave a little skip. After my "talk" with Principal Grant I was paranoid that everyone was out to lynch me.

"Nothing."

"Okay, what did your *sister* do to Andrew?"

Huh. Grant hadn't thought to ask me that.

"Nothing permanent," Wren answered from her place beside me. She had changed clothes since this morning and was wearing a long boho skirt, peasant blouse and a floppy hat. Her feet were bare. Who needed shoes when your feet didn't actually touch anything?

I was going to miss shoes when I died.

I barely looked at the living girl walking beside me. "I don't know what you're talking about. I haven't seen him since the fire alarm this morning." When we'd come back to class he was gone. I hadn't asked Wren what happened and I didn't want to know. My sister was normally quite gentle, but she was dead, and the dead took offense easily. Andrew had screwed himself when he'd suggested I should have been the one who died.

"Come on, Lark." Roxi stopped on the cracked sidewalk. Weeds poked up through the concrete near my feet and I nudged them with the toe of my secondhand pink-and-red Fluevog shoes. "I've known you since we were five. I know you're not crazy, and I know Wren is real. I'm not the only one, either."

My eyes narrowed. "Could have used you when everyone else thought I was a liar...or nuts."

Wren stood behind Roxi, studying her. "She seems sincere." She didn't care who I told about her. She only cared about me. But I cared about *us*.

"I told everyone who would listen that I didn't think you were crazy."

I looked her dead in the eye. "Gotta think that wasn't too many people."

Roxi blushed. She was even pretty with her face all red. "No." She started walking again. I fell into step beside her. "Still, I wanted you to know I believed you."

"A little late coming." Wren walked on Roxi's other side, still studying her as though the girl was a dress she'd like to try on. "Nice thought, though. I think she means it."

"Thanks," I said, looking straight ahead. My grandmother's house was just down the block. I could feel relief loosening my shoulders. I'd only been out of some sort of care for the past few months, and being back to school had exhausted me with all the noise and bustle. All those bodies conditioned to respond to the sound of a bell reminded me a little too much of the "hospital" my mother had abandoned me to when I had refused to say that Wren was all in my head.

When I had tried to die to be with her.

I didn't think Mom believed I was crazy, either, but it was easier than saying she hated me because Wren talked to me and not her.

"Is she with us now? Your sister?"

I cast a distrustful glance at her. Was she trying to trick me into saying something wrong? You give people messages from dead relatives, fight a few ghosts on school property, try to kill yourself and all of a sudden you're Trouble. Huh.

"What do you think?"

I tried not to laugh as Wren jumped in front of her and shouted, "Boo!" My thoughts were getting too morose, and she knew it.

Roxi shot me a shrewd glance as she walked right through my sister—and shivered in the early September sunshine. "I think you're not about to discuss her with someone you're not sure you can trust."

"I'm a fairly private person."

"That's just a pretty way of saying you're antisocial."

I grinned as my sister laughed. "That, too." I liked this girl. I really hoped she wasn't playing me.

"I like this girl," Wren commented. "I really hope she isn't playing us."

That thing they say about twins being on the same wavelength, feeling the same thing, thinking the same thing? It was true, and the whole dead-vs-living thing just cranked it up to eleven. The only reason I was alive was because Wren had felt something was wrong and had come looking for me the night I'd partied with a bottle of vodka and a razor blade. Good times. And I felt her anguish the entire time I was locked up and she couldn't do anything to help me.

She'd done more than anyone else. More than our parents or any sanctimonious doctor. And I had been so pissed that she'd played a part in saving me, because I had thought death would finally put us in the same world.

It wasn't my time to die, she'd said—as if she had any way of knowing.

We walked in silence for a bit, my grandmother's house coming steadily closer. I'd only lived there a few days—since Dad had dropped me off with a guilty look and my own credit card—but it already felt more like home than my old house had in a long time. We'd lived in this town since I was three, but after my...accident, my parents had moved to Natick up in Mass. Mom needed to run away, while they decided I needed to endure daily torture at the hands of my peers. Whatever. I wasn't bitter. Much. And at least here I didn't have to see the look on her face when my mother looked at me. Not that she looked at me very often.

"So," Roxi began, ending my pity party, "want to hang out later?"

My inner alarm went off, screeching "abort!" over and over. "Uh…"

"I'm going over to 'Nother Cup at eight. It's open-mike night. Kevin McCrae's playing. You know him, don't you?"

Oh, yeah. I knew him.

"Yes!" Wren screeched in my ear. "Say yes! Say yes or I'll bring Mr. Havers over to visit."

Mr. Havers was the old dude who liked to haunt for the hell of it. He had few teeth and was as bat-shit crazy as a dead guy could be. And he smelled like a horse. "Yes," I said through clenched teeth. "I know him. That sounds great. I'll meet you there?"

"Sure." Roxi grinned. "It will be fun."

"Yeah. Big fun." Could I sound any less sincere? An evening spent around more staring people with my sister rhapsodizing about Kevin McCrae—the one person other than me who could hear her. And the one person I wanted to see less than Mace. Woot. And I was such a fan of coffeehouses with blatantly unclever names.

But when was the last time I'd been out? When was the last time I'd spent time with people my own age who weren't dead or mentally unstable? Or the last time I had to worry about curfew? Did I even have a curfew?

We stopped at the foot of my grandmother's driveway. The smooth pavement led to a large slate-gray Victorian with eggplant trim. Large maple trees grew along both sides of the drive, forming a canopy that was just starting to show a hint of color.

"Your grandmother drives a Volkswagen Beetle?"

There was no missing the little car—it was purple. "Yes."

Roxi squinted. "Are the taillights shaped like flowers?"

"They are." I didn't mention that the interior was green. Chartreuse. Nan had it custom done.

The dark-haired girl nodded. "Pretty." She glanced down at her feet. "Listen, I know you don't want to talk about it, but I'm really glad Mace found you."

She forgot to add "lying in a pool of your own blood with your wrists sliced open."

"Thanks."

Roxi nodded as she lifted her head. "Okay, so I'll see you at eight."

"Sure."

She grinned. "Great. See you then." She turned to walk away, then stopped. She glanced over her shoulder with a lingering smile and looked somewhere over my right shoulder. "'Bye, Wren."

My sister stood at my left, but the effect was the same.

Wren's eyes widened, and I wondered if Roxi would ever know how much those two words meant to her. How much the thought meant. Wren lifted her hand and waved, even though Roxi had already set off down the street.

We walked up the lane, finally alone.

"What *did* you do to Andrew?" I asked.

Wren shrugged. Her blouse slid down on her shoulder. "Scared him a little, that's all. I told you, nothing permanent."

"Then why wasn't he in class?"

"He had to go home."

"Why? And please don't say he was bleeding from the eyes."

She shot me an indignant glance. "He peed his pants." Yes, the scariest person I knew said "peed."

"That's it?"

"Isn't that enough?" she shot back.

I held up my hands. "Just making sure."

My sleeves had fallen down my arms when I raised them, and Wren grabbed my left forearm before I could lower both. Her thumb was like velvet against the satin of the scar that ran down the throat of my wrist. Tears filled her bright blue eyes.

"It's all right," I told her.

"Did it hurt?" she asked. Wren didn't have much of a concept of physical pain, having never experienced it. She had no scars and she never would—not unless there was something in the afterlife that neither of us knew about. She'd never asked me about them before.

"Not as much as I thought they would."

"I'd take them if I could."

"But you can't." I gently pulled my arm away. "They're mine." And the only thing other than our hair that set us apart as two separate people instead of two halves of one.

chapter two

WREN

Sometimes I watched Lark sleep, just to make certain nothing happened to her. She didn't know that I did it or she wouldn't have closed her eyes. She said I "creeped" her out when I did things like that. What else was I supposed to do? I didn't sleep—I didn't need to. I had tried to once, but I got bored. As a child I'd figured out—with Lark's help—how to pass through books so that I could actually read them. Thankfully our grandmother had a fabulous library—not as good as the one in the Shadow Lands, but it was more than adequate.

When we were little, Lark asked me if I lived in Heaven. I told her I didn't know. I still didn't. It was an untruth that the dead had all the answers. We just had different questions.

The truth of where I "lived" was that it was big and peaceful and muted. No bright colors—except for my hair—no loud noises, no strong smells. Certainly nothing like the wave of deliciousness that greeted me when I phased through the door of our grandmother's kitchen. My sense of smell wasn't that developed, but spending time in this world had helped strengthen it, and what I smelled was *good*.

"Oh," I said. "What *is* that?"

"Peanut butter cookies," Lark told me. "Best smell in the world."

"Can I have one?" I sounded so pathetic, and I was. We both knew the only way I'd ever taste that delicious scent was if Lark let me in, and I'd already violated her space once today.

My sister smiled, indulging me like she always did. She had such a big heart, especially where I was concerned. "Sure." I forgave her for asking what I'd done to that boy in her class. It wasn't as though she didn't have reason to ask, especially after what I'd done to that orderly in the hospital our parents had put Lark in. I scared him so bad they took him away sobbing. He never came back, but I visited him from time to time.

"I didn't hurt him," I insisted, needing her to know the truth. I didn't have to tell her who or what I was talking about. She knew. Lark just nodded. She didn't like to talk to me in front of other people anymore. I understood why, but it still hurt sometimes. Other times it made me angry. People got hurt when I got angry, so I tried to stay calm.

"Hello, girls," Nan greeted us. "Hug."

She was five feet tall and slim with a head of thick hair dyed a color almost as bright as mine. According to Lark she didn't look like a grandmother, but Charlotte Noble *felt* like one.

Lark hesitated—she always did. It was my fault, this distrust she had of people, even those who should have her complete faith. Just by being, I'd made her life so much harder than it should have been. She didn't like to hug, and I wished I could hug everyone I met. When we first came here, Lark let me in so I could feel our grandmother's arms around me. Today, I simply moved through the tiny woman, letting her sweet warmth sift through me.

To my delight, Nan smiled. "Wren, you're like walking through a patch of sunshine, dear. Lark, just come hug me and get it over with, girl. I won't bite you."

I watched, anxious as the two most important women in my existence embraced. Was it my imagination, or did Lark relax a little? True to her word, Nan didn't bite. I'd been nervous for a moment.

Out of the corner of my eye I saw a flicker of something in the next room—just a passing shadow flickering in the afternoon sunlight. Was there someone else in the house? I moved slowly into the room, hoping to catch our visitor, but there was nothing, not even a trace of spectral energy. That was disappointing. It would have been nice to meet another ghost—a friendly one.

In the Shadow Lands I had form and substance, but in the living world I was nothing more than a projection. It was annoying. In the Shadow Lands I could eat a cookie—if they existed there. The dead didn't need to eat. We didn't get our strength from food.

We got it from the living. Humans left a trail of life energy like slugs left slime. Maybe not the best analogy, but it was almost like they exhaled a little bit with every breath. We drifted along sucking that up. Sometimes a ghost would get greedy and siphon from a person. Heightened emotion meant more life force. Ghosts particularly liked the taste of fear. That was why so many hauntings were terrible things.

Fear tasted like my grandmother's cookies smelled.

I looked around one more time, but there was nothing out of the ordinary. Maybe I had spent too much time in this world and my eyes had started to play tricks on me, or maybe I was becoming as suspicious as Lark.

I wished she had talked to Mace earlier. We—I—owed him so much for saving her life. When I saw her lying on the floor, and what she had done, I panicked. I couldn't help her except to hold her wrists and try to stop the bleeding. I needed help, and I cried out to anyone who could hear me.

Kevin McCrae had heard me. Some people were more attuned to the frequency of the dead than others. In the human world they were called mediums. Where I came from, they were called "doors." Kevin was a door I could open, and I didn't even knock first. He hadn't even known who I was when I tore into his mind like a madwoman, begging for his help. He didn't live close to us, but his friend Mace did. Kevin called Mace and asked him to check on Lark, then Mace called 911.

Kevin and I kept in contact after that night. Not a lot, but some. He was the only person other than my sister to have ever known I was in the same room, and he was the person I'd run to when Lark wasn't there.

He was the reason I wanted to go to the coffee shop that night. Lark knew it, of course. But my sister didn't know *all* of it.

Oh, and I wanted to know what Roxi was hiding. There had been sincerity in her invitation, but there had been something else, as well. It was easy enough to assume that the secret was something she thought might convince Lark not to go if she revealed it straightaway. That made me suspicious.

"Anything exciting happen today?" Nan asked as she used a spatula to move the warm cookies from baking sheet to plate.

Lark and I exchanged glances. She *knew*.

"That *lovely* Principal Grant called today." I didn't believe *lovely* was the word she really wanted to use. "Told me you'd gotten called to the office because you'd scared a young man badly enough that he wet his pants and had to go home."

Lark glared at me. I shrugged. "I'm not sorry I did it."

"I didn't do a thing to him," Lark said.

"I didn't think you did." Suddenly, our grandmother looked right at me. "You owe your sister an apology, young lady."

My jaw dropped. I knew she couldn't see me, but this *thing* of ours seemed to come from her side of the family, because she was definitely sensitive to the Shadow Lands.

"She does?" Lark asked, speaking for both of us.

Nan nodded. "I know you didn't hurt that boy, and that your sister's intentions were good, but you got the trouble for it. You'll always get the trouble for it. Wrenleigh, you need to think of these things before you act. I know you want to protect Lark, but now you've made things difficult for her, so you need to apologize for that."

There was no way she'd have known if I apologized or not. I could have broken every window in this house. I could have made her sorry she'd tried bossing me around. Neither of those things were going to happen. I was chastised. She was right.

"I'm sorry," I said to Lark. "I didn't think. He hurt you and I just wanted to hurt him back."

My sister nodded. "I know. It's okay."

But it wasn't, was it? I knew Lark had forgiven me—she always did—but her life would have been easier if I hadn't always been doing things she needed to forgive me for.

Nan smiled. "That's a good girl." She held the plate of cookies out to Lark. "Take one for your sister, too."

Lark plucked two cookies off the cooling plate, gathered up her school books and announced that she was going to do some studying before dinner.

"Liar," I accused.

Lark ignored me. "Nan, is it okay if I go out later? Roxi Taylor invited me to open-mike night at 'Nother Cup."

There was no denying how much this pleased Nan—her face lit up. "Of course it's all right! Do you want to take the car?"

Horror filled me. "No!"

But my sister smiled. "That would be great, thanks." Because a white-haired girl driving a purple car wouldn't stand out at all. God, it was a good thing I was invisible to most humans because I'd wish I was if I had to drive in that car. Fortunately, I didn't have to depend on human modes of transportation.

As we climbed the stairs to our room, I thought I saw something again—a flash of black in my peripheral vision. I whipped my head around, but there was nothing.

"You okay?" Lark asked. "You're not mad at Nan?"

She sounded a little...afraid. "No! Of course not. I thought I saw something."

"I didn't see anything."

Of course she hadn't. She could see a lot of things, but she still had the limited eyesight of a living person; they were notoriously shortsighted. "Probably nothing."

"You know, if you want to go to the coffee shop tonight, I don't mind if you go without me."

I looked at her, lips twisting. "And miss seeing the reaction to you driving a grape jelly bean? I don't think so. Besides, you promised Roxi you would go."

"Yeah, I know." She stared straight ahead as she climbed the rest of the stairs. "It would be rude of me to bail on her."

I didn't add that it would also be stupid for her to stay home and try to send me away. I wasn't bound to Lark, I could come and go as I pleased, and tonight it would please me to be there with my sister to make certain no one tried to hurt her. If anyone gave her a hard time—even if it was Kevin— I'd risk Nan's wrath and make certain they regretted it for a very, *very* long time.

LARK

So. Many. Hipsters.

I walked into 'Nother Cup expecting to be punched in the face by a wave of pretention, and I wasn't disappointed; it almost dropped me on my butt.

I wasn't proud to admit that I'd changed my clothes before leaving the house. I wore a black-and-white sleeveless dress with a Peter Pan collar and a pair of chunky black-and-white-striped Mary Janes. I'd pinned my hair—as white as my collar—into a messy updo and smeared on some black liner and red gloss. *The Addams Family* meets *Mad Men*.

"Stop fidgeting," my sister commanded with a scowl as I

straightened my dress. She was wearing something romantic and flowy, with her brilliant hair in curls. She looked gorgeous—and no one could see it.

"No one says *fidget* anymore," I muttered, turning my head so no one else could hear.

Wren pointed across the fairly crowded shop to a low table surrounded by plush leather sofas and paisley chairs. "There's Roxi. Do you see Kevin? I'm going to see if I can spot him." She took off before I could answer, slipping in and out of people like they were wisps of smoke.

Only, she was the wisp. I needed to remember that. She was as real and solid to me as anyone here, but only to me.

I ordered a chai latte—which took forever—and made my way through the throng toward the stage area. I was practically on top of the table when I saw who else was there.

I knew I should have stayed home.

"Lark!" Roxi jumped up and hugged me. "You guys, this is Lark. Lark, this is Gage, Ben, Sarah and Mace."

Okay, so I didn't really know Gage, but I recognized him from school. Looking at Mace still made me want to puke. Sarah seemed friendly enough. The one who really got me, though, was Ben, the guy I'd seen in the principal's office earlier. Maybe I could ask him what his sister had meant about letting him wait a little longer. And where he'd gotten that black eye.

And why when he looked at me I felt he knew me. Really knew me.

I gave them all a halfhearted wave. "Hey." The only empty chair was the one near Roxi. Unfortunately, it was also next to Mace. He wore a white shirt over a black T-shirt with dark

jeans and boots. Great, we were coordinated. I think he noticed, too. His mouth lifted a teeny bit on one side. It was a
pretty lame-ass smile.

Sarah—the girl I'd seen with Mace earlier at school, smiled
across him at me. She should really have a bandage on that
scratch. She must have been new to school. I didn't recognize
her from before I went to Bell Hill, where they'd loaded me
with pills and therapy. Thank God they hadn't tried an exorcism.
"Hi," she called over the noise of the crowd. "I love your shoes."

She seemed sincere, and my biggest vanity was my fashion
sense. I smiled. "Thanks." I had gotten them at Goodwill and
painted them with leather paint to freshen them up. It had
been a real bitch taping off the stripes, but worth it.

Wren plopped herself down in my chair, phasing through
my right leg so that we were literally joined at the hip.
"Kevin's about to perform," she squealed.

I didn't reply, of course, but I put my hand on my leg and
patted so she'd feel it. I didn't want to encourage the crush—
it wasn't like anything could have come out of it when he
couldn't even see her.

A short bald man stepped up onto the stage and up to the
mike. "Thank you all for coming to open-mike night here at
'Nother Cup. Our first performer is Kevin McCrae."

Thunderous applause met this announcement, along with
several hoots and whistles. Mace was one of the loudest, which
surprised me. I watched him as he shouted out his support,
a grin on his face.

Mace turned that grin on Sarah, who whistled, then Mace's
gaze met mine. I watched, helpless, as the joy melted from
his face. Superfabulous for my ego, that was.

Did he remember how I'd looked that night? All decked out in a white cami and pj pants, my arms sliced open and blood in my hair? Did he remember that I'd looked him in the eye and begged him to let me die? Of course he did. He'd begged me not to die on him. Finding someone in the middle of suicide wasn't something a person forgot. He'd told the police that he thought he'd heard something. As my next-door neighbor he'd decided to check in on me, knowing my parents weren't home. He found me on the floor of my bathroom, my wrists cut. He called 911 and tried to stop the bleeding with towels.

But Kevin had been the reason he'd found me. Kevin was a medium, and Wren had made contact. I didn't feel guilty because he knew about me. I felt guilty because he knew how badly I'd upset Wren.

Mace opened his mouth to speak—what the hell could he possibly have to say?—but a chord from Kevin's guitar stopped him, thank God. I jerked my attention toward the stage, because my sister was squealing like a freaking idiot.

Kevin McCrae was a freshman in college. He was tall and well built, with longish curly dark hair, incredible blue eyes and glasses. I thought he looked a little too much like "thoughtful-sensitive man," but if Wren liked the look of him, who was I to judge? After all, I was trying really hard not to stare at Ben.

He did a couple of covers—Beatles tunes and something by Nirvana. He played well and had a fabulous voice. I hated to admit it, but I enjoyed his set—until his last song.

"This is a song I wrote," he said in his low, slightly raspy voice. "It's for Wrenleigh."

I swear to God my heart freaking stopped. I tried so hard not to glance at my sister, but it was hard when she was right there—part of me. I could feel her nervous energy fluttering inside me. There were very few people in the town, let alone this room, who would have known Wren's full name. You would have to go to her grave to see it.

Kevin McCrae had written a song about my sister? Just how well did they know each other? How well *could* they know each other? I forced myself to listen to the lyrics. Something about hearing ghosts for so long, but then one so beautiful he was in awe of her came to him.

Barf.

And then Kevin looked right at me as he sang, "Did you think of how much it would hurt her when you cut to the bone? I felt her pain calling out to me like it was my own."

He might as well have gotten off the stage, walked up to me and smashed his guitar over my head. I couldn't believe it. I just sat there, shocked and frozen like an idiot, my face burning.

Screw that. I tried to stand up, but Wren held me to the chair. She'd known. She'd known about the damn song. She'd known he was going to sing it. Everyone at this table knew what he was singing about.

I never thought my sister would sit and watch me be humiliated, the past shoved in my face one more time.

"Get out of me," I whispered.

"Lark," she pleaded. "Just listen to the song, please."

Wren was preternaturally strong, but I wasn't without my own talents. If she had a little extra power where the living was concerned, then I had a little more influence over the dead—or at least more experience. I gathered up all the hurt and anger inside me and pushed it at her. It must have surprised her, because she let go easily, lifting out of me to hover a few feet above the table. Show off. I'd have been sprawled on the floor if she shoved that hard at me.

I jumped to my feet and ran, elbowing my way through the audience.

"Watch it, cow," a girl dressed all in white snarled.

I could snarl, too. "Get out of my way."

She smirked. "Say please."

What was this, a CW show? This kind of drama just didn't happen in real life, did it? I took the plastic top off my cup and dumped what was left of my latte down the front of her. She gasped. Actually, it was more of a roar, but I'd already shoved her aside and kept moving. I didn't stop when I stepped out into the warm September night but made a beeline straight for my borrowed purple Bug. Nan had been so excited at the prospect of me making friends. God, she was even more naive than I was.

I pressed the button to unlock the car and climbed in, tossing my purse onto the passenger seat. For a moment, I sat there, forehead against the steering wheel. How could I have been so stupid? Hadn't I learned anything? God, I was so deficient. I was going to have to switch schools because I was too young to drop out. I could probably have gotten into one a town or two over. Maybe. My past would have caught up with me sooner or later, it always did, but for a little while I could have hidden.

I started the car and lifted my head. I'd just slipped the gear into Drive when someone stepped in front of the bumper.

The headlights made them look ghoulish, but even ghoul-ish, Mace was gorgeous.

I put down the window and stuck my head out. "Get out of the way."

"Give us a minute, will you?" he asked. "We just want to talk to you."

Roxi appeared by the window. "Please, Lark. I can explain. It was my idea."

"Explain this." I flipped her the bird. Then, to Mace, "Move, Ryan."

Roxi's hand grabbed my shoulder. Her grip was tight, desperate. "Please."

I ignored her as I revved the engine, trying to scare Mace. He knew I wasn't going to run him over, though. Jerk. The others stood there with him, clustered in the headlights with anxious expressions on their faces—not what I'd expect of people wanting to mess with me. And my sister was finally there, just on the edge where I could barely see her. I wasn't in any danger from these people or she would have been full-on Amityville right now.

Unless she was in on it.

And that really was crazy. A genuine insane thought.

I turned off the car and stepped out, holding the door open between me and them like a shield. "What's going on?"

Kevin had joined our group, too. He looked at me like I was something he'd just scraped off the bottom of his shoe. I didn't even know the guy. What was his damage?

Roxi stepped forward, hands held out in front of her, imploringly. "Lark, no one meant to hurt you tonight. I'm sorry if you feel like you've been ambushed."

I raised a brow. "You mean I haven't been?"

"I told you to be straight with her," Ben growled. He was all frowny and serious, not quite so pretty, but even more hot. He turned to me. "We asked you here to talk to you."

I glanced at Roxi. "Not to be my friend, then." Shouldn't have said that. Made me sound whiny and pathetic.

She looked like I'd slapped her. "I meant what I said."

I wanted to believe that, I really did.

"This is stupid," the darker guy—Gage—said. I remembered him from elementary school. His last name was Moreno. "You guys watch too much TV. She can't help us, because there's nothing going on."

Help them? With what?

I turned my attention back to Ben, but my gaze caught on Sarah instead. "You should get that scratch looked at," I told her. "It looks infected."

It was as though I was a hunter with a semiautomatic and they were a herd of deer. They all froze, staring at me.

Sarah's hand went to her face. "Really?"

"Yeah. You should at least put a bandage on it. Some Neosporin."

Gage stepped forward, rolling up his sleeves. "What about me? Do I have scratches, too?"

Long, jagged furrows ran the inside length of each of his forearms. They rose up in thick, scarlet welts that oozed wetly under the streetlights.

I made a face. "What the hell have you been into?" I asked them, but I shouldn't have asked. Hell, I shouldn't have let them know I could even see them. I knew my mistake as soon as the light hit his arms in the right way, allowing me to see that tar-like tinge that clung to the wounds.

"Oh, hell," I whispered. "You pissed off a ghost."

No one else could see their scratches. Even they couldn't see them, but I bet they could feel them. Some ghosts were nasty that way.

"Oh, Lark," Wren whispered. "This is bad."

"Did it get all of you?" I asked.

"Not me," Kevin said, but the rest nodded.

I glanced at each of them. I didn't want to get involved in this. But...shit. I couldn't just walk away. They had no idea what they'd gotten into.

Roxi shot a fierce look at Sarah. "I told you Ben was right. I told you something happened that night."

Sarah's jaw was slack, her eyes wide. Her fingers were still pressed to the wound on her face. "It's not possible," she whispered. "Ghosts aren't real."

"There's one here right now," Kevin informed her hotly. Huh. Mr. Sixth Sense all ready to snap to my sister's defense. I liked him at that moment. A little.

Gage shook his head. "This is so fucked up."

I turned to Ben. "How did you know?"

He shrugged. "I felt it."

"You believe in this stuff?" Mace demanded. He looked from Kevin to Ben like he felt betrayed by them. "That's just great."

"And you don't?" I asked. "Come on, Mace. You're smarter than that."

He glared at me. He blamed me, I think. He'd been living in perfect ignorance before being dragged into my world.

Gage stood there, rubbing at his forearms. He looked scared and confused. "Ghosts are real?"

For a second, there was silence. Then, I said, "Yes." There went that promise I'd made to keep myself out of trouble. To keep my head down and not attract attention.

"We have to help them," Wren insisted.

I glanced at her. "Can't help them if they don't want it," I replied.

Gage was watching me. "Who are you talking to?"

I sighed. "My sister. She's dead."

He paled a little. "Oh, shit. The stories about you are true?"

Roxi patted him on the arm. "It's okay."

Mace and Sarah exchanged glances, then looked at Gage, Roxi, Ben and Kevin. None of them wanted this to be true. In fact, I expected them to protest a little harder, but they weren't stupid. They knew something was off.

"Can you help us get rid of it?" Roxi asked, her hand over her stomach.

"Yeah," added Gage. "What do we do?"

Okay, so they were ready to admit that something was wrong. That meant that they were open to believing in ghosts, and that for the first time in my life I was with people who just might believe *me*.

I didn't know everything about ghosts, but I knew more than they did. I knew more than most people did. And Wren knew way more than me. Still, she and I just sort of figured things out as we went along. We weren't exactly experts.

"We're all they've got," my sister whispered. Kevin's gaze jerked in her direction. Just how sensitive was he to her presence?

"Where did you find it?" I asked. Cool fingers curled

around mine and squeezed. My sister, giving her approval. I had an awful feeling that this was going to bite me on the ass.

"Fairfield Cemetery," Sarah replied.

I shook my head. And closed the Beetle's door. I wasn't going anywhere just then.

"Lark, that's not right," Wren insisted. "Do you hear me? I said it's not—"

I shot her a glare. "I *know*." Did she think I'd forgotten about Kevin and his little song during this drama?

"Are you talking to your sister again?" Sarah asked hesitantly.

I tried to smile. It didn't work. "Yes."

"Her name's Wren," Kevin said, stepping into the circle. He shot me a glance. I gave him the finger. He'd flapped his lips about my sister enough already.

"Ghosts don't haunt cemeteries," I informed them. "Cemeteries are sanctuaries. There's nothing there but bones and peace. Ghosts need something to hold on to—a person, place or thing. When ghosts need to feed they go back to a place they knew in life where they might find the living. Your ghost is from somewhere else. Where else have you been that's close to there?"

They all looked around, shaking their heads.

"At least one of you has been somewhere else. Maybe you walked across property near the graveyard? Trespassed somewhere?"

That shared glance was all the answer I needed. "Where?" I demanded.

"Haven Crest," Gage said, voice hoarse and face white. "The old...hospital. We cut across the grounds one night."

I made a face at his choice of term, which I knew had been

for my benefit. Haven Crest had been an asylum in the most horror-movie sense of the word. Every kid in town knew about it by the time he or she was ten. Some even dared to brave its rusted gates. I knew better. I saw what was there. Those memories kicked my heart into overdrive and brought back other memories, of pills being forced down my throat as the ghosts of Bell Hill looked on, some of them eager for a chance to "play" when my senses were dulled and I couldn't fight back.

"You're on your own," I told them and pivoted on my heel. "Good luck."

"Wait!" Roxi cried. "You're not going to help us?"

"I can't," I told her. "I'm sorry." And I really was.

"Lark, we have to help them," Wren insisted, but I turned away.

Someone grabbed my arm, but it wasn't Wren. It was Mace, and he looked angry. And afraid. Of all the people to grab me, to make me look them in the eye, why did it have to be the one who had saved my sorry life? Yes, they'd locked me up after he did it, but I was here because of him. I *owed* him.

"You can't tell us we need your help and then walk away," he said.

I shook my head as though he'd been the one to remind me of that fact. "I won't do it. You can't make me go there. Do you know what that place is? Do you know what it's like to be surrounded by ghosts that don't have any sense of right and wrong? To be strapped to a bed and unable to fight when creatures who get off on pain come to play?" Tears filled my eyes and I refused to be ashamed of them. "You don't know, and I can't do that again."

"You're right," he said. "I just know this." And then he shoved my hand under his shirt, flat against the smooth, muscled wall of his chest. I gasped at the heat there—the burning ridges that scorched my palm. He had the scratches, too.

Heat raced up my arm. No, it was like my arm was on fire. I cried out. Wren reached for me… My head snapped back—eyes, too.

Pain. Blood. Suffering. Terrible images filled my brain, each moving too fast to be sure of what I was seeing. I heard screams and laughter, tasted blood and tears. And I burned.

Then I saw them—Mace, Roxi, Gage, Sarah, Ben and Kevin—all of them. They were dead—ripped apart by something with huge claws. Their blood covered the floor of what looked like an old medical ward. Rats scurried along the edge of the growing crimson pool.

Mace's face—what was left of it—turned toward me. Something had ripped out his eyes, but I knew he could see me. "You," he rasped.

And there was Wren, clacking like a vulture, squatting among all the gore. Black clots of blood matted her hair, stained the skin around her mouth. I watched in horror as she lifted unnaturally long, bloody hands. Each finger had become a wicked razor-sharp claw, and from those claws dangled a cluster of eyeballs—like an upside down bunch of small, macabre balloons. I saw Roxi's eyes and Mace's eyes, and Sarah's. They all turned to stare at me accusingly.

My sister grinned at me before popping one of them into her mouth.

I screamed.

chapter three

WREN

Lark slumped against Mason at exactly the same moment a police officer got out of his car on the other side of the parking lot.

"Crap," Ben muttered. "Is that Olgilvie?"

Someone else swore.

I barely glanced at the tall, heavyset man in uniform walking toward us. I was more concerned about my sister. What had happened when she'd touched Mason's wounds? "Lark?"

Mason held her up. He couldn't see me, however. To his friends he said, "Stay calm. Let me do the talking."

Sarah looked panicked. "How are we going to explain her?" She gestured at Lark. "She looks drunk."

It was obvious that everyone thought we were in trouble, so I did the only thing I could think of. I stepped into my sister and took over her body for the time being. People called it possession, but I didn't like to use that term in regards to Lark. Thankfully, she was just asleep. I opened my eyes—Lark's eyes.

Mason looked down at me. He frowned. "You're not her," he whispered.

I managed a small smile, impressed that he could tell the difference between us—most people couldn't. "You can let her…me, go now. Thanks."

He dropped his arms like I was on fire. I stumbled, but managed to catch myself. Wearing Lark was fairly comfortable, but I wasn't used to having substance in this realm. Limbs were heavy, clumsy. I braced my hand against the roof of Nan's car.

By that time the police officer—Olgilvie—had reached us. "Evening, kids. Had a report of a girl accosting another with a cup of hot tea. Then I heard a scream. Everything all right up here?"

"Yeah," Mason replied. "Just messing around."

Olgilvie ignored him and came straight toward me. Did I know him? He looked familiar. Had he been there the night Lark had hurt herself?

He peered at me with narrow dark eyes. "You're that Noble girl, aren't you? Charlotte's granddaughter."

I nodded. God, even Lark's head was heavy. How did the living walk around like this all day?

His shoulders straightened, like a rooster trying to make itself taller. He tucked his thumbs into his belt. "Are we going to have trouble again, Miss Noble?"

Again. I wanted to explain to him that *we* had never had any trouble, but that *we* certainly could if he wanted. I wanted to make the little hairs on the back of his neck stand up on end.

I wanted to make his bladder quiver. A girl screams and he shows up talking like she'd done something wrong? Shouldn't he be asking if she—I—was all right?

A skinny young man with a lot of hair and jeans that were too tight stood beside the officer. It was obvious he was one of my kind—not just because he looked out of place, but because he looked right at me and winked.

"No," I said, looking away from the ghost. "We're not going to have trouble."

The policeman nodded, rocked back on his heels. "That's good, because I have friends at Bell Hill. If I think for a minute that you're a danger to anyone in this town I won't hesitate to give them a call."

Lark would say something snarky—my sister got defiant when threatened—but I couldn't think of anything. I was too angry. How dare he bring up that awful place. Lark hadn't done anything and this man talked about sending her back there? He looked at her as though he thought she was a criminal. Trouble. Just what did he think she was going to do? She'd hurt herself, not anyone else.

"She didn't do anything," Mason said, with a frown. "Why don't you back off?"

The officer obviously didn't like his tone. "You watch your tone, Mace."

"No." The boy who had rescued my sister, and earned my eternal gratitude, folded his arms over his chest. "There's nothing going on here, so maybe you should go find some real trouble, because *I* won't hesitate to call my father—you know, your boss—and let him know that one of his officers is bullying a teenage girl for no reason."

The older man stared at Mason, who stared back. Oh, I wished Lark could have seen it! If I liked Mason Ryan before, I adored him now for standing up for my sister.

"Someday, you're not going to be able to hide behind your daddy the chief anymore." Olgilvie pointed a thick finger at him. "I'm going to be there when that happens."

Mason shrugged. "Then I guess you and I will have trouble. *Someday.*"

The officer stepped forward, jaw tight. That was when I put myself, or rather Lark, between the two of them. I probably shouldn't have done anything, but it was the only way I could think of to end this situation before it became any more out of control.

And the only way to get the ghost to go away.

"You hid behind your father when he was chief, Opie."

The color drained from Olgilvie's face. "What did you call me?"

"That was what they called you, wasn't it? The kids who liked to tease you?" Sometimes I knew things about the living, but in this case, the name had come from the ghost with him.

I smiled a little, moved closer to him, so only he could hear what I said next—the secret his companion shared. He staggered backward after I spoke to him, looking at me like I was something unnatural, which I was, of course. I was glad Lark wasn't awake to see it, because too many people had given her that same look over the course of her life.

The officer turned and walked away. He looked unsteady. The younger man's ghost walked beside him.

"What did you say to him?" Mason asked when it was just the group of us again.

"Something only he and a dead man knew," I answered. And that was all I was going to say. Things taken to the grave were taken there for a reason. By revealing it, and scaring the officer away, I'd basically indebted myself to the ghost haunting him. If the ghost ever needed a favor, I was obliged to reciprocate. No need to bring anyone else into that bargain.

I had bigger things to worry about. "Can someone help me? I need to wake up Lark."

With the exception of Mason, they all looked at me in... well, it wasn't quite horror. Surprise? That was when I finally let myself look at Kevin. My heart skipped a beat.

"Wren?" His voice was hoarse.

I nodded. His eyes were so blue, even in the dark parking lot. The breeze blew dark curls around his face. Such wild hair. It didn't occur to me to speak. I just wanted to look at him. God, I could touch him if I wanted.

After that first connection when Lark had hurt herself, I didn't expect to talk to Kevin again, but he reached out to me a day or two later. And when my sister had shut me out, he was the one person I could talk to about it. It took some time, and it wasn't easy, but we got so that we could communicate fairly easily. He couldn't see me, couldn't touch me, but he could hear me.

"Oh, shit," Gage said, staring at me. "That's a ghost in there? Dude, that's...fucked up."

I blinked. There were other people with us. I hadn't exactly forgotten them, they just hadn't mattered all that much to me. Sometimes the living faded into the background, there were just so many of them.

"Where do you need to go?" Mace asked.

"Someplace private. Quiet. Not here," I replied.

Kevin came forward. "My place. My parents are away for a long weekend."

His house! Oh, no. Lark was going to kill me when she woke up. I didn't care. I wanted to see his house. I wanted to touch the light switches he touched. Walk the floors he walked. I wanted to smell his toothbrush. Maybe try on his clothes. I didn't care if it was weird—I spent 99.9 percent of my time incorporeal, damn it.

"I need someone to drive," I said with a wince, gesturing to my grandmother's hideous car. "I can't."

"I'll drive you," Kevin offered.

Oh, Lark, please stay asleep. Just for a little while longer. Please, please.

"Are you sure? It's an ugly car."

He smiled, and it was like watching the moon rise from behind the veil. So bright. "I don't mind."

Mason clapped him on the shoulder. "We'll meet you there, man."

The keys were already in the…thing. What was that called? The ignition? I managed to clomp around the back to the passenger side. Kevin opened the door for me. I smiled. "Thanks."

I pulled the seat belt across Lark's body and buckled it. No need for both of us to be ghosts. Kevin climbed in, fastened his belt and then started the engine. He glanced around at the interior.

"Wow," he said. "It really is hideous."

I laughed. "Isn't it?"

He grinned, adjusted the stick thing and then made the

vehicle move. "It's weird, being able to actually talk to you, and have you be more than a voice in my head."

"I know." I sneaked a glance at him. "It's nice." There were so many things I wanted to say to him, but they all seemed so foolish now that I had the chance. We'd talked a few times over the past year and a bit, but this seemed much more…intimate. I could touch him if I wanted. Smell him. Feel his warmth.

I never realized just how cold I was all the time.

"Do you think Lark will help them?"

"Yes." It wasn't a lie. "She'll do what's right." It just took a little prodding to get her there sometimes.

"Good." He turned his head toward me just for a second before looking back at the road. "I can't believe it's you in there. Earlier that face looked like it wanted to kill me."

"She felt ambushed. The song…"

"Did you like it?"

"*I* did. Lark felt like it was an accusation."

"It kind of was. She put you through something terrible."

"She thought she was insane, Kevin. Living with me made her feel that way." I couldn't have expected him to understand.

His jaw tightened. "No. She let *people* make her feel that way. I know what that's like, and it's not your fault."

He was sweet, but he really *didn't* understand. "We can't be friends if you hate her." It hurt to say the words.

"I don't hate her. I just think she made some bad choices."

It sounded like something Lark would have said. As much as I liked him, this was my sister we were discussing. He had to be an only child, because he obviously didn't know that the only person who could say anything bad about Lark was me. "She didn't do it to hurt me. She did it so we could be together." I had never told anyone that. In fact, Lark and I had only ever talked about it once—shortly after she cut herself. There had been that brief moment when we had actually been together behind the veil. She'd been dead for a few seconds.

It had been wonderful. I never had and never would tell her just how much. Lark and I could touch, but there was always this invisible barrier between us. We were in different worlds, even if they overlapped. To have her with me finally was incredible—and wrong. She didn't belong in my world, and I couldn't have let her stay.

Kevin glanced at me again. "Okay." He only said that one word, but it seemed to mean so much more than that. I smiled.

"Can I...?" I swallowed. "Can I touch you?"

The car swerved as he jerked his head toward me, then back again. "Now?" His voice was strained.

"I just want..." I leaned over and wrapped one of his curls around my finger. His hair was silky, springy—exactly like I'd hoped it would be. I laughed. "I've never felt hair other than Lark's before."

And this was different from when Lark was awake and I shared her body. Despite the heavy limbs and awkwardness of them, they felt like mine. I was in control, not my sister, and it...it was *wonderful*. And strange. So strange.

I pulled my hand away, but he caught it and twined his fingers with mine. His hand was warm. Strong. My heart slammed hard against my ribs. Was I going to vomit, or burst into song? I couldn't tell.

And it wasn't my heart, not really. It was Lark's heart. I

had to remember that. This wasn't my body. In this realm I didn't have a body. I wasn't real.

But I let Kevin hold Lark's hand all the way to his house anyway.

LARK

My eyes opened. The first face I saw other than my sister's belonged to Mace. Funny, but his face was the last thing I remembered seeing before I passed out. God, that vision of Wren eating eyeballs had been gross. Not something I ever wanted to see again.

"Where am I?" I demanded. "Whose bed is this? And why do I smell toothpaste?" I swear on her grave my sister blushed.

Kevin's freakishly curly head appeared over Mace's shoulder. "You're at my house. My bed."

Well, ew.

"You fainted," my sister informed me. "I had to wear you for a bit—there was a police officer."

I opened my mouth, then closed it again.

"It's okay," Wren continued, strangely giddy. "They know about me. We're friends."

At the same time, I heard Roxi say, "Your sister possessed you when the cop showed up. It was awesome."

Oh, great. Okay, so Wren possessing me seemed to convince everyone that I'd be on board with helping them, but what the hell had my sister done while running around in my body? I glanced at Kevin, my gaze narrow. She better not have made out with him. I sat up. My head swam a little. I reached out to steady myself, my hand clamping on to something warm and hard.

It was Mace's shoulder. As soon as my brain settled I jerked my hand away.

"You okay?" he asked.

I nodded, avoiding his gaze. He needed to go away. He was too much of a distraction for me. I couldn't seem to think around him. All I could think about was that he'd seen me at my weakest, and I could never change that. I owed him my life, and I couldn't change that, either. That meant that regardless of what I thought of the others, I *had* to help him. I had to do everything in my power to save him. I might be a living, breathing girl, but I knew ghosts—I could fight them and hurt them—and I had one on my side.

So, I was going to walk into an asylum. A haunted one. I wanted to mention—just in case there was any confusion on the subject—that asylums and hospitals and jails didn't have one ghost, or even half a dozen ghosts. Most of them, especially the old ones, could have hundreds of ghosts. When I was thirteen my parents took me—and Wren—to London. The Tower of London freaked me out. Wren had to return to the Shadow Lands—where she lived when she wasn't with me—because the ghosts wouldn't leave her alone.

There was a different energy to ghosts when they were in this world. The ones that stayed here had issues, and they were agitated, while Shadow Land ghosts were generally more calm. At least that was what Wren told me. I wasn't there long enough to find out for myself, not really. But the Shadow Lands was like a stepping-stone between dimensions—a place between earth and Heaven, reincarnation...whatever.

"What happened to you earlier?" Roxi asked. She was perched on the dresser near the foot of the bed. Mace and

Sarah were on the edge of the bed and Gage and Ben stood against the far wall. My sister was with Kevin. I didn't like that very much, but at least he wasn't looking at me like I was Hitler. In fact, he seemed really confused when he looked at me.

Oh, God. She'd made out with him. Didn't she? She was so lucky she was already dead.

"I don't know," I told her honestly. "I had some kind of vision."

"Of what?" It was Kevin who asked.

"I don't want to talk about it."

"It could help us."

I scowled. "I said I don't want to talk about it."

"But it could help," he insisted.

I clenched my jaw. "It won't." I gave him a look that said if he pushed it I'd punch him in the face.

Instead of continuing the argument, he tilted his head. "That bad?"

I resisted the urge to snort. "I passed out." Was that bad enough for him? And why was he suddenly being all understanding? I thought he hated me.

"Sorry 'bout that," Mace apologized. "I didn't know that would happen."

I shrugged. "Didn't think you would have."

He looked down—at my hand, the one he'd shoved under his shirt. My fingers twitched. I closed them into a fist. "I need to see where you were attacked."

He didn't even blink. "Okay. Let's go."

"Now?" His girlfriend blinked enough for both of us. "You're going now? She just woke up."

Mace rose to his feet and so did I. "He wants to make sure

I don't change my mind," I remarked with less humor than I intended.

He shot me an unamused look. "Maybe I just want to make sure my friends and I are back to normal as soon as possible. I have to think that spectral wounds aren't good."

He was right, they weren't. In fact, they could be life threatening. It was weird, but he didn't seem to doubt for a moment that I could fix this, even though I had no freaking idea of how to do just that. "Let's go, then."

Wren came toward me. God, there were a lot of people in the room. So many of them depending on me to help them. I didn't do well with responsibility. "I'm coming with you."

I shook my head. "You're not going anywhere near that place until I've checked it out." I turned to Kevin. "Do you have a can of salt I can take with me?"

"Sure," he said. I had to admit that I liked not having to explain myself. I followed him to the kitchen—everyone else tagging along behind. He took a large can of salt from the pantry and handed it to me. It was full, the seal not even broken. It was a cheap but effective weapon against spirits. I wasn't sure why, but I didn't care so long as it worked.

"If you're not back in an hour we're going to come looking for you," Ben said. He'd been pretty quiet up until now. Then again, he and Wren could have chatted up a storm and braided each other's hair while I was out of it, for all I knew.

I shot him a grim smile. "If we're not back in an hour we're dead."

That brought the mood down.

"Why would you say that?" Sarah demanded. She turned to Mace. "Why would she say something like that?"

"Because it's true," I retorted.

My sister looked embarrassed. "Lark…"

I held up my hand. "We'll be fine. I'll have your friend back in one piece, I promise."

"You're our friend, too," Roxi said softly.

I snorted.

"If you want to be," Ben added.

There was something in his gaze that freaked me out. He freaked me out—almost as much as Mace, but for different reasons. "Morbid curiosity?" Why else would he seem to be so interested in me? He was probably one of those guys who secretly crushed on goth girls. "Let's go."

I pivoted on my heel, toward what I hoped was the back door. Outside I stomped toward Nan's car.

"We're taking my car," came Mace's voice from behind me.

I swerved toward the Jaguar. It was old and black—cool without screaming, "I have a huge wang!" Good thing he was driving, because I had no idea where the keys to the Beetle were. Whoever drove it here must have still had them.

I tried the passenger door. It was locked. Great. The thing predated auto lock, so I had to wait for him to come around and unlock it for me. I stood there feeling like a loser.

When Mace reached me he didn't immediately unlock the door. He stood there watching me. Finally, I lifted my chin and met his gaze with a belligerent one of my own. "What?" I wished I'd worn heels so I could be more at his eye level. I found him…intimidating.

"Just so we're clear, *my* interest in being your friend isn't morbid curiosity." His tone smarted with indignation. "*This* is morbid curiosity." He grabbed my right arm and yanked my sleeve up.

"Hey!" I cried, pulling against his grip. He was way stronger than me and held my arm tight, turning it so that the scar there was fully visible—a long, smooth ridge against my pale skin. He touched it with his other hand—a gentle stroke. It was a violation.

"Don't," I choked out. I was tempted to hit him with the can of salt.

His gaze lifted and locked with mine. "That was the scariest day of my life, finding you like that."

"Oh." A genius with words was I. Being the center of my own little world, I'd thought only of my own shame, my own feelings. It never occurred to me how finding me must have affected him beyond his opinion of me.

He continued, still staring into my eyes, still holding my arm. He didn't touch my scar again, though. "Nobody has ever scared me more than you have—that day, and then tonight when you passed out."

My throat was tight—probably because my heart had jumped into it. A smart-ass retort came to mind, but I couldn't bring myself to say it. "What do you want from me, Mace? An apology? Fine, I'm sorry."

The muscle in his jaw twitched. "What I want is for you not to treat me like I'm one of those assholes who doesn't understand you or treats you like you're crazy."

I yanked on my arm again, but he held tight. I knew that if I pretended it hurt he'd let me go. Here was the twisted part—I didn't want him to let me go. It had been so long since someone, especially a guy, had touched me. "What are you, then?" Did he really expect me to believe that *he*, of all people, didn't think I was nuts?

His nostrils flared slightly. "I'm the guy who kicked in a window to get to you. The guy who found you in a pool of your own blood and wrapped your arms in pillowcases to try to stop the bleeding. I'm the guy who prayed for you to live while you begged me to let you die. I don't want your apology."

"What the hell do you want? Gratitude? A freaking medal?" I wasn't yelling, but I was close.

"What do I want?" His fingers tightened on my arm. "Jesus, Lark. I want you to forgive me!"

chapter four

LARK

I stared at him. "What?"

Mace stared back. There was maybe three inches between us—just enough that I could look at him without going cross-eyed. He took a step backward. I was glad he did, even though my arm felt cold when he let go. "I want you to tell me that I did the right thing."

"Oh, Mace." I felt like I'd been punched in the stomach. He looked haunted, and I knew all about that. "Yeah, you did. You did the right thing."

He looked away, raking a hand through his thick hair. He stood with his back to me, hands on his hips. I thought I heard him sniff. What was I supposed to do? I couldn't hug him, I wasn't very good at it. Should I say something? What?

Then he turned. He didn't look at me. "Let's get going." He unlocked the Jag and opened the passenger door.

"Thanks," I murmured as I slid inside.

Mace closed the door, then crossed in front of the car to climb in the driver's side. We buckled our seat belts and he started the engine. Neither of us spoke during the drive to the graveyard. It was secluded and we could park there while poking around close to the asylum grounds without getting too close. Mace would be a magnet for the thing that had marked the group of them. With any luck I'd be able to get a feel for it, or at least get an idea of what we were up against. If our luck went bad, the thing would come for Mace, and maybe kill both of us.

My fingers tightened around the can of salt. Mace and the others had put their faith in me, were depending on me. Stupid of them, really. Even though I knew most of them wouldn't have anything to do with me in any other circumstance, I felt like I had to at least try. Besides, it wasn't as though I was scared of dying. Been there, done that.

Fairfield Cemetery edged up against the grounds of Haven Crest—the asylum had a huge amount of land that the town was apparently thinking of reclaiming. Yeah, good luck with that. They'd better burn, salt and bless every square foot.

"Want to get the gate?" Mace asked when we pulled into the graveyard lane. I unfastened my seat belt and climbed out. There wasn't any traffic on the quiet side road, although it was after eleven. The only light was the Jag's headlights casting long, eerie shadows through the wrought-iron bars. There was a chain draped around the rungs, but it was just for show—not locked. I removed it and pulled open the gate so that Mace could drive in. He stopped and waited for me to replace the chain. Then we continued into the graveyard.

"There are other people here," I remarked after we drove by two cars parked some distance apart.

"They won't bother us," Mace said, looking straight ahead.

"How do you know?"

He shot me a disbelieving glance, as though it should be obvious. "They're busy."

Suddenly, I understood. Embarrassment heated my face. How could I have not figured that out on my own? "How romantic," I muttered.

Mace shrugged. "It's private. Personally, I think it's disrespectful." He laughed drily. "You probably think that's stupid, huh?"

Now I was the one looking at him like he should know better. "The person I love most in the world is a ghost. I think I have a unique perspective on respecting the dead."

He tilted his head. "I guess you do."

I stared at him. "Do I agitate you?"

"Yeah. Yeah, you do." He pulled the car under a large maple tree and put it in Park. He turned to look at me. "But I think you like having that effect on people. Keeps them from getting close."

I scowled. "You sound like a shrink."

He smiled. Actually, it was more of a smirk. "Guess I agitate you, too." Then he unfastened his seat belt and got out of the car. I had no choice but to follow him, and for once, I had no smart-ass comeback.

It was dark in the cemetery, but it was a clear night and the moon cast everything in a silvery light. I recognized our surroundings as we walked deeper into the stone garden. "Do you mind if we make a stop first?" I asked. Cemeteries weren't just calming to ghosts—they were calming to me. There was a sense of peace here, and I needed a minute to center myself.

"Really?" He arched a brow. "Are you serious?"

"It will just take a minute." Without waiting for his response, I veered right, down a worn path, and kept walking until I reached a familiar stone angel bowed over a matching bassinet. Both were smudged with age and dirt, with patches of moss clinging to them. Someone had left a bouquet of flowers—like the kind you got at the grocery store—on the small, flat headstone that was set into the grass. I couldn't see the name on the stone, but I didn't need to. I knew whose grave it was.

"Someone's been here," I said—like it wasn't obvious.

"Kevin," Mace replied. "He's been coming every couple of weeks ever since it happened."

No need to say what "it" was. My opinion of Kevin rose a little. Before I had tried to kill myself I had visited this sad little plot once a week, making sure it looked good, cleaning the stone. This was my first time back since returning to New Devon. I would have to thank him for taking care of Wren's grave while I was gone.

"Is this the stop you wanted to make?"

I nodded as I picked a bit of moss from the angel's head.

"Sorry I gave you a hard time about it."

I shrugged. "They bought room for me, too."

"What?"

I crouched down and moved the flowers so that he could see the headstone. "My parents."

Mace peered over my shoulder. "Shit."

"Yeah." I traced the letters of my own name, carved there

beside Wren's. Unlike her, I had no expiration date below mine. I couldn't even begin to articulate how I felt about having a grave all ready for me to move in whenever I needed it. "You know, I'm okay with not being there yet. I meant what I said earlier—you did the right thing. Thank you."

He cleared his throat. "Yeah. You're welcome."

I stood up. "Okay, let's go. Take me to the spot where you guys sneaked onto asylum property." The old hospital campus was locked up at night, but kids from New Devon had been sneaking in for as long as I could remember. I couldn't remember any stories about people getting hurt, though I'm sure there were some. Maybe Mace and his friends had pissed off a ghost, but the more likely explanation was that recent construction on the site had stirred something up. Ghosts weren't big on change. My newfound "friends" had simply stumbled in at the wrong freaking time.

Or something there was getting stronger.

We walked back along the path, then took a right on the main trail. It wasn't long before we reached the stone wall. It had crumbled in spots, but was about eight feet tall, and topped with rusted barbed wire. The grass was tamped down around one particularly large tree. Someone had nailed boards into the trunk a long time ago—we're talking the '70s from the look of the wood. The bark there had been chipped and worn away from years of traffic.

"There's a rope ladder on one of the branches," Mace explained. "We climbed the tree, then went down the ladder."

"Awesome," I muttered, looking down at my cute shoes that were so not made for climbing trees. Neither was my dress. I felt completely ridiculous.

"Want me to go first?" he asked.

"Unless you want to be scarred for life by the sight of my granny panties, you'd better." They were boy panties, but who could tell the difference in the dark.

He gave me an odd look, then scampered up the tree like he'd been born to do it. I followed a lot less gracefully. My shoes had smooth soles, so they couldn't grip the homemade ladder. I still had the salt, too, so I was only holding on with one hand.

"Ow!" Damn splinter in my palm.

Mace's hand appeared before me. "Your hand or the salt—give me one."

I gave him the salt. I didn't want him to get the idea that he was my freaking knight in shining armor or something.

Once I made it to the branch he was on—a limb thick enough to hold both of us—he held on to another branch for support and walked out over the wall. I inched along behind him. It would be just my luck to fall and break my fool neck on the asylum side. By the time I got to the rope ladder, Mace was already on the ground, holding the rope steady for me. There wasn't any graceful way to descend a ladder that swayed and diped with every movement. I swore the entire time down—under my breath, of course.

"You've got a mouth like a sailor," Mace commented when I joined him. The grass was brown and flattened by dozens of feet. That was good.

I opened the salt and began pouring it. "Met many sailors, have you? Is there something Sarah should know about you, Mace?"

"I love me a man in uniform," he quipped. "What are you doing?"

"Making a salt circle around you."

"Why?"

I didn't look up. "Because this thing has had a taste of you and will be able to sense you're here, and I don't want to have to explain to Sarah that it took you on my watch."

"Your concern is touching, Lark. Really."

It wasn't his sarcasm that made me look up, though I appreciated his skill at it. "I owe you. That means I'm going to do everything I can to keep you alive. You okay with that?"

"Yeah, I think I am." His gaze locked with mine. We stood there, staring at each other. Awkward.

A cold breeze brushed my bare legs. I turned my head in its direction. "Feel that?"

"Yeah." Out of the corner of my eye I saw his hand go to his chest as if it hurt. The ghost was coming.

I checked the ring I'd poured around him—it was a good, thick mound of salt that could withstand a spectral wind. Good.

I took a deep breath as my hair began to stir. In Bell Hill I'd faced several malevolent spirits, and I'd done it stoned on antidepressants and antipsychotic and antianxiety meds. I could deal with one in a field.

Even if it was the one who had sent me a vision of my sister eating eyeballs.

The chill cranked, raising goose bumps on my arms. My hair rose at the roots. This thing was hungry and pissed. It wasn't even trying to be stealthy as it came at us. It had sniffed out Mace and was eager for another taste.

Honestly, I couldn't say that I blamed it—aggravating as he was.

There was no one way to describe encountering a ghost. Yeah, there was the cold, but that was about the only thing they had in common. Every ghost—in my experience—had their own energy and their own weaknesses. I guess I knew this stuff because of Wren, or because of our situation, or maybe because of my brush with the other side. So maybe I didn't know *why* I knew these things, but I did know when there was a ghost around, and I could usually tell how strong they were.

This one was strong. Old and strong. And angry. I could feel its rage in my bones, in the pressure of my teeth grinding together. It swirled around me like a snarling dog trying to catch my scent. It hadn't bothered to take form, and it looked like nothing more than a swarm of flies circling me. If those flies had frozen razor blades for wings, that was.

"Lark?" Mace looked concerned.

"I'm good," I shouted over the noise of the ghost. He probably couldn't even hear it. My heart hammered in my chest. *What are you?* Its voice was like screeching brakes in my ears.

I ignored it. Holding my hands out to my sides, I sifted the ghost through my fingers, inviting it to reveal its personality. It was like a thousand paper cuts as its angry energy flicked over my skin. I'd felt ones that were like sandpaper, an itch, even feathers, but not this. I would be left bleeding afterward—no invisible wounds for me. Fortunately, I didn't wound like normal people. Scratches like Mace's hurt me, but didn't last—I assumed because I was connected to the dead. That didn't mean I was willing to go through it again.

Come on. Show yourself. Images began to swim in my head—flashes of blood. Screams. It was what I'd seen when I touched Mace but sped up and fragmented. This was the right ghost, all right. Now I just needed to hold on a little longer so that it could show me something useful. Something personal.

The ghost withdrew from me, as though it could read my intent. *Crap.*

I watched as the buzzing black vortex of dark energy leaped at Mace. It smacked against the protection of the salt like bugs on a windshield. Its roar of rage shook the ground beneath my feet. I could tell that Mace felt it, too. It was a warm September night and his breath came in puffs better suited to late November. The ghost charged again. This time, the line of salt quivered beneath the assault.

Not good. It had lost interest in me for the time being and was going to snap at Mace until it managed to break the circle. All it needed was a hair's width of a crack and it could get in. I couldn't risk that.

I cupped my right hand and filled it with salt. Damn, but it stung when it hit those cuts. My eyes watered. I stepped forward and flung the salt at the ghost. The breeze caught most of it, but the spirit hissed in pain.

"When I tell you to run, I want you to get back to the graveyard as fast as you can," I told Mace, pouring more salt into my stinging palm.

"What about you?" he asked.

"I can save myself tonight, thanks." I closed my fist around the salt and drew back my arm, "Now run!"

He didn't argue, he just did what he was told, which actually kind of surprised me. Not too many people would trust that I knew what I was doing. Or maybe he just wanted to get the hell out of there.

I flung the salt just as the ghost reared back to give chase. The tiny grains got caught up in the wind, and barely grazed the spirit. It wasn't enough to scatter it, but just enough to piss it off. Great. It whipped around, gathering itself into a vaguely humanoid form. I couldn't tell if it was male or female, and right then it didn't matter. I barely had enough time to pour more salt into my palm as it lunged. Instead of throwing the salt, I wrapped my fist around it, drew back, and punched the ghost in the "face." The force of the blow reverberated all the way up my arm. It was like hitting a brick wall. My fist opened and salt poured out.

The ghost hung suspended in the air for a second and then exploded into black dust and salt shrapnel. I turned my head to protect my eyes and caught the blast on the cheek. Ouch.

I didn't waste any time, either. I'd only wounded the thing. It wouldn't take it long to regroup and come after us again, and this time it would be *really* mad. I didn't want to face that kind of anger with nothing more than a can of kitchen salt and cute shoes. I ran.

The rope ladder was harder to go up than down, and my bloody hands didn't make it any easier. Neither did the pounding of my heart. I was going to die of a heart attack if I didn't get to hallowed ground quick.

Mace waited for me on the Fairfield side of the wall and helped me down from the tree. It wasn't until I was on the ground that I realized how badly I was shaking.

"Are you okay?" he asked.

I nodded. My teeth were chattering.

He grabbed my hands and turned them palms up. "Shit."
"I'll be f-fine. We g-gotta go."

We ran to the car. I honestly didn't know how I managed it on my wobbly legs. Mace practically shoved me into the passenger seat. I was still fumbling with my seat belt when we tore out of there, headed back to Kevin's.

"You saw it, right?" he demanded. Other than being pale and a little wild-eyed he'd come out of this in surprisingly good shape. I'd seen grown men turn into bawling babies in the presence of lesser specters. "What was it?"

I leaned back in my seat. My heart was finally slowing down. "I don't know," I told him, looking at my bloody hands. "But for all our sakes, I'd better find out."

WREN

Lark was in trouble. I could feel it.

"They should be back by now," Ben stated, watching out the window at the night. He sat at the kitchen table drinking a cup of coffee. It smelled really good. Lark let me have coffee with her sometimes. It smelled better than it tasted. He took a drink, then turned to look at his friends. "Shouldn't they?" He was worried about Lark—I could feel it. Did he have a crush on my sister?

Kevin rubbed a hand over the back of his neck. He was worried, too. The light above his head reflected in his glasses, preventing me from seeing his eyes. "They've only been gone half an hour."

Gage helped himself to the box of donuts that sat on the table. "Think they went to the asylum?"

"They'd have to climb the tree," Roxi remarked.

My sister had not been dressed for tree climbing.

"In those shoes?" Sarah shook her head. "I should have lent Lark my sneakers."

The bunch of them traded looks that increased my anxiety. I had promised Lark that I would stay there so she didn't have to worry about me, but that didn't seem like such a good idea anymore. I wanted to go to her. I knew better, though. Despite my worry, it wouldn't have been a good idea for me to suddenly show up where she was. I would attract more ghosts. Lark and I together could possibly attract them all if we didn't take precautions, for which we didn't have the provisions on hand. In my wanting to help I might have only made things worse.

Like I had in Bell Hill.

Still, if I couldn't go to her, I could reach out. "Normal" twins often had an incredible bond, but Lark and I weren't normal—at least not in the common sense. Most humans were bound to the earth by the physical anchor of their bodies. Ghosts were often bound by their remains. There wasn't much left of me in that little grave, but Lark's body was made up of the same DNA, making her body almost like my own, which was why I could possess her so easily—and how I could find her without really trying. All I had to do was let go of the place I was in and let my consciousness (because, really, that was almost all I was in this world, along with some potent energy) reach out to the one that was the most like mine.

Something brushed up against me—not physically, of course. It was like another consciousness rustling against mine. Just a tickle and then it was gone. I didn't know what it was and I didn't care. Probably just another ghost. Maybe one near my sister.

I found her. Latched onto her.

My heart—and I do have one, just not in the mortal sense of the word—fluttered desperately inside me. My sister was afraid. Lark, who was always so foolishly brave, who defiantly stared down danger and dared it to come for her, had encountered something dark. Something that scared her despite the fact that she didn't fear death.

And she'd done it for me, because I wanted to help these stupid kids. Because I wanted them—Kevin—to like me. Because I wanted friends. They just wanted out of the mess they'd blundered into. And they had no idea of what that mess was all about. And while my sister might not fear death, I very much wanted her to live. I wanted to witness every day of what ought to be a very long life.

I pulled back, returning to myself. I looked at the teenagers gathered in the kitchen. They looked worried. And bored. Why weren't they talking about how to get themselves out of this mess? Why were they so ignorant of my kind and the damage we could inflict? From what I could tell, television was positively crammed with programs about so-called ghost hunters. Surely there had to be information available? And yet, here they sat, staring at one another, or the walls. Even Kevin seemed at a loss.

If Lark got hurt because of them...

"Do you feel that?" Sarah asked, lifting her head. She was a gorgeous girl, with all that blond hair and bright blue eyes. The wraith's infection would make short work of her looks.

Ben glanced at her, his dark hair falling into his eyes. "It's cold."

Roxi shivered. "It's really cold."

"Wren?" Kevin was on his feet, coming to stand in the middle of the kitchen, not far from where I was. "Is that you?"

Oh, dear. It *was* me. My emotional state was making me manifest. Kevin's breath came in visible puffs. Sarah rubbed her arms. The others looked at each other.

And then they looked at the cupboards as the doors flew open. Cutlery rattled as the drawer jerked out. The overhead light began to flicker.

They were worried now. Afraid now, but not for Lark. For themselves.

One of the lightbulbs above Kevin's head cracked.

"Move!" I yelled at him.

He heard me, lunging out of the way just as glass exploded and rained down where he'd been standing.

"What the hell?" Gage half ducked, arms over his head. "What's her problem?"

"I'm sorry," I said. "I'm sorry. I'm sorry." This was so embarrassing.

"I know you are," Kevin replied. The one benefit of a manifestation was that I was easier for mediums to hear and communicate with. He turned.

He looked at me. I mean, right at me. He *saw* me. I have to admit, my hand went to my hair. I had no idea what I looked like at that moment—I could have tentacles or rot-face, something horrible, meant to terrify.

Kevin smiled a little. Probably no rot-face, then. "I know

you're worried about Lark. We're worried, too, but I need you to relax, okay?"

Roxi looked in my direction. "Yeah, Wren. We're worried about her, too." Then, to Kevin, "Anything we can do?"

"Ghostly shoulder rub?" Ben suggested. Kevin frowned at him.

I laughed. Maybe these people were my friends after all. At least they hadn't run away screaming.

"It's warming up again," Sarah remarked.

Kevin took a small broom and dustpan from one of the lower cupboards I'd opened and started cleaning up the glass from the lightbulb. I closed what drawers and cupboards I could, but the more calm I became, the less strength I had. Gage came over and watched as I closed the cutlery drawer. I could feel the infection that was taking hold of him. It was like a hot, greasy smear over his soul.

"That is *so* cool," he mused. "I wonder if she'd help me clean my room?"

"No," Kevin and I chorused. I knew he heard me because he smiled, but his gaze didn't quite reach me. I guess him seeing me once was all I got. I'd been lucky to get that.

Gage shrugged. "Whatever."

That was when the door flew open and in walked Mace and Lark. I took one look at my sister and froze. I'd been too distracted to feel her near. Her hair was a mess, her clothes were dirty—she had a huge run in her tights—and her hands were bloody. But more concerning than even that was the look on her face. I'd seen that expression before. I'd seen it when she was in that awful place. It was a face that said things were bad, and that she was prepared to fight, quite possibly to the death.

I didn't like that face—her ghost-fighting face. I wanted my sister to live a long and happy life, and I wanted to experience it with her every step of the way.

Sarah hugged Mace. He winced when she pressed against him. Ben clapped him on the shoulder. Out of all of them, I noticed the infection less in Ben. I didn't know why, but some humans had a stronger resistance to spiritual wounds. It didn't seem to have to do with religion, but with the strength of their soul.

"Oh, my God, your hands." Roxi's dark eyes were as big as saucers as she stared at Lark's bloody fingers. "We've got to clean those. What happened?"

"It attacked you, didn't it?" I asked, following my sister to the sink.

"Your ghost wanted a little taste of me, too." Lark turned on the water and stuck her hands beneath the faucet. She hissed when the warm wet struck her skin. "It looks worse than it is."

It could have been worse; we both knew that. My sister had experienced worse. She healed from these sorts of wounds quickly, but they could still hurt her.

"So, did you get rid of it?" Gage asked.

Patting her hands with paper towel, Lark turned to him with a scowl. She was in more pain than she let on. Pain and uncertainty always made her cranky. "What do you think? Do you feel like it's gone? Or do you still have a little sweat at the base of your spine?"

The boy drew back, hiding a little behind his shoulder-length black hair.

"You don't have to talk like we're idiots," Sarah insisted hotly. "Or like you're superior because you know something about ghosts. We didn't ask for this."

Lark tossed the rust-stained paper towel in the garbage. "No? So you hadn't heard stories about Haven Crest before you decided to go for a midnight stroll on its grounds? You don't really expect me to buy that crap, do you? You all went there looking to have a little scare, maybe find a ghost. Well, congratufuckinglations, you found one."

Ben straightened. "Hey..."

Lark held up her hand. "Look, I get it. I know you didn't ask for this, but you got it, and you've asked me to help fix it. Well, if you want my help, don't frigging lie to me. Don't tell me you weren't hoping for something to happen, and don't get all defensive when I call you on it." She walked right up to Sarah and looked down at her. "You want to think I'm a bitch? Fine, but I'm the only thing standing between you and a pretty crap death, so you'll forgive me if sometimes I get a little superior."

I think everyone in the room held their breath for a second while the two of them faced off. I got the distinct impression that Sarah was not accustomed to being "talked back to."

"All right," Sarah said, holding my sister's gaze. She smiled. "What next, bitch?"

Lark actually grinned, which seemed to be a surprise to everyone but me. "We need to find out who we're up against."

"A lot of people died in that place," Kevin reminded them. "That's not going to be easy."

Lark held up her hands. A myriad of tiny cuts stood out against the pale of her skin. "Yeah, but our guy has a thing for razors."

The whole bunch of them smiled at each other—as though they'd made some sort of fantastic discovery. As though everything was going to be all right.

But it wasn't. I could have told them that.

chapter five

LARK

"It's an old ghost. Strong. Angry. This isn't the first time it's hurt people, but it's been dormant for a while and now it's hungry."

It was just Wren and me. We were at home, in my—our—bedroom. I was in bed and she lay beside me on top of the covers. Nan had been asleep when we got home so I didn't disturb her, but in the morning I planned to be up front with her about what was going on. I loved a good lie as much as the next person, but I didn't want to lie to the one person who wanted me and had put her reputation on the line to support me.

Plus, Nan had lived here her entire life. She knew about the town and its history. Maybe she knew about its ghosts, too.

"Why didn't you tell the others this?" There were things Wren really understood about being mortal, and then were things that still gave her trouble—like the difference between a lie and bending the truth for someone else's benefit. She was learning, though.

"They didn't need to be any more afraid than they already were." Sometimes when people were really scared they did really stupid things. "If I want them to help me—us—stop this thing, I need them smart."

My sister smiled teasingly. "You want their help? Or *Mace's* help?"

I rolled my eyes. "Please. That's just too uncomfortable to even joke about. There's got to be stories around about this thing—it's too powerful for someone not to have pissed off before this. Hopefully we can narrow it down to one or two ghosts, but then we're going to have to go inside Haven Crest."

Wren's expression grew serious. "Can you do that?"

I shrugged. "I have to. I'm the only one who can see the dead and talk to the living." How poetic that sounded. "Other than Kevin, and I don't think he's ready for that." I wasn't being snotty, just truthful.

"I'm going with you."

My first thought was to tell her no, but I realized that was stupid. I nodded. "We're stronger together."

Her smile took up most of her face—seriously. It was like the freaking Cheshire cat.

"That's really disturbing," I told her—her teeth were almost the size of dominoes. "Stop it."

She laughed, and let her features go back to normal as she snuggled up against me.

"You didn't make out with Kevin when you were driving my body, did you?"

She looked put out. "No!"

Now I grinned. "Are you mad because I asked, or because you didn't think of it at the time?"

"Both." Yeah, it never occurred to her to lie, either.

I laughed.

"It's not funny!" Wren declared, soundlessly jumping off the bed. "If you like a boy you can see him whenever you want, and he can see you. I have to borrow you or manifest for him to see me!"

My laughter died. "Manifest? When did you manifest?" She didn't lie, but she could conveniently not mention things.

She looked sheepish. "Earlier tonight. It must have been when you got hurt. I felt you were in trouble and I couldn't stop it."

Well, crap. I hadn't even worried about that. I'd seen her do her crazy-ass ghost thing before, but that was just it—I had been there with her. I should have realized it could happen without me present. Hell, it probably happened easier without me around.

"Are you okay?" I asked first. And then, "Did anyone get hurt?"

She shook her head, vibrant hair bouncing around her shoulders. It wasn't fair her having that hair. Maybe I could dye mine. Mom would never let me, but Nan might. "No. A lightbulb blew up. That was it."

Okay, that was a relief. When I was in the hospital I once saw her take out a couple of windows. An orderly got pretty cut up. I wasn't too upset about it—I wasn't upset at all—but it had been pretty freaky to witness. I've never been afraid of Wren, but sometimes I was afraid *for* her.

"The glass almost hit Kevin," she confessed. She looked wrecked over it. "I could have hurt him."

"But you didn't," I reminded her. Something in her expression bothered me. She looked way more upset about this than I figured she ought to be. Usually she only looked this way when she'd done something that affected me.

Oh, *hell.* Someone should really smack me in the head. The guy had been looking after her grave the entire time I was gone. You didn't do that for a random ghost you met once. That was a caring gesture. That was something you did for someone you cared about.

God, she was so freaking good about forgetting to mention things. But this was big. This was part of her life she'd purposefully cut me out of. That hurt. A lot.

"How long have you been seeing him?" My voice was hoarse around the huge lump in my throat.

She didn't try to deny it. "As often as I can. Most of the time he doesn't even know I'm there. But tonight, when I manifested? He saw me then." Was she about to cry? "He actually saw me."

I didn't know how to feel about this. Oh, I knew how I felt—sad, happy and slightly afraid. Angry, too. I wanted to rant and rave about being locked up in that place while she flirted across dimensions, but how could I do that when flirting was something I could do anytime I wanted and she was the one trapped and unable to reach out? And why was I so afraid that she would abandon me for Kevin, when she *couldn't* abandon me?

So maybe what I was feeling was worry. Nothing good could come of this. They could chat and flirt and do whatever it was they were doing. He might tell himself that he couldn't hurt her because she was dead. They might even tell themselves nothing could come of it, but someday Kevin was going to meet a living, breathing girl and break my sister's heart.

I was still pissed that she hadn't told me about him. "Why didn't you say anything?"

She sat back down on the bed, barely disturbing the blankets. "Haven't you ever wanted something just for yourself?"

"Not really," I replied. "I've always had you, so I didn't need another secret." I'd thought that I was enough for her, too. Just me and Wren against the world, right?

Wren smiled. "Kevin's the only person other than you who ever heard me." Then her smile faded. "Those times when you shut me out, or were too drugged to acknowledge me, I went to him. You'd never left me before—not like that. He made me feel less alone, and he made me believe that you would come back."

Great, so now I owed him for that. More important, I owed Wren. I swallowed against the lump in my throat. "I didn't mean to leave you, I just let them make me forget for a little while." Lame.

"And then you wanted to protect me from the ghosts."

I nodded. "Then that." Several of the more malicious ghosts in Bell Hill had decided that they wanted Wren to join them, become one of them. There'd been a time when I'd been terrified they would succeed, and that she would leave me forever to be a vicious, hurtful thing. It wasn't something I liked to think about. That was why the vision of her with the eyeballs had really freaked me out.

"Are you mad at me?"

"No." I meant it. Maybe I was jealous or whatever, because even my dead sister seemed to be able to get a guy, but I wasn't mad.

Cool fingers curled around mine. "How are your hands?"

I opened them up so she could look. The cuts weren't so angry anymore and were already scabbing over.

"You could have gotten hurt."

"Nah," I argued. "Not during the first dance. It just wanted to check me out. I don't imagine Haven Crest has seen anything like us before."

"Do you suppose anyone has seen sisters like us before?"

"I don't know. Probably?" I mean we were pretty freaky, but we couldn't be the first or only ones. Could we? "I mean, there have been twins in dad's family before."

Wren tilted her head. "I wonder…" Apparently that was all she was going to say.

"Mmm." I glanced at the clock. It was getting late. "I should do a little research on Haven Crest."

"Can I help?"

"You can rub my feet."

She rolled her eyes at me, but that didn't stop her from schooching down to the bottom of the bed and setting one of my feet in her lap. I sighed. Wren gave the best foot rubs.

An hour later, my eyelids starting to droop after reading crap account after crap account of "spirit activity" at Haven Crest, I bolted upright. "I found something."

Wren looked up from her own reading. She liked to read my textbooks and was already deep into the play we had to read in English class. "What?"

"It's from a diary of a girl named Maybelline Scout who

was born in 1900. 'May 2, 1918—Recently I visited my friend Anne at Haven Crest hospital. She's been in a steady decline since the death of her fiancé, Russell, fighting the Germans.'" I glanced up. "Anne would have been sixteen or seventeen at that time. Can you imagine being engaged at that age?"

Wren shrugged. "Iloana was fourteen when she married her first husband."

Iloana was an old woman Wren sometimes talked to. She'd had several husbands apparently. I often wondered if Iloana hadn't helped all of her misters into their graves.

"Keep reading," my sister commanded.

"'My sister Honoria, who was always sensitive to spirits, was with me, which resulted in being a horrible mistake. A few unpleasant spirits haunting the hospital found Honoria and began to make sport of her—and poor Anne, whose mental state was already frail. I had never seen a ghost before that day, but I saw that one as clear as glass—a man with a straight razor...'" I stopped. Swallowed. My tongue was suddenly dry as sand. "'...hurt my sister badly, and provoked her to the point that she attacked both Anne and myself with a sort of violence uncharacteristic of my dear sister even at her worst. I struck the spirit with a poker from the fireplace, which banished it, but not before it left me with a vicious wound for my trouble. As for Honoria, it took two days for her to return to herself. Anne, I'm afraid, never recovered, her sanity quite undone by the experience.'"

Silence hung between us, thick and tense.

"That doesn't mean it will happen to me," Wren protested.

"No?" I looked her right in the eye. "Wren, if the ghost

did that to someone who was alive but sensitive, what will it do to you?"

She scowled. "Nothing worse than what it might do to you," she shot back. "That girl was obviously unprepared for the sort of energy that saturates places like Haven Crest. After Bell Hill, I know to take precautions."

"Do you?" I asked. "I don't mean to be a bitch, but neither of us have gone up against anything like this before. Bell Hill was a relatively new facility, with modern treatments. We're going to be walking into a place that lobotomized people with a spike through the eye, chained them up like beasts and performed experiments on their patients like they were little more than lab rats. There's going to be a lot of pain and suffering."

My sister looked me dead in the eye with a gaze that told me not to bother arguing. "We don't have a choice, Lark."

"Sure we do. We don't go."

Wren's eyes widened. "We can't do that!"

"Yeah," I said with a humorless laugh, "we can."

"We promised them we'd help them!"

"No promise is worth putting you in danger—putting both of us in danger. It's stupid."

"It could kill them."

"Only if it gets really bad." Even as I spoke I cringed. I sounded like such a cow.

"We can stop it. We're the only people who can."

I looked at her. "Why do you care? It's not like Kevin was with them. He'll be fine."

"The rest of them won't be."

"It's their own fault."

She bristled. My bed trembled. "I can't believe you'd be so cruel."

"You going to freak out?" I goaded. "This is what I'm worried about, Wren. You can't even keep your shit together with me. How are you going to stand up against dozens of angry ghosts? We're not going in."

Wren went still—statue still. No human could be so motionless. "Even at my worst I'll still stand up better against any number of ghosts than they will alone. And you will, too. We're doing this, Lark. We're not going to lose the first friends we've had in a long time."

And that was how she won the argument, because she was right. "We'll need to make sure we take extra precautions—and teach them how to protect themselves, too. Maybe your boyfriend knows something helpful."

She brightened at the mention of him. Silently, I gagged. I was self-aware enough to know I was jealous. Come on, there had to be something wrong if your dead sister got more play than you did.

"I'm going to bed," I announced. "It's late." I wasn't really tired, but I didn't want to talk anymore—argue anymore.

My sister looked disappointed. After sixteen years I'd think she'd be used to me having to sleep. "I guess I'll keep reading." She'd loved books ever since she realized that all she had to do to read them was phase into them. I wasn't sure how it worked, and I didn't care so long as it kept her entertained.

I shrugged. "Whatevs."

"Maybe I'll go see Iloana."

Another shrug. "I'll see you in the morning. You can catch me up." I set my laptop on the table beside the bed and pulled the blankets up around me. I turned off the light. Wren didn't need it anyway—ghosts had their own natural luminescence.

"Good night," Wren whispered.

I sighed. She was almost impossible to stay annoyed at. "Night."

I rolled onto my side. It was a warm night, but the breeze through my window was just cool enough. I didn't expect to fall asleep as fast as I did. As much as I needed rest, I didn't enjoy sleeping. Sleeping brought dreams with it, and my dreams could get freaky.

But that night my dreams weren't freaky. I would have welcomed freaky. Instead I dreamed that I was the ghost and Wren was real.

Everyone seemed much happier with that situation—including Wren.

Including me.

WREN

I didn't read, even though I should have. I didn't stay in the house, even though I should have. I should have spent my time trying to figure out a way to keep myself from hurting my sister and new friends, but I didn't do that, either.

Instead, I went to Kevin. I could lie and say I went to him hoping he had answers, but I'd rather not say anything at all. I didn't see the point in lying when you can just stay quiet.

If there was one thing I could say was my favorite part of being a ghost, it was just how easy it was for me to get around. Lark had to walk or drive, but all I had to do was think about where I wanted to be and I could go there. Lots of ghosts were bound to one or a few locations, but I was different. A lot of us who died as babies are this way—we have nothing to bind us, nothing that we hold on to or let hold on to us. All I had was Lark, and she didn't need me to be glued to her side, so I wasn't. If she knew she had the power to bind me she'd use it, so I didn't think anyone would blame me for not sharing that information with her.

Well, except for Lark, of course.

I understood her concern—what happened at Bell Hill with those ghosts hadn't been fun. But did I stop her from doing what she thought she needed to do? No. She needed to stop being so overprotective and treating me like I was fragile. In case she hadn't noticed, I was the one who was the supernatural creature out of the two of us. I was stronger than she gave me credit for.

The ghosts at Bell Hill hadn't been able to make me like them, even though they'd tempted me. It felt really good to give in to that darkness, but not good enough. My bond with Lark saved me then, and it would be strong enough to save me again—not that I'd need it. I was stronger now—I'd made sure of it.

Kevin was in bed when I arrived. I thought he might be asleep, but he was reading. Propped up against a mountain of soft pillows in a T-shirt and sweatpants, he repeatedly bent the toes on his left foot, cracking them in an almost steady rhythm.

"You shouldn't do that," I said.

He looked up from his book, frowning. He looked very edgy and dangerous when he frowned, and I liked it. This was an odd reaction, I thought, but I seemed to like everything about him, so his frown might as well be added to the list.

"Wren?" He glanced around, as though expecting to see someone else. "What are you doing here?"

I hadn't thought that maybe he wouldn't be as happy to see me as I was to see him. Why would he be? He had friends and a life. And it wasn't like he could see me. There'd been that brief moment earlier, but that was it. Maybe he thought I was a complete lunatic after that.

"I'm sorry," I said. "You're busy. I'll go."

"No!" He jumped off the bed. "I'm not busy. You don't have to go. Stay. Are you okay?"

"I'm fine. Sorry about earlier. I lost control."

He shrugged, smiling a little at a point just over my left shoulder. He couldn't see me. Something inside me sank. "It was just a lightbulb. Besides, it was pretty cool after it stopped being scary."

I moved closer to him. "Cool? Really? I thought maybe you wouldn't want to see me anymore."

"Are you kidding? Of course not. It was actually kinda hot."

I'd long ago stopped wondering at the language of the living. Temperature wasn't something that had a large impact on my existence, but I'd never figured out how it was possible for something to be both hot and cool, even though I'd heard Lark use these same terms as though they were interchangeable. What I did know, however, was that *hot* was very often used to describe something as sexy. I didn't mind that.

"Did I look awful?" It was a vain question, but I had to know.

"You were gorgeous," he blurted. "You *are* gorgeous."

"Oh." There was a fluttering in my stomach. I still felt these things even though I technically had no form in the human realm.

"Is that okay?" he asked. He looked worried.

I giggled. Lark would be so disgusted with me being so stereotypically girlie. "It's more than okay."

He grinned. I grinned. "I wish I could see you now," he said.

I reached out for him, settling my hand on his arm. We'd worked on this the past couple of times I'd seen him—which hadn't been as frequent as I would have liked. "You can," I told him. "You just have to *look*."

The contact helped. I had to focus all my energy on the point where our skin met, but it was enough. I felt myself shiver through the veil, energy taking form. I knew it was working when Kevin gasped.

Our eyes met. I smiled at the wonder in his wide gaze. That was worth the tension pressing down on me—the struggle it took just to make myself visible to him. "Hi."

His jaw closed. "Hi." His fingers reached for my face, only to pass through me. I shivered at the trail of warmth he left behind, saw the disappointment in his eyes as the connection was broken. At least he'd seen me—really seen me—even if only for a second.

"Can I try something?" I asked. My voice sounded low and strange.

"Sure." He didn't ask what, just trusted me. I wished my sister would give me the same benefit of the doubt. Okay, that was unfair. Lark trusted me more than she trusted any-one, but that wasn't always saying much.

I stepped closer. And closer. If I needed to breathe, I would have taken a deep breath. But I didn't need to breathe, so I hesitated just for a second. This might go far beyond Kevin's sense of "sure."

I slipped into him, beneath his clothes, through the warm layers of flesh and muscle and blood, into that warm cavity deep inside all humans. I didn't know if it was his soul, but it was a place that welcomed me, that closed over me like... well, I didn't know what, but it was beautiful.

His breath caught.

Breathe.

He inhaled. Exhaled.

Is this okay?

"You're inside me." His voice cracked.

Do you want me to leave? I hoped he wouldn't say yes.

"No." He sat down on the bed, then stretched out on the mattress. I could feel his heart racing. I could feel *him.* "No, I want you to stay."

And so I did. Even when he fell asleep, I stayed with him a little while, exploring him at a spiritual level. I didn't leave until I had to. Kevin was still asleep, but my sister would be awake soon. I didn't want Lark to ask me where I'd been, or what I'd been doing. This wasn't something I wanted to keep from her because she'd be mad. It was something I wanted to keep from her because I wanted it to be just mine. Private. With Kevin I wasn't a ghost, I was a girl, and that wasn't something I was about to share.

Not even with Lark.

chapter six

LARK

I woke up a couple of times before getting up for good Saturday morning. Once was around four and the second time right around seven. Both times it took me a second to figure out what was wrong. I was alone—totally alone. That hadn't happened since Bell Hill, and for that reason it made me anxious that my sister wasn't in the room with me.

I knew where she was.

The third time I woke up it was just after nine. I hadn't slept well for the six hours that I'd been in bed, but it was good enough. This time my sister was sitting at the window, staring out.

"Hey," I said, tossing back the covers. "You been at that all night?"

"Good morning!" She flashed me a sunny smile. "Did you sleep well? I was thinking that maybe I should check the library in the Shadow Lands for any information on Haven Crest."

Some of my annoyance—and hurt—faded. I hadn't thought of that. I would have never thought of that. "Yeah, that would be a great idea. Worth a shot."

She looked so relieved—probably because she thought I hadn't noticed that she hadn't answered my question. "Do you want me to do that now?"

I shrugged. "Mayzel." I'd picked up the term from my friend Jess in Bell Hill. It was slang for "might as well." Drove me nuts, but I still used it. "I have to eat and shower."

"Okay." She watched me for a few seconds. "Are you all right?"

Guilty much? It wasn't who she saw, or even that she was sneaky about it—it was that she was purposefully shutting me out.

Over a guy.

"It's morning," I replied drily. "No, I'm not all right. I need coffee."

She didn't look convinced and I didn't care. I'd die for Wren, but right now it stung and I didn't want to look at her. I felt left out. The feeling wasn't new, but the fact that it had been caused by my sister was.

She left while I was pulling on my robe. After a promise that she'd see me later, she simply disappeared into thin air. Just faded out of this world into her own. To be honest, I was glad to be alone.

I went downstairs to the kitchen. Nan had breakfast ready—she fed me like I was a lumberjack. I sat down at the table to a plate loaded with bacon and eggs and fried bread. So good. She sat down across from me to a plate just as full. The woman was slim, but she ate like a monster.

"Where's your sister this morning?" she asked as she poured me a cup of coffee. "I didn't hear you talking to her on your way down."

I chewed a piece of bacon and swallowed. "Shadow Lands. Hey, Nan, do you know if there's ever been anyone like Wren and me in the family before?"

She thought for a moment. "I remember hearing stories about my grandmother, that she was 'different,' for lack of a better term. My father called her eccentric, but I don't know the full extent. I'm afraid he didn't talk about her much. Would you like me to see what I can find out?"

"That would be awesome, thanks." Did I sound too desperate? Look too eager?

She smiled at me and watched me for a moment—almost long enough for me to start squirming. "It's okay if there's never been anyone like the two of you before, you know that."

I nodded. "It would just be nice to have some information if there was."

"There are several trunks in the attic that have been in the family for generations. I'll take a look after breakfast."

"Can I help?"

She shook her head. "Why don't you go out? It's a beautiful Saturday. Go have some fun."

Fun. It had been a while since I'd experienced that. Maybe Roxi would want to get together, or that cute Ben... I dumped some sugar in my cup. "Hey, Nan, there's something I want to tell you."

She smiled as she lifted her cup to her mouth. "Let me guess, you've stumbled upon someone who needs your help with a ghost and you don't want me to worry about you?"

What the hell? "Uh…sorta." I added cream to the cup. "How did you know?"

"Lucky guess. I figured it was only a matter of time. People like you are always going to stumble upon people who need them. Unfortunately, I can't promise I won't worry. I do appreciate you telling me, though."

I squirmed. "I didn't want to keep it from you."

She reached across the table and took my hand. She was strong for an old chick. "You're allowed to have secrets, Lark. I'm here to listen whenever you want me to, and I'll do anything I can to help you, understand? This is your home, and I'm not going to send you away for being who you are."

Unlike my parents. She didn't need to say it—I could see the pain in her eyes. My father—her son—had told me I couldn't stay with them anymore. He didn't want me, so he'd told me it was too hard for my mother and sent me to live with *his* mother. I scared him, and we all knew it.

But I didn't scare Nan.

Crap. My throat closed so tight my breath squeaked. My eyes burned. I tried to stop the tears, but I couldn't. I hadn't cried in… Well, I didn't remember the last time I'd felt that familiar salt sting on my cheeks. Next thing I knew, my grandmother was standing next to me, holding my head against her stomach as I sobbed, clinging to her like she was all I had left in the world.

Other than Wren, she was.

After I finished soaking her shirtfront and recovered from the embarrassment of it, Nan and I finished breakfast. Wren was still gone, so I decided that I was going to go out in pursuit of this "fun" Nan spoke of. I went out to the garage, found my old kayak that had been stored there when we moved to Mass and strapped it to the hood of the dreaded Beetle. Then I made the short drive to nearby Marle Lake. I was just strapping on my life vest when another kayak joined my very girlie one on the launch.

"Never pegged you for a pink girl," came a familiar voice.

Behind my sunglasses, I closed my eyes and silently swore. I glanced over my shoulder at Mace's smirking face. He stood just behind me in a T-shirt, board shorts and sandals. "I'm full of surprises," I replied. "You, on the other hand, are exactly the sort of guy I'd picture owning a black one. No skull and crossbones?"

"Thought that might be a bit much." He glanced around, as though looking for someone. I looked, too. Was Sarah with him? I didn't know if I would be happy or disappointed if she was.

"Hi, Wren," he said. "If you're here."

I almost smiled at the self-conscious tone of his voice. "She's not." And really, I didn't know whether to be impressed or pissed that he thought to say hi to her. I mean, he had yet to say hello to *me*.

Mace seemed surprised. "We're alone?"

"Again," I reminded him. "Careful, people will start to talk about you spending time with the crazy girl."

He met my gaze——or at least I think he did. I couldn't really see his eyes behind his sunglasses. "I think I can handle it." He nodded at the lake. "Want me to give you a push?"

I made a face. *"No."* And then, because I realized how I sounded, I added, "Thanks anyway."

He chuckled and gave his head a little shake. Wow, didn't

need to be a genius to figure that one out. He had obviously just realized how obnoxious I was. "Yeah, okay."

I sighed, and turned back toward the water. Did fate have it in for me? Why did it insist on shoving Mace in my face every time it got the chance?

I shoved my kayak into the water and hopped in, just barely getting my feet wet. I picked up the paddle and dipped one end into the water, then the other, finding my rhythm. I loved it out on the lake. Usually Wren was with me, perched up on the bow, trailing her feet through the water—or water through her feet, I guess. I didn't miss her yelling, "I'm the king of the world!" like she did practically every damn time.

Mace's boat glided up alongside mine. "So, you're not going to talk to me?"

I didn't look at him, but kept my gaze focused on the far shore. "You want to talk?"

"Don't you?"

"Sure, Mace. What would you like to talk about? How you found me sliced open like a trout, lying in my own blood? Or the fact that an angry-ass ghost ripped you a new one?" Sometimes I pushed the "bitch" button before I could stop myself.

"Are those my only choices?" If sarcasm was water he'd be drowning right now. "Because I think we've done both to death."

I chuckled at his choice of words. "Okay, you pick, then." I had settled into an easy pace now, slicing through the water. "Obviously, I suck at conversation."

"You?" I didn't have to look to know he was smirking again. "But you're so friendly and open."

Normally I'd tell him to fuck off and paddle away, but I

didn't. I actually smiled. "Yeah, yeah. You can't think of a topic, either, can you?" How sad were we?

"Not so, buttercup." *Buttercup?* "I'm dying to know what your future plans are. Rock star? President? Goodwill ambassador?"

I laughed. I couldn't help it. "Therapist. I really just want to *help* people, you know?"

He grinned, teeth flashing in the sun. God, he was really gorgeous. Like, unfairly gorgeous. And the more time I spent with him, the less that fact intimidated me. "Well, you're so caring and giving."

"What about you?" I adjusted my pace to match his, and we drifted along side by side. "Are you going to follow in your father's footsteps?"

He snorted. "Not likely."

When he didn't say anything else, I prodded, "So?"

"You seriously want to know?" He seemed surprised by the idea. To be honest, I was a little surprised, too. I actually wanted to know, and normally I didn't care about other people that much. Not when I could count the ones who had cared about me on one hand—on the first two fingers of that hand.

"Yeah. I want to know."

"History prof."

I never would have guessed that in a million years. Funny thing was, I could easily imagine him in front of a room of people, holding their attention. "Cool. Any particular period or civilization?"

"Mostly European—Second World War."

I nodded. "I think you'd be good at that."

Mace stopped paddling, and I had to stop so I wouldn't lose him. "Did you just pay me a compliment?"

Heat rushed to my face. Thank God for the sun. "Don't let it go to your head."

"My heart, buttercup. I'm going to let it go straight to my heart."

I didn't like to be teased—it felt too much like mockery—but I didn't feel like Mace was making fun of me. What I did feel like was returning the honesty. "I want to be a shoe designer."

He started paddling again. "I can see it."

"I've never told anyone that," I blurted. Now, why the hell did I do that? "Not even Wren." I was sure she knew, though. She saw me drawing shoes all the time.

"Neither have I."

We paddled in silence for a bit—a comfortable silence. It was...weird. Nice.

"I was thinking," I began as we reached the opposite shore and began to turn, "that we might find answers faster if we all go together and researched Haven Crest."

"Good idea. I'm free this afternoon."

I blinked. "Okay."

"I'll call Kevin and the others. Meet at 'Nother Cup?"

I'd rather eat glass than have Kevin around. It wasn't that he was a jerk, though he could give me a run in the obnoxious race, it was that I didn't trust him with my sister. "Provided no one calls the cops on me again, that should be fine."

"Don't worry. I've got an in with local law enforcement."

I rolled my eyes.

By the time we made it back to shore it was almost noon.

Mace helped me strap my kayak to the Beetle, even though I said I didn't need his help. I felt compelled to help him lift his boat into the back of his father's truck.

"Give me your phone," he said, holding out his hand.

"Why?" I didn't know why I was so suspicious. What was he going to do? Change my ringtone? Criticize my choice of apps?

He gave me an impatient frown. "Hand it over, buttercup."

I took my phone from the pocket of my shorts and slapped it into his palm. "What's with this 'buttercup' crap?"

"You don't like it?" He wasn't even looking at me as he tapped away on the screen.

I shrugged. "Just wondering where it came from." Great dodge. I couldn't very well tell him that part of me liked it very much.

"I dunno. It suits you."

"Is that supposed to be a good thing?"

He laughed as his own phone rang. A man's muffled voice shouted, 'Answer your phone, idiot!"

"Nice," I commented. "Filled with self-loathing much?"

Mace only smiled. Then, he tapped my phone again and gave it back to me. The man's voice cut off. "Now you have my number and I have yours."

I stared at the phone. His number. I only had Nan's. Roxi had given me hers but I hadn't added her to my contacts yet. "Thanks."

"Sure." He started around the truck. "So, I'll see you around two at 'Nother Cup?"

"Sounds good." I turned to open the car door.

"Hey, Lark?"

I turned. He was looking at me over the top of the truck, the open door helping him balance as he stood on the threshold. "Yeah?"

Mace smiled. "We should do this again sometime." Then he dropped down into the seat and shut the door. The truck's engine roared to life as I stared dumbly. Then he was gone with nothing but a little puff of dust as his tires stirred up the sandy road.

What the hell had just happened? Had Mace Ryan and I just become friends?

WREN

The Shadow Lands were a lot like the living world, but less vibrant. The only way I can think to describe it was a perpetual twilight, caught between night and day. Everything was muted, but there was something shimmery about the place. It sounded like it ought to have been depressing and dark, but it was actually a beautiful place. Magical. I was real there—tangible. I'd forgotten how good that felt, I'd been spending so much time in Lark's world.

I wished she could have spent more time in mine, but she'd have to have died for that to happen, and I wasn't in a hurry to repeat that experience again. When Lark had tried to kill herself... No, she hadn't tried. Lark had succeeded in killing herself, at least for a short time. When Lark had killed herself it had felt like someone ripped my soul out. It hurt so much. Maybe it hurt because it wasn't her time. Regardless, it had pushed me into a state of manifestation that allowed me to reach out to Kevin—the first medium I'd found—and make him understand me. I was getting better at that now. I didn't need to get so upset to communicate, but I still had a lot to learn.

I wished I had someone to teach me, instead of figuring it out on my own, but the Shadow Lands were a huge place—just like the living world. My corner of it wasn't terribly populated, and those who were there weren't actually social. Ghosts were a lot like the living that way.

Though, I always wondered—how had I managed as a baby in this place? I didn't need to eat or drink, but surely I'd required some sort of care? It hadn't been Iloana who'd cared for me because I remembered the moment we met. So, who had it been, and why had they abandoned me just when I started having questions? I had no memory of anyone being there, but I'd never felt alone. Maybe there was someone who watched over dead children. To be honest, I'd never really cared enough to find out. I'd had Lark, and that was all that mattered.

I walked down a fairly modern street and turned a corner onto a Victorian alley. Pavement gave way to damp cobblestones and gas streetlamps. I loved this section of town, though it could be dangerous. Some humans—creatures—carried on in death as they had in life. Contrary to how humans seemed to act, death didn't make saints of them all. If you were unpleasant in life, you were probably unpleasant in death.

It wasn't just that the Shadow Lands looked like another time and place—it *was* another time and place. All of time and space existed here in various incarnations. There was a strange part of town not far from here where the ghosts weren't human. I didn't know where they came from. There were creatures like that all over—and strange little neighborhoods where they carried out their afterlife. And everyone usually kept to themselves. I used to find that safe and comforting, but now I blamed it for my ignorance of this world and my place in it.

A horse and carriage rattled past—they did that sometimes. I walked to the end of the alley and turned another corner onto another cobblestone street. This one was lined with fancy buildings—the kinds lords and ladies would have lived in. It inclined slowly up a low hill, and at the top of that hill sat a large stone building with huge columns and wide steps leading to the door.

The library.

I walked up the steps and through the double doors. There were a few spirits around but the cavernous building was much bigger on the inside than the outside. I didn't believe the laws of physics applied to the dead at all. There was a front desk, a few tables, and then rows of books that stretched on for miles and rose as high as a skyscraper. It went on for eternity.

Where did I even start to look?

"You look lost" came a voice from beside me.

I turned my head. A beautiful woman with long white hair like Lark's stood beside me. Her eyes were like ice, glittering brightly. She smiled, and I felt compelled to smile back even though something about her scared me a little.

"I came here to do some research," I admitted. "It's a little...overwhelming."

"Come with me."

I followed her to the desk, careful not to step on the hem of her long, opalescent gown. Sitting there was what looked like a small ivory horn mounted on an ebony stand. "Say what you want into this, and it will be brought to you."

I looked at her. "Really? That's it?"

She nodded, still smiling that serene yet sharp smile. "That's it."

"But how does it know to bring me the right one? What if there are books written by different people with the same name?"

She shrugged. "The library knows."

Lark would have called her a liar, but I didn't quite have the nerve. Instead, I decided to trust her. I leaned toward the horn and said clearly, "Haven Crest."

It was as though the building came to life—nothing quite so dramatic—but I could feel a vibration beneath my feet, like a giant creature far below had just woken up. In the distance I heard a whisper—was it something moving, or simply a sigh? It was coming from one of the stacks. I turned my head and watched as a small speck came toward me, growing ever larger. It was a spirit from some race I couldn't identify—a wraithlike creature with several arms and no discernible face. In its fingers it held several leather-bound volumes, which it placed on a podium at the end of the aisle.

The woman gestured for me to collect the books. "Ask and you shall receive."

"Weird," I whispered.

Soft laughter followed. "Indeed. I am glad to see you availing yourself of this world, Wrenleigh Noble. I had begun to fear the living held more appeal for you."

I went still. Slowly, I turned my head to look at her. She was watching me, still smiling. "How do you know my name?"

"I know all about you, Wren. I have ever since you first came here."

What? How was that possible? I'd never met her before. Had I? Was she one of those I'd wondered about just a few minutes ago? Someone who cared for dead children? "Who are you?"

"Emily." She said it like it ought to make sense to me, but it didn't.

"Nice to meet you, Emily." It seemed the right thing to say. "Thank you for your help."

I thought she might leave then, but she didn't. "What did you want to know about Haven Crest?"

"History," I replied. Lark must have rubbed off on me, because I thought twice about telling her everything. "Interesting stories. That sort of thing."

She smiled. "Let me guess, some children from the town have gotten themselves into trouble with a ghost from there."

I kept my eye on her. "How did you know?"

Emily shrugged. "Because they were doing that in my day, as well."

"You're from New Devon?" This was good! Wasn't it? If she was here, then she wasn't tied to the asylum. This place was like a halfway house for the dead, but those who haunted a place usually put so much of their energy into the haunt they couldn't come here—or they wouldn't. Haunting was a big commitment, meaning the spirit was very attached to that person, place or thing and didn't like to leave.

She tilted her head. "You really don't know who I am, do you?"

"Should I?"

"I suppose not. You haven't seen me since you were very young. Yes, I am from New Devon. What would you like to know about the unfortunate place known as Haven Crest?"

"Inmate information. We're looking for a ghost that might have used a straight razor as a weapon when it was human."

"A cutter?" She arched her eyebrow. She really did remind me of Lark. "That's something like the needle in the haystack, is it not?"

I shrugged. "It's a place to start."

"I suppose so. And these are things you and your sister must figure out for yourselves if you're going to traffic in both worlds." She walked over to the podium and picked up one of the volumes the library had brought forth. Then she offered the book to me.

"I shouldn't interfere, but take this."

It was huge. As far as places to start went it was one big shiny haystack. "What about the other volumes?"

"You don't need those."

"But there might be information—"

"*Wren.*" She put her hand on my arm, squeezing hard with her fingers. She glanced over her shoulder, as though worried someone might be watching. "*This* is the book you need."

I stared at her. She was so familiar and yet a complete stranger.

"Who are you?" I demanded. "Why are you helping me? Why now?"

"I'm a friend," she insisted. "And I'm helping you now because I am able. I'll explain everything when I can. Promise me you'll be careful."

She didn't even wait for me to promise before she simply

disappeared. One moment she was there and the next she was gone, leaving me holding the book she'd given me with a stupefied expression on my face.

"Helpful," I muttered. "Helpful and *weird*." My sister was definitely rubbing off on me. Holding the book to my chest, I closed my eyes and let this world slip away. It was like peeling back layers of spiderwebs—only not so sticky. For a moment, I existed in between dimensions. It was always tempting to just stay in that void where there was nothing but peace. I didn't stay, though. I didn't even linger. I opened my eyes to the familiar sight of my sister's bedroom—our bedroom.

I was alone. Where was Lark? And more important, what had we gotten ourselves into?

chapter seven

LARK

"Melanie's cousin bought the house. She said they had to rip up the carpet in that bedroom. Her blood soaked right through to the floorboards."

I froze a couple of feet away from the table where my new "friends" Sarah, Ben and Gage sat. Was Sarah talking about my old house? About me?

"You shouldn't repeat that kind of shit," Ben said.

"You're just saying that because you've got a thing for her," Sarah goaded.

Ben leaned forward on the forearm he rested on the table. "No, I'm saying it because I'm not a gossipy bitch."

I could kiss that boy.

I had two choices. I could be ashamed of what I'd done and walk away, or I could say fuck it. I pulled out a chair and sat down. They seemed really surprised to see me. "Actually, my parents had the carpet changed before they even sold the house. I don't know if there's a stain or not—I was locked up in Bell Hill at that point."

Sarah flushed. Now who was ashamed, bitch?

"You don't owe us an explanation," Ben reminded me. I looked at his mouth. Definitely kissable.

Sarah played with the plastic lid of her cup. "I didn't mean to be a bitch. You're just…" She met my gaze. "You're the only person I know who ever had the balls to actually, you know, *do* it."

"You mean try to kill myself?"

She nodded. I doubted her sincerity, but at least she'd apologized.

"If the idea of slicing your wrists open isn't appealing, you're probably not too keen on dying. Balls has nothing to do with it. I just really wanted to die."

Gage perked up, dark eyes brightening. "But Mace saved you."

I opened my mouth to congratulate him on his ability to tell me what I already knew, but never got to say a word because Sarah's head had snapped up and she was looking at me like I was contagious. "*Mace* saved you?"

"Yeah." How could she not have known that little tidbit? Maybe Melanie ought to have filled her in.

God, I wished I had a chai.

She looked completely pissed. If I was her I'd be more concerned about that narsty-assed scratch on her cheek. It was starting to look bad. In fact, none of them were looking too hot. Their wounds may not be visible to norms, but the circles under their eyes and their pale skin were.

"He never told me about that." And obviously she wasn't

impressed. How long had they been dating? And just *how* did you work finding someone practically dead into conversation?

Out of the corner of my eye I watched Ben leave the table. "To be honest, Sarah—"

"It wasn't any of your business" came Mace's voice from behind me. I didn't have to look to know that he had his gruff face on. And where did he get off finishing my sentences?

Sarah flushed, but her chin came up defiantly. "Everyone else seems to know."

"They didn't hear it from me." He sat down in the empty chair between me and her.

"That's true," Gage said. He had little drops of sweat beaded on his upper lip and pink splotches high on his cheeks. Was he running a fever? It was a warm day, and maybe his coffee was too hot, but I didn't think that was it. "Word got around about it, but Mace never said anything about any of it. To anybody. We were all pretty pissed at him, too." He chuckled—it turned to a strangled wheeze when I looked at him. "Sorry."

"Forget about it," I said, my gaze locked with his. I really didn't want to talk about it. "You feeling okay, Gage?"

He shrugged. "My little brother's sick—kept everyone in the house up half the night. I'm beat."

Maybe it wasn't the ghost riding him, then. These kinds of infections—and I'd only ever seen one like it before—were a ghost's way of marking humans as their own personal buffet. The ghost left a bit of themselves behind and that allowed them to feed more easily on the life force of their victim.

Ben returned to the table. He set a paper cup in front of me. It was a chai latte—I could smell the spicy deliciousness. How had he known? And why was he being so damn nice?

I lifted my gaze—right into his as he sat down. Out of all of them he looked the healthiest. I mean, aside from that healing black eye. He wasn't bulky, but he was definitely ripped. His snug T-shirt showed off his tanned, muscular arms. Made me wonder where the ghost had gotten him, and if he'd let me look…

I picked up my drink, the sweet-spicy smell filling my nose as heat filled my cheeks. "Thanks."

He nodded. "Sure." But we both knew that thank-you was for a whole lot more than just tea. He had to know I'd heard what he'd said to Sarah.

I turned to the others. "If any of you want to know about what I did, you might as well ask and get it out there so we avoid embarrassment later."

Gage looked around the table, as though waiting for someone else to go first, but Ben was frowning at Sarah, who was glaring at Mace, who was staring at the table.

"Look," I said, gesturing my cup at Sarah, "I appreciate that Mace hasn't talked about me to everyone he knows. Why don't you just be glad your boyfriend has some integrity, find comfort in knowing he'll never post pictures of your naked ass on the internet and take your bitchy attitude down a notch?" I stopped for a breath—and to take *myself* down a notch. "I'm not ashamed of what happened or why I did it, but if I find out any of you have spread gossip about me around the school, if you tell anyone about Wren, you're on your fucking own with this ghost. Got it?"

"That goes for me, too," Kevin announced as he sat down across from me. He set a laptop and a stack of hard- and soft-cover books on the table. Some of them had library tags on the spines, others didn't. Some looked fairly new and others looked like they had nothing more than spite holding them together.

Sarah muttered something under her breath.

"What?" I demanded.

She glared at me. "I asked if there were any other threats you want to make?"

I held up my hands. "I wouldn't gossip about you. I'm just asking for the same respect for me and my sister. If you can't give me that, then just say the word and I'm out of here."

"That sounds like a threat to me." She leaned back in her chair and folded her arms over her chest.

Would my foot fit down her throat? It was really, really tempting to let the ghost have her, let her try to save her own ass, but I couldn't do it. For all my tough talk, I wasn't going to let someone die.

Not even someone who despised me for no good reason.

"Whatever," I said. Then I turned my back on her. "Where's Roxi?"

"Grandmother's," Gage replied. I figured he would know. He and Roxi seemed pretty tight. "She's going to meet us when she's done."

"Where's Wren?" Kevin asked.

I wanted to ask him how he knew she wasn't there—goad him a little. I wanted to tell him it was none of his damn business. I wanted to tell him to leave my sister alone. "She's doing some research. She'll be back soon." I assumed she would— she'd been gone for a few hours now. That might only be a few minutes in the Shadow Lands, or it could be six days. Time just didn't follow any set of rules there.

"I brought my books on spirit communication and hauntings," Kevin informed us. "I don't know how much help they'll be, but it's a place to start. I'm still new to this whole medium thing, but I know a guy in Southbury who might be able to help us."

I wouldn't have thought of Southbury as a hotbed of ghostly activity, but hey, Ed and Lorraine Warren had based their paranormal investigation business in Monroe, and they were the ones who had investigated the house in Amityville. That movie *The Conjuring* had been based on one of their cases.

"How did you get into this?" I asked him.

He shrugged, his gaze guarded behind his glasses. "I saw things when I was a kid, you know?"

"Yeah," I said drily. "I know."

Was that actually a smile? "I'm not nearly as gifted as you, but I caught glimpses of ghosts. I could sense them, and sometimes they told me things."

Gifted? He thought I was gifted? I could have fallen right out of my chair if I didn't think everyone would laugh at my underwear.

"Anyway, I never thought much of it until the day you..." He cleared his throat. "The day Wren found me. It was like having someone scream in my face after a lifetime of whispers."

I smiled. "She's like that."

He looked me in the eye, his dark blue eyes serious. "She was terrified, and I had no idea what the hell was going on."

Not much wonder he wasn't my number-one fan. "I'm sorry you got dragged into that."

"Don't be."

Okay, fine. "I started digging into Haven Crest history," I confided, wanting to change the subject before I could get jealous again. "Seems it's been nasty for a long time. I need to find out the possible effects the place can have on Wren and me, given our connection to the other side. Ghosts can be real bullies, especially when they're all crammed into one place."

Sarah laughed. "The other side. You sound like one of those ghost-hunting shows."

I turned to her. "The dead, then."

"How are you going to find that out?" Ben asked. "I can't imagine you can just look it up on Google."

I took a sip of my latte. It was perfect. He'd even gotten them to add a shot of vanilla. Would he think I was crazy if I proposed to him? "Well, we could do a séance, or we take a trip to Haven Crest."

They all looked at each other.

"Wouldn't that be dangerous?" Gage asked.

"Yeah, but we're going to have to do it eventually. We'll have to go there to destroy the ghost. It would be safer to have a séance first."

"That's still contact with the ghost, isn't it?" Ben asked. "How is that safer?"

I took another sip. "Because we'll be on our own territory, and because Wren, Kevin and I can form a protective barrier against the ghost."

Mace finally spoke. "How can we contact it if we don't know who it is?"

Ah, good question, and one I was hoping no one would ask. "We don't need to—it will come if you guys call it. And then I'll know who it is."

"How?" That was Kevin. "What if it doesn't give its name?"

"I don't know how, I just know that I'll know." That was the lamest answer ever. It was also totally honest. I really didn't know why or how I could figure out who a ghost was.

"I'll see it as it looked in life," I told them, trying to find a better explanation. "I'll be able to talk to it. Plus, Wren will be there, and she'll be able to interact with it in ways I can't."

"What if it tries to hurt her?" Kevin asked.

His concern was actually sweet. I grimaced. "It can't hurt her—" at least, not like he thought "—she's already dead."

He looked as though I'd just kicked his puppy.

"This is so *weird*," Sarah remarked, shaking her pretty blond head. "And I thought my family was strange."

I stared at her. There had to be a disconnect between her brain and her mouth. She just didn't think before she spoke. Or maybe she did.

Ben defused what might have become a situation. "My uncle George used to walk around town in a top hat carrying his pet duck under his arm."

"Don't worry," I told him. "I hear duck-carrying skips a generation."

Brown eyes stared into mine for a second before he grinned. "Good to know."

Okay, I was starting to crush on him a bit. I managed to smile back before it felt as though a piece of me that was loose got pushed back into place. The world slipped into a tighter focus, and I was a part of it.

Wren was here.

Kevin looked up—he felt her, too. I stared at him. *Jerk.*

When he looked at me, one of his eyebrows arched. Oops. Guess I hadn't done a very good job at hiding my thoughts.

"Be nice," Wren said, tugging on a lock of my hair that I had somewhat contained behind a black headband—it made a nice contrast.

Kevin smiled. Oh, great, he could hear everything she said now?

"Don't look at him like that," she went on. "And no, he can't hear me all the time when I talk to you. You and I have our own frequency."

I didn't ask how she knew that, I simply trusted that it was true. I wouldn't suggest that she and I could read each other's minds, but each of us understood how the other thought.

Ben obviously noticed a change in me. "What's wrong?"

"Nothing. Wren's here."

"Hi, Wren," he said, with a little wave in her general direction.

My sister looked thrilled at the attention. It hurt to look at her, because that foolish grin told me just how lonely she was. I wasn't enough for her. I wanted to be, but I wasn't. She was in this world because of me, but she couldn't interact with it like I could. If I weren't already halfway crazy, being in that situation would send me all the way over the edge.

The others greeted her, as well. I didn't know if it was to suck up to me, or because they were actually happy she was there, and I didn't care. It made Wren feel good, and that was all that mattered.

"I found a book on Haven Crest in the Shadow Lands," my sister informed me. "I think it'll help us."

I repeated that to the table.

Kevin scowled. "How can you bring something like that into this dimension? You shouldn't be able to do that."

Wren looked surprised by his tone. Hurt. My eyes narrowed. "Might want to adjust your attitude, Sixth Sense."

He shook his head, but he didn't look at me—he looked at Wren. "Sorry. I mean, how is it possible that you're able to do that?"

Wren shrugged. Kevin smiled a little. He really could see her. Or at least, he could sense her.

For the benefit of the others who weren't so ghost-abled, I said, "Sometimes Wren and I can do things we shouldn't be able to do. We don't know why. Neither of us came with an instruction manual."

"No one expects you to know everything," Sarah said. Gotta admit, that was a surprise. "But thanks for sharing what you do."

"You're, uh, welcome." I had a great career in public speaking in my future.

Out of the corner of my eye I saw Mace reach down and entwine his fingers with hers. For a second she was stiff and cool, but then her hand closed over his. Obviously she forgave him for not telling her about finding me. And obviously he forgave her for being awful about it. I envied that. And I hated them a little bit for it, too.

"Did she bring the books with her?" Mace asked.

I shook my head. "No. She can bring them into this world, but she can't transport them once they're here."

He nodded. "So, what do you want us to do?"

The bunch of them stared at me. They thought I had the

answers. They expected me to have the answers. They *trusted* me to have answers. Damn, that was…unnerving.

"Can you do a search on Haven Crest ghosts or hauntings? I've got to think some of the stories have gotten out over the years. Look for anything that has to do with razors in particular." Then to Sarah and Gage, "Maybe you guys can look up incidents or attacks at Haven Crest over the years? Each take a couple of decades to make it go faster."

Their thumbs started flying over the screens of their phones.

"What can I do?" Ben asked.

"You and I are going to go shopping for supplies."

"Want some help?" Kevin asked.

I shook my head. "Go through your books for ways to protect ourselves. Anything that stands out make a note or send Wren to me. Or call." Yeah, calling was probably more convenient.

Everyone seemed on board. I took my chai with me, and as we walked out of the shop, Ben gave me a hesitant smile. "We're like the Scooby gang or something."

"Or something," I replied drily. But my heart gave a stupid little flip. Other than group therapy at Bell Hill, I'd never been part of anything before. Ever.

I really hoped I didn't get any of them killed.

Self-checkouts prevented so much embarrassment.

Ben and I went through the twelve-items-or-less line with ten cans of salt, a bottle of iron supplements, a bottle of fennel and a jar of cloves.

"You have thirteen items," the woman at the next check-out commented, looking pointedly at the salt as I scanned it through.

I grabbed a pack of gum, dragged it over the scanner and tossed it on the belt. She didn't say another word.

"You're such a rebel," Ben remarked, his eyes twinkling. He bagged our purchases. "Do we really need all this?"

"We will. You should salt the windows and doorways in your house."

"Yeah, because that's not hard to explain."

He had a point. "At least the windows and the threshold of your bedroom. It will keep the ghost from getting you in your sleep if it decides to come visit."

He shook his head, a lock of dark hair falling over his forehead. "I don't need it."

"Because you're such a badass?" It was snarky of me, but why was he here if he didn't want my help?

He stopped bagging and turned to me with the bottle of cloves in his hand. "You know, if you knocked that chip off your shoulder you'd be able to see beyond yourself and realize that we're not the assholes you seem to think we are. Sarah's not a bitch, she's just scared and guilty because it was her idea to go to Haven Crest. And your buddy Mace? He got really pissed at her for it. Made her cry. And no, I'm not a badass, but I have a grandmother who likes to put *pujok* all over the house to protect us from evil spirits, so I feel relatively secure. Oh, and it wasn't Kevin's or Roxi's idea to ask for your help, it was mine, so you can be shitty with me over it. But I probably didn't have to tell you any of that, did I? Because you know everything."

I stared at him as he tossed the cloves into one of the bags.

He drew a deep breath, nostrils flaring, then let it out before looking at me again.

"Wow." I scanned the last can of salt. "You found my place and put me in it. Well done."

He sighed. "I didn't mean to be a jerk, but we don't expect you to save us, Lark. We just want your help saving ourselves. And to be your friends."

"That's what I don't get," I told him, digging out the credit card Dad had given me from my wallet. "Why would any of you want to be my friend? You never did before."

He froze. In fact, he looked furious. "Grades four through seven."

I frowned. "What about them?"

Ben's jaw twitched. "Those were the years I invited you to my birthday parties and you never came."

I stared at him. "Are you high? You never... Wait. Are you Benji Ross?"

His face flushed, and I felt heat rush to mine. Oh, crap. Benji Ross. Chubby little dude who I'd always thought was a weird kid. Quiet. Wow. He'd obviously had a growth spurt since I'd last talked to him...and improved his social skills.

My shoulders sagged. He looked so embarrassed, and I... "I'm such a shit. Ben, I'm sorry."

He gave a stiff nod. "Forget it. Are we done here?"

I swiped my card through the machine, signed and followed him out of the grocery store.

"I can take some of the bags," I said.

"I've got them," he replied, staring straight ahead.

I tossed him the keys to the car. "I forgot something. I'll be right back." I turned and ran back inside.

When I came out a few minutes later, the bags were in the backseat and Ben was in the front listening to the radio. I climbed in and handed him an envelope.

"What's this?" he asked.

"Open it."

He did, and I held my breath as he read the Happy Boo-lated Birthday card I'd gotten him with a little cartoon ghost on it. When he laughed, I sucked in a lungful of grateful air.

"You really are a shit," he said. His smile faded a little. "Thanks."

I smiled back, heart thudding hard against my ribs. "Are we good?"

He nodded. "Yeah. We're good."

Those words made me happier than I would have thought. I guess I wanted friends more than I realized. Or maybe I just couldn't stand knowing I'd hurt Ben's feelings years ago. It wasn't a good feeling.

On the way to Nan's, we drove through where I used to live—Mace's neighborhood. Funny, I never really knew him until he saved my life. He'd always been fairly popular, and I had always been fairly…not. His house was one of the nicer ones on the street—an old Victorian that had been restored. A gorgeous house, and the kind I tried to avoid if I could. Old houses tended to contain old ghosts.

After a big lawn and low stone wall was the house I'd called home until Bell Hill. It was big, but not a mansion, with a ve-randa practically covered in plants. The new owners had made it really pretty. My mother had kept it a bit more…bland.

"Did people really talk about me bleeding through the car-pet?" I asked as we passed.

"I didn't," Ben replied.

No, I bet he hadn't. Him and Mace. "Thanks."

"Why did you come back here?" he asked after a moment's silence. "I would think this would be the last place you'd want to be."

"I didn't have much choice. My mother didn't want me anymore." I couldn't believe I'd told him that.

"Let me guess, because you can see Wren and she can't?"

"Yeah." The fact that he'd nailed it freaked me out a little. "So, my Nan took me in, and the school took me back, provided I behave and don't act like a crazy person."

"Doesn't helping us go against that?"

I flashed a halfhearted grin. "See, you were right about me being a rebel."

"I think you're more than that."

"I have no idea what I am."

I saw him glance at me. "You're not afraid."

"I'm afraid of a lot of things." Wow, it was True Confessions day for me. "Being afraid pisses me off."

"You must be afraid a lot."

I laughed. He grinned.

Ben was quiet until we pulled into Nan's drive. "I thought about eating a bullet once. My uncle found me with the gun and made me learn Tae Kwon Do instead. Beat me senseless, but it worked. Twisted, huh?"

I turned the keys and the engine cut out, leaving us in silence. I turned to him. "After I cut my wrists I thought about calling for help, but I couldn't get to the phone." Really, why was I telling him this? To make him feel better, or me?

"At that point you were committed."

I smiled. "No, they committed me after I got out of the hospital." Cue laugh track.

He glanced down at his sneakers. "No one else knows about the gun."

"And no one else ever will," I promised, and then opened the door.

Nan was there when we entered the kitchen. She said hi to Ben, asked if we needed or wanted anything and then made herself scarce. I loved her for trusting me enough not to hover.

"I'm going to grab the book," I told Ben. "I'll just be a second."

When I walked into my room, the book Wren had brought back with her was on the floor, where she would have dropped it as soon as she returned to this dimension. She had a very difficult time holding on to things in this world unless she used me to help her.

I bent down and reached for the book. As my fingers touched the soft leather cover, a tingle ran up my arm. I didn't know if it was in welcome or warning. All I knew was that this book was not of this world and it wanted to remind me of that fact. I had to be very careful with it and not let anyone else handle it. God knew what its energy might do to someone not linked to the dead.

I gathered the book up and held it to my chest—it was like holding a box of droning bees against me. It wasn't painful, but it wasn't exactly pleasant, either.

Ben was on his cell when I entered the kitchen. He stood with his profile to me, one hand in his pocket. He really had changed since we were little. Would I feel so bad for being such a bitch to him if he wasn't so gorgeous? Honestly, I didn't want to give that too much thought, because I was pretty sure I knew the answer, and it didn't look good on me.

"Okay," he said to the person on the other end of the conversation. "We'll meet you there." He pressed the disconnect button and looked at me. "Kevin wants to have the séance at his house."

"Good idea, since his parents are away." Nan was great, but I figured even she would draw a line somewhere. Calling the dead into her house would probably be it. "We can mix up the ghost repellent there, too."

"Ghost repellent?" To say he was incredulous would be an understatement.

"The groceries we bought. Ghosts are allergic to them, especially when they're mixed together."

That seemed to make sense to him. "Give me a lift back to the coffee shop? I need to get my car."

We decided that I should drive with him so Nan wouldn't be without a car. She drove us back to the coffee shop, asked me to text if I was going to be late and gave me a wink before driving off.

"She thinks we're on a date," I murmured. Even though I was standing there with bags of the weirdest groceries ever, and she knew there were ghost shenanigans going on, some part of my grandmother believed I was a normal teenager. That was nice.

"Don't expect me to put out," Ben joked, taking the bags from me. "I'm pretty, but I'm not easy. I'll put these in my car."

Hmm, I thought as he walked away. *That's too bad.*

Maybe there was a little normal in me after all.

chapter eight

WREN

I wasn't much of a help with research, but I watched over shoulders as the others tapped away on the keyboards and screens of their electronics. Amazing gadgets, really. I never tired of the living and their technology.

Although, I noticed that the living didn't have a library that would *bring* you the book you wanted.

I wondered if Lark had found the book, and if she would bring it with her. Probably it would be for the best if no one else touched it. I didn't know what sort of effect its energy might have on the living. I was fairly certain Lark would be all right, but I couldn't say for sure, which made me nervous.

Speaking of which…I needed some time with my sister. Alone. I hadn't really lied to her that morning when I told her I'd been in her room all night. I'd only spent a few hours with Kevin before guilt had driven me home. But never mind that. I wanted to know what had happened while I was gone, and if Kevin had said anything about me. I also wanted to know why Lark had chosen Ben to go with her.

While Kevin and Gage discussed the best way to protect the group against ghosts—which apparently involved a phone call to someone named "Chuck"—I got my chance to do a little snooping.

"Can I talk to you?" Sarah asked Mace. "Privately?"

Mace wore that half surprised, half annoyed expression that most boys seemed to have when they were interrupted from doing something they thought was important. "Now?"

"Yeah," she said—as though there wasn't anything more important—"now."

He didn't look happy about it, but he stood up and followed her out of the shop. I drifted through the nearest wall and caught up with them outside. They had walked around back where they could have a little privacy, but not too close to the Dumpsters.

"What?" he asked, hands on his hips.

Sarah folded her arms over her full chest. The wound on her cheek stood out sharp and red, and her aura vibrated brightly with tension. Poor Mace. "Do you have a thing for Lark?"

His eyebrows shot up, then lowered into a scowl. "Seriously? You dragged me out here because you're jealous?"

"I'm not jealous of some white-haired freak," she shot back.

Careful, sweetie. That freak's my sister, and she's got nothing *on me.*

"Hey, don't call her that." My opinion of Mace went up another couple of notches.

"I'm sorry," Sarah sneered. "Did I insult your girlfriend?"

She really was jealous. Lark would have such a laugh over this.

"She's my friend." He didn't sound convinced. I understood. Lark didn't go out of her way to make herself likable. "Our friend. She's helping us get out of this mess."

"What mess? Other than a sore stomach or cheek, what else has this supposed ghost done?"

Mace stared at her as though she was joking. "So, I suppose you're not having nightmares?" He frowned again. "And of course you haven't experienced any weird stuff—like hearing someone talking to you or feeling like you're being watched even when no one else is there? You haven't felt like you're coming down with a flu that feels like it's in your bones?"

"That's just paranoia. This ghost stuff has freaked us all out. That's it. It's nothing."

He shook his head. "You weren't there the other night. I saw what it did to her. I felt it. She's putting herself in danger by helping us."

Sarah snorted. "Please. She's doing this because she's horny for you. Or Ben. She couldn't care less about the rest of us."

The Dumpsters trembled. Neither of them seemed to notice. Bet she'd notice if I picked one up and crushed her with it. She wouldn't be half so pretty with her insides smeared all over the pavement.

"Don't be stupid." He just looked disgusted now. "I'm going back inside."

She grabbed his arm as he walked past. "Mace...wait."

He stopped. "What?"

"I'm sorry." Her shoulders slumped. "I'm just scared."

I watched as he seemed to debate for a moment, then put his arms around her. He was a good guy. Too good to date a girl that was manipulative, which was why I was going to keep an eye on Sarah. Sometimes being haunted changed people, especially if the ghost was able to influence them. It wasn't quite possession, but it was close.

I left them standing there when she lifted her head in an invitation for him to kiss her. I drifted to the front of the building and looked around. There was a young woman walking down the road that was one of my kind—the sort people called a Woman in White. I wondered how many people had stopped to offer her a drive over the years? And in the distance, I saw a man dangling from a tree branch, swaying in the breeze like a lazy cat's tail. Didn't he get bored just hanging there?

My sister was standing near the door of the coffee shop when I came around. She turned and looked at me with a raised eyebrow. She was probably wondering what I was doing out there. Unfortunately, Mace and Sarah chose that moment to walk around as well, their arms around each other. I shrugged and smiled. She'd ask me about it later—and give me a lecture about eavesdropping. I'd heard it before.

The couple paused as Ben joined Lark. I smiled at the change in Lark's aura when Ben stood next to her. She liked him.

"Get everything?" Mace asked.

"I think so," Lark replied. "How goes the search?"

"We found three people sent to Haven Crest because of razor-related crimes. Gage's still looking to see if there are any more."

Lark nodded, her jaw tight. I knew she was miffed that the two of them were out here when there was work to be done. My sister was a little...obsessive when she put her mind to something, and sometimes she expected everyone else to jump on board. I told her she'd be a lot less angry at the world if she didn't do that. She told me to...well, do something sexual to myself, and then I'd probably be less annoying.

My sister started for the door of the coffee shop when another car pulled in beside us. It was an odd thing that looked like someone had smooshed a car and truck together.

"Hey, Chuck," Mace said when a tall, thin man with black hair down to his waist and a tanned complexion climbed out of the vehicle in a cloud of smoke. Lark smirked as she sniffed the air. I sniffed, too. I'd smelled that acrid scent before, but couldn't place it.

"Mace," the man greeted in a deep, lazy voice. "I have something for Kev. Is he inside?"

Mace nodded. I moved closer to the man, still sniffing, trying to identify what was so amusing to the other four. Suddenly, the man looked right at me. Then at Lark. "Miss, does this little red-haired girl belong with you?"

Lark stepped back as though he'd slapped her. It wasn't very often that someone saw me—even less that they acknowledged it. My sister looked at me, and me at her. Then she turned to Chuck. "Yes."

He nodded, then said to me, "Miss, I don't mind if you come closer, but you should know that I've got a good quantity of iron on my person, and I don't want to cause you unnecessary discomfort."

Well, wasn't that sweet? Most people didn't even know that iron had an effect on ghosts, much less worried about it. "Thank you."

He glanced at Lark. "What did she say? I can see her, but I can't hear her."

Poor Lark looked a little dumbstruck. "She says thanks."

Chuck nodded. "Sure thing. Nice to meet you." Then he smiled at me and went inside.

Mace shook his head. "That was weird."

My sister wasn't so amused. "Who is that guy?" The unspoken question was whether or not he was a threat to me.

"That's just Chuck. He's harmless."

Lark shot him a sharp glance as she made to follow after the man. "No one who can see Wren and knows how to hurt her is harmless." She yanked the door open and stepped inside.

Sarah smiled a little as they followed. Sometimes I was glad I wasn't alive because I didn't have to deal with all the strangeness that came with being a mortal teenager. So much insecurity and pettiness. Honestly, I'd rather spend a day with a raging poltergeist than a teenage girl—other than Lark, of course.

Inside, Chuck was at our table, handing Kevin a small burlap pouch. Kevin gave him a couple of twenties and thanked him.

"You guys be careful," Chuck cautioned, then he left. He nodded at me as he walked away. I waved.

Kevin emptied the pouch on the table. Nine iron rings clanked against the laminate. They were made from old nails.

Sarah stared at them. "What are these for?"

"Iron weakens ghosts," Lark explained, picking up one of the rings and sliding it onto her finger as she sat down. "Not bad, Sixth Sense."

Kevin glanced at her. "Gee, thanks."

I poked her. She poked back, though I'm sure it looked like a twitch to anyone watching. At least she didn't poke me with the hand wearing the ring. That would have been uncomfortable.

"What have we got?" she asked.

Gage, dark hair hanging in his eyes, took a drink from his enormous cup of coffee. "Okay, so far we've found three potential BBGs."

BBGs?

Lark smiled slightly. "Big bad ghosts?"

He grinned. He was cute when he smiled and got the hair out of his eyes. "Exactly. Eva Mortimer, Josiah Bent and Thomas Stark."

"What did they do, and do they tie into any hauntings?" Lark asked.

Gage continued, "Mortimer was a nurse who apparently went nuts one night and sliced some patients up. Bent killed six young girls with a straight razor, and Stark liked to carve himself and anyone else he could hold down with a hunting knife."

Kevin leaned forward, finger flicking over the screen of his phone. "Eva Mortimer claimed she was made to do what she'd done by the ghost of an old patient, but she didn't say who before she slit her own throat. Nasty. She died in 1932, and a lot of people say they've seen her on the grounds. Some kids that broke in in the '80s say they saw a man with a blade coming at them, but they didn't say if it was a razor or a knife."

Gage piped up next. "But in 1966, a girl who was admitted as a patient insisted that there was an older man hovering over her at night, and that he kept telling her he wanted to cut her up."

Lark nodded. "The entity I encountered felt male, but I couldn't tell for certain. It was definitely angry—and mean. Mortimer sounds more like a victim than who we're looking for."

"My aunt and some of her friends sneaked in about fifteen years ago," Roxi added—she'd arrived while Lark was gone. "She said one of the other girls insisted that a ghost slashed at her with a knife, but they thought she was making it up since she didn't have any wounds."

Not ones that were visible to the living, at any rate.

"What happened to her?" Lark asked.

Roxi shrugged. "I don't know." She was lying. Or at least, there was something she wasn't telling the rest of them. Were Lark and I the only ones who noticed? If I had to guess I'd say that one of the aunt's friends died shortly after that trip to Haven Crest, but Roxi didn't know if it was the one who was attacked by the ghost or not, and didn't want to upset her friends.

Lark looked at me, and I knew she was thinking the same thing. Then she turned back to the table. "Everyone take a ring. If our ghost manifests around you and you see it, the ring will help fight it off. I have a salt-and-iron mix for you to carry, as well. Also, when we summon the ghost, you need to at least pretend you're not afraid and that you mean no harm. Ghosts are attracted to fear and negative emotion. It makes them aggressive."

"Like when your sister freaked out at Kevin's," Sarah said. "She picked up on our worry about you and Mace."

I would have liked to manifest right then and punch her in the face. She hadn't been worried about Lark at all.

"No," Lark corrected her. "It was Wren's worry for me that caused her to manifest, and you're lucky. If it had gone the other way you'd all be in much worse shape right now." I wished she hadn't said that.

"Wait." Gage put his phone down. "You're saying your sister is dangerous?" And *that* was exactly why I wished Lark hadn't said it.

Lark frowned at him. "She's a *ghost*. You don't need to be afraid of her, but her power is something you should remember and respect."

He shook his head, long hair brushing against his face as he looked in my direction. "Glad you're on our side, badass ghost girl."

I laughed. Lark smiled.

"So, what's the plan?" Mace asked, bringing everyone back on track.

I could tell from the way Lark looked at him that she was surprised by his gruff tone. "We go to Kevin's, summon the ghost, find out what we're up against, and then we go to Haven Crest, I find the remains and destroy them. That's the simple version."

"Why do we even need to summon him?" Sarah asked. "Isn't that just asking to be attacked again?"

"It's the only way to be sure we have the right ghost," Lark said. "It will come out for all of you."

"But it came out for just you and Mace, didn't it?"

"But I didn't see it. With all of you there I think it will be forced to manifest."

Mace put his arm around his girlfriend. "You don't have to do it."

"Yeah, she does," Lark announced. "You got into this together, you stay in it together."

"What difference does it make if one of us doesn't hold hands around a table?" Mace demanded. He and Lark glared at each other. If this was one of those soap operas my mother liked to watch, they'd kiss.

"You think Ben or Roxi or Gage want to do this?" my sister asked. "If Sarah doesn't have to do it, no one has to, and then it will end up me and Wren looking for a ghost-needle in a fucking ghost-haystack. And I'll be in the Haven Crest graveyard digging up and burning all three graves just in case. That's if I'm lucky."

"I'd help," Kevin volunteered.

Lark didn't look at him, but I did. I smiled. My sister kept her gaze locked on Mace, who stared back. "That's great, but you weren't there the night they got jumped, so while your abilities might be helpful, there's no guarantee you'd find the right one, either."

"We're all doing this," Gage proclaimed, his dark gaze traveling from one of his friends to the next. "That's all there is to it."

Sarah glared at him. "You guys want to punish me because you blame me."

What was her...? Oh. Oh, I understood. "Lark, make her put on one of the rings."

Lark glanced at me, but didn't hesitate. She picked up one of the rings and handed it to Sarah. "Put this on."

The other girl shook her head. "I have a metal allergy."

My sister smiled, but it wasn't a nice smile. "Put it on."

"No."

By now the whole table was watching—a couple of customers from other tables were, too.

"Lark, what the hell?" Mace asked.

Gaze narrow, Lark kept her attention on Sarah. "She's being influenced by the ghost."

The others all turned their heads to stare at the blonde girl. "That's stupid," Sarah protested.

Lark glanced at Mace. "Noticed any strange behavior lately?"

Of course he had—like not even twenty minutes ago. He took his girlfriend by the hand, and then held that hand out. "Put the ring on, Sar."

She jerked back, hands clenching into fists. "Make me, Daddy's boy." *Uh-oh.* Sarah's voice had changed. "Lark…"

My sister held up her hand. "I hear it. Sarah, you need to put this ring on for your own protection."

The other girl turned her head to look at my sister, and when she did I could see hatred burning in her eyes. "*You.* They should have kept you at Bell Hill. Should have fried that weak little mind of yours."

"Shut up, Sarah," Mace warned.

"That's not Sarah," Lark informed him, her gaze unwavering. "Who are you?"

Sarah grinned and leaned toward her. Everyone was frozen still now. "I'm the one who's going to devour your little friends."

"No, you're not," Lark replied. "I'm not going to let you."

"You can't stop me, youngling." Sarah's voice was low and rough—mannish. "I'll suck the souls right out of them and lick my fingers when I'm done. Maybe if your sister's a good girl I'll let her have the eyeballs." She looked right at me then and winked.

I froze. How did she…?

Lark leaned closer. "You stay away from my sister, you sorry sack of shit, or I swear to God, I'll burn your bones one at a freaking time."

Suddenly Sarah's hand whipped out and wrapped around Lark's throat. Roxi cried out. People at the other tables gasped. One even stood up. This was going to get out of control very quickly.

I lunged forward, into my sister. The iron ring in her hand hurt me—like something being shoved under my skin, jagged and sharp, ripping back and forth. I didn't leave her, though. I put all of my strength into that hand and lifted it to the one around Lark's neck. My sister struggled for breath and I forced her throat open as I pried at the fingers trying to crush it. Sarah might be a conduit, but she wasn't a match for the real thing. She shouldn't be a match for Lark, either, but then this was probably exactly what my sister had had in mind, because normally she would have already punched Sarah in the face. I pried one of the supernaturally strong fingers up, and Lark shoved the iron onto it.

Sarah hissed, and then her shoulders slumped, as though something had let go of them. Let go of her. Her hand fell away from Lark's neck and my sister gasped for breath.

The strangeness I saw in the other girl's aura earlier was gone. "She's good," I said.

Lark nodded. She saw it, too—only not the same way I did. "Feeling better, Sarah?"

The blonde girl nodded. "I am. What happened?"

"The ghost was influencing you. It was doing a good job, too."

"This is a powerful ghost," I said. Lark merely glanced at me. I didn't need to tell her that. She was worried, I could see it.

"Anyone else feeling weird?" she asked.

Everyone took one of the rings and put it on without hesitation. Maybe I imagined it, but I thought Gage perked up a little.

One of the counter staff approached our table. She wasn't much older than Kevin and had an apologetic look on her round face. "Guys, you're disturbing some of the other customers."

"Drama club," Gage quipped. "We're practicing. Sorry."

"Yeah," Lark said drily. "Drama. Sorry, we'll leave." My sister stood. The others gathered up their belongings and followed her out. Everyone in the shop watched them go, whispering. Lark did not need this kind of attention.

It wasn't until we were outside that I realized I hadn't needed to worry about the book at all—no one had tried to touch it, not even Sarah. No, the only thing I needed to worry about was a violent ghost who had killed before and was looking to kill again.

A ghost who knew my secret.

chapter nine

LARK

"You still want to go through with the séance?" Kevin looked at me like I was nuts. No big surprise there.

"Yeah," I replied. "I think we have to after what happened to Sarah." The ghost was powerful if it could do a grab and go from a distance like that. "It could influence any of them." I didn't tell him what else I feared—that the ghost had no intention of letting them go. It was going to play with them and drain them, because this ghost had plans.

How did I know that? It was just a hunch, but a strong one. The recent construction at Haven Crest had stirred something up, and now it was threatened by the changes in its habitat. Ghosts weren't big on change, and they responded to threats the same way people did—fight or flight.

I was going on the assumption that our ghost meant to fight.

"I've never done this before," he admitted.

I could have made a crude joke about taking his séance virginity but Wren was there and she wouldn't have liked that. "Wren will help you. I need you to help anchor her, too."

"I'll be fine," my sister insisted, but she was just going to have to deal with my paranoia. I'd seen ghosts try to influence her before. I knew she was stronger now, but I wasn't going to gamble on that.

"Can I help you with that?" He nodded at the cans of salt and baking supplies I had strewn on the top of his kitchen counter.

"Sure." I handed him a can of salt. "Dump this into the food processor. So, what do you want to know about the séance?" It wasn't like I was an expert. I'd done two in the course of my life, and one had been by accident.

Kevin opened the can of salt. "What do you need me to do?"

Wren came forward to join us. "You summon the spirit. You order it to come to us."

He glanced in her direction, and I knew that he could hear her as well as I could. "Won't that piss it off?"

"Mediums are like catnip for ghosts," I explained. "They are attracted to you because you're a way for them to make contact and show off. I don't think our guy will be able to resist. And we'll have protection around you so he behaves."

"I won't let him hurt you," Wren promised. I felt awkward overhearing her make such a promise. She really cared about him, and that wasn't good. They could never be together.

Kevin smiled at her. "So, I call it and then we trap it?"

"Pretty much," I replied. "We won't be able to hold it for

long, but hopefully long enough to find out who it is and how to stop it."

He dumped the salt into the food processor. "How do you stop ghosts?"

I shrugged. "There are a few ways, but the only way to really get rid of one is to salt and burn the remains."

"What if there are no remains?"

"Then you burn whatever it is they're attached to," I said, handing him another can. "Put this one in, too."

"Do you really think we can do this?"

I measured out some cloves so each batch of salt would have an equal amount. "Yes. We can do it, I just don't know if time is on our side. If there are remains, great. If not, then we have to find what is left behind, and that's the bitch of it."

"Then let's hope there're bones."

I gave him a slight smile. Finally, it felt as though he and I were on the same side.

We worked quickly and pretty efficiently, if I say so myself. I ground up all the cloves and the fennel and dumped each into the food processor one batch at a time. Kevin ran the processor, and then we both scooped the mixture back into the salt cans.

"Weird to think this works against ghosts," he remarked.

A few feet away my sister wrinkled her nose. "I hate it."

"Then stop hovering," I told her. "You'll make yourself sick."

She stuck her tongue out at me, but drifted from the room when Kevin told her he didn't want anything to happen to her.

Barf.

Once all the cans were filled, Kevin and I took them to the dining room where everyone else was.

Sarah sat at the table, scratching at her cheek. Normally that wouldn't be a big deal, except she was digging at the wound left by the ghost. It weeped black, the skin around it raw and red.

"Stop!" I ordered. Shit, it had really done a number on her when it had used her as its puppet.

She jumped and glared at me. "What the hell?"

"You're going to make it worse."

"It itches!" As if to prove her point, she clawed at it some more. I winced.

I grabbed her hand and pulled it away. Could she feel that ghostly wet on her fingers? Could she smell it? Because it smelled pretty damn foul.

She pressed my fingers to the mess that was her cheek. Oh, gross. It was hot and slick, like sticking my fingers in bacon grease congealing in a pan. I pulled back, but she held firm. She was a strong girl.

"Ahh," she sighed. "That's better."

I watched—and I promise I'm not making this shit up—as the wound lost some of its angriness. It was as though it sucked that awful black back into itself, tucked the raw edges of torn flesh back together a little. WTF? Could I heal wraith marks, or was I only making it stronger? And how was I doing it?

When she finally let me go I ran to the kitchen and scoured my hand with a metal-mesh scrubber—the kind Nan used on pots. I used it until my skin stung and then threw the scrubber in the garbage. I dried my hands and returned to the dining room.

"Are you okay?" Ben asked. He was frowning—like he was really worried about me. Sweet, but I wasn't the one any of them should be worried about.

"Yeah, thanks." I glanced at Sarah. She had this goofy look on her face—like she was a little stoned. "Are you?"

"I feel good. You must be magic or something."

Not magic, but definitely something.

I just wish I knew whether it was good or bad.

"Okay, everyone sit down," I instructed. As they did I handed each of them a can of the salt mixture. "Pour this in a circle around your chairs. Make sure the line isn't broken at any point." Then I jerked my head toward the door so my sister would follow me, and not have to be present while the salt was out.

"What's wrong?" she asked as we stood just outside the door.

"I want you to promise you won't try to be the hero to-night."

Wren looked affronted. "That's rich, coming from you."

I sighed and folded my arms over my chest. "If things get bad, you jump into me, okay?"

"You mean if I feel like I'm going to lose control."

Touchy much? That meant she was worried about it, too, but the last thing I wanted to do was get her agitated. "I mean if things start to go south for either of us. We're stronger to-gether, and we don't know what we're up against." But we both knew it was nasty.

She turned her head and peered into the dining room. I followed her gaze. Kevin.

"So, you and Kevin can communicate pretty well, huh? I mean, he can see you now."

"I guess."

She didn't want to talk about it, and I realized something at that moment. I realized that it wasn't my business. If she wanted to tell me, she'd tell me. Maybe she thought I'd be angry, or maybe she simply didn't feel the need to share this one thing with me. She was entitled to one thing of her own, wasn't she? Yes, she could get hurt. In fact, I was entirely certain she was going to get hurt big-time, but she deserved her privacy—just like everyone else.

"Look after him," I said. "He volunteered for this, and he has no idea what he's getting into. He might need your help."

"I know."

"No, you don't. I'm telling you to protect him before me."

She turned back to me, a frown on her face. It was funny that I found her face pretty, but mine not so much. "No one comes before you."

"Tonight they all do."

Her hand settled on my shoulder—I hadn't even seen her move. "Helping them is one thing, Lark, but putting yourself at risk is another. They're not your responsibility."

"No? Then whose are they?"

"Their own."

That was easy for the dead girl to say. The one who had been so hot to help them in the first place. I didn't say that out loud, of course—it was mean. And she was only saying these things because she remembered things from Bell Hill. When people asked how I knew things about ghosts, I let them think I was just brilliant or whatever, but the truth was that everything I knew, I'd learned the hard way.

"I'll be fine," I assured her. Right, because I'd never said *that* before. But I was fairly confident I would be all right. I'd put salt around my chair, too, and I'd wear the iron ring in my pocket if I had to. "Just promise me you'll watch out for the others."

She nodded. "I will."

We returned to the dining room where the group was gathered around the table. There was a chair left for me at the head of it—opposite Kevin and between Ben and Mace.

I sat down in the chair—someone had already poured salt around it for me.

"Should we turn off the lights?" Gage asked.

"Not if you want to see," I replied.

He looked disappointed. "Do we hold hands?"

"Place them on the top of the table so that your pinkies touch the person's next to you." Guys sometimes got weird about having to hold another guy's hand, but not just that, I wanted the iron of their rings to be visible and easily accessible if needed.

"Ready?" I asked.

Murmurs of "yes" sounded around the table as they placed their hands pinkie to pinkie. They looked terrified, and I didn't blame them. I was a little nervous myself. I'd be an idiot not to be.

"I need you all to think about that night at Haven Crest when you were attacked," I told them. "Think about how it felt, the energy you encountered. Sarah, it's already tried to manipulate you, so I want you to think about how that presence felt in your head, okay?"

She nodded, face white. There were dark half circles beneath her eyes, and the scratch on her cheek looked like makeup, it was so bright against her pale skin. "Okay."

"Go ahead," I said to Kevin. He was the one with the ability to summon ghosts. I attracted them, but I couldn't single out a particular one unless I knew exactly who I was looking for, and even then, I couldn't focus like he could. He could channel the energy of the people around him into finding their spirit and call it to them. That was how mediums managed to contact people's dead loved ones.

He closed his eyes. He wasn't wearing his glasses. Wren stood behind him—outside the salt line. He wasn't wearing the iron ring because it might interfere with his abilities, so she was there to give him a little extra protection just in case our ghost decided to break with tradition and tried to hurt him.

"I know you're out there," Kevin said. "I know you're watching or hovering, whatever you do. We got the message you sent through Sarah earlier, and now we invite you to show yourself. If you want to be the big bad, show your face. Unless you're a coward."

Okay, so, not the way I would have done it. Although, antagonizing the ghost was probably the fastest way to call it forth.

Nothing happened. Everyone—except Kevin—glanced around the table at one another. I tried to keep my attention on Wren. She flickered for a second like bad TV reception, then was whole again.

"It's coming," she said.

"Kevin," I commanded. "Keep going."

And he did. "Come on," he whispered. "Come scare us. Show yourself. You know you want to."

The lights turned off and on. The table shook. Ben's little finger slid over mine like a hug.

"You can do better than that," Kevin goaded.

It was like all the air was sucked out of the room by a giant vacuum. Everything went quiet and perfectly still, like we were all frozen where we sat. And then a man appeared behind Sarah.

Gage jumped and swore.

"Nobody move," I cautioned, keeping my gaze focused on the ghost. "Gage, is your salt circle intact?"

"Yes, boy," the ghost mocked in a raspy voice. "Check your circle."

Gage's normally tanned face was chalky, eyes wide like inkwells as he peered down at the floor.

"It's good," he croaked.

That was a relief. Poor Sarah looked as though she might pass out. She clung to Mace and Kevin like they were the only things holding her in her chair. Kevin actually seemed surprised that the ghost had come.

Our spirit was a middle-aged man. Not bad-looking, but far too crazy-eyed to be really handsome—kind of like Bruce Campbell in some of the scenes in *Army of Darkness*. He had dark hair and dark eyes and was dressed in old-fashioned clothes. He wasn't my first apparition, so I was able to study him without the same shock and fear as the others. I filed every little detail about him away in my memory.

He had bloody hands, and there was arterial spray across the front of his blue shirt.

"Look at you all," he said, smiling as his dark gaze swept around the table. "Little lambs." He leaned his head close to Sarah. "Hello, my dear."

Her eyes widened, but she was too terrified to even make a sound.

Lambs? Farmer, maybe? Or a preacher. "Tell us your name," I commanded, pulling his attention away from Sarah.

The ghost shot me a glare. "Bossy little bitch, aren't you? No, I have no intention of telling you my name." Then he turned his head and smiled. "You must be Lark—prickly little scar-girl. And you—" he turned to Wren "—you're the Dead Born. Oh, I've heard so much about the two of you."

"From who?" I demanded.

But it was Wren who had his attention. He drifted closer to her. My sister held her ground, even though I wished she'd come closer to me.

"Look at you," the ghost murmured as he approached. "You pulse with life even though you're so thoroughly dead. Not like you're other half—the walking dead."

Okay, so that stung. It also made a lot of sense. Wren watched him like a gazelle watching a lion.

"So powerful," the ghost went on. "You don't even know how much. It's almost charming." He stared at my sister as though she was an angel—or a demon.

"Hey!" I snapped. This was my show, not his. "Old Mac-Donald—you need to step off."

The apparition turned its head. "I beg your pardon?"

"Not mine you need to ask for," I told him. I gestured to those around the table. "You need to let them go."

He seemed to find this amusing. "Or what?"

"Or I'll salt your bones and turn them to ash."

He smiled. "Such bravado. How will you find my remains when you don't even know my name, little girl?"

"Josiah Bent," Kevin said, and I knew from the ghost's expression that he was right. Wren put herself between the two of them.

I smiled. "So, I guess I'll be finding your remains now, asshole."

Bent reared back, his face contorted into a monstrous, ugly mask. Somehow he conjured a straight razor—a long one that gleamed under the light. He whirled around, slashing the blade toward Roxi. She cried out and ducked. Gage thrust his arm—the one not protected by iron—in front of her.

"No!" I shouted, but it was too late. If Gage hadn't moved he would have stayed within the salt circle and Bent wouldn't have gotten him, but all I could do was watch as that razor sliced across Gage's arm.

Gage screamed.

I jumped out of my chair, pushing it back so the legs ripped through the salt, destroying my protective barrier.

"Hey, dickwad!" I shouted.

Time slowed as Bent turned toward me.

"Lark," Wren said softly—a warning. "What are you doing?"

I smiled at Bent. "You don't scare me."

He lunged then, coming at me with the wrath of a tornado. I drew back my right fist, and smashed the iron ring on it right into the middle of his face.

See, I can make contact with any ghost, not just my sister. I had managed to keep that pretty much to myself until now.

Bent scattered—exploded into a thousand jagged wisps, and was gone.

Silence filled the room. Everyone looked at each other, then to me. I was looking at Wren, who was still and quiet.

"Is he gone?" Sarah asked.

"He should be," I said.

But Kevin shook his head. "No. I still feel him. He's—"

Suddenly Bent took form again—this time right behind Wren. He grinned at me as he wrapped his arms around her.

"No!" I screamed.

But it was too late. Bent was gone.

And the asshole had taken my sister.

chapter ten

LARK

"Where are you going?" Ben asked when I jumped up from the table. Everyone else was still trying to figure out what had just happened.

"Haven Crest," I replied. "He took Wren."

The room fell silent at that pronouncement. Kevin looked as though I'd just punched him in the face. "What?"

I barely glanced at him. I was too busy shoving cans of salt-mix into my bag. "Bent took Wren. I'm going after her."

"I'm going with you," Ben said.

Kevin's jaw tightened. "So am I."

"We all are," Roxi joined in. "Right?"

"I don't care who comes with me," I told them. "But I'm going. Now."

They followed me out of the house—Ben was right behind me. "I'll drive," he said. I didn't respond. Of course he was driving. I'd left Nan's car at home.

I went straight for his MINI Cooper and tossed my bag on the floor on the passenger side. Roxi and Gage jumped in the back as Ben slid behind the wheel. Sarah and Mace would have to go with Kevin.

"Uh, hey," Ben told me as he slipped the key into the ignition. "I got you something."

I frowned. "Okay." Couldn't it wait? My sister was in danger.

He reached behind his seat and pulled something out.

"A stick?"

He held it lengthwise. Then I saw the twists in the metal. "Wrought iron," he said. "The paper wrapped around it is a *pujok* my grandmother made for you."

I grinned. "A ghost-beating stick!" Oh, I hoped Bent gave me a chance to use it on him.

He laughed. "I guess. My mom's an artist. She works with metal. I brought a couple extra, but you can keep this one."

"Thanks." It was actually one of the most thoughtful gifts anyone had ever given me—given the circumstances. "And thank your nan for me."

Ben smiled, and my heart did this funny little dance.

Roxi and Gage sat in the backseat and made out most of the way to the graveyard. I couldn't believe it. Ben turned on the radio to cover the face-sucking sounds behind us. Really? In the movies danger always makes people sexy, but this just made me want to smack them. I knew that Wren was more important to me than them, and that to them she was a ghost and should be able to protect herself, but they didn't know about Bell Hill and how I'd almost lost her.

"Are they always like this?" I asked.

Ben glanced in the rearview mirror and grimaced. "This just started earlier today, I think."

I turned my head to look at him. He was smiling. "Really?"

He nodded, smile growing.

I laughed. Couldn't help it. "That's messed up."

It was a short ride to the graveyard. Kevin pulled his car into a spot right beside Ben's. It was a busy night—lots of cars with lots of steamed-up windows.

Everyone had their rings on, and those who hadn't brought something made of iron took one of Ben's sticks. I handed out the cans of the salt-iron cocktail. "Don't use it unless you have to," I said. "We don't want to waste it—no telling how many we'll be up against. If you're attacked or feel threatened, let some fly." This whole thing could be a trap, and I knew that. I also didn't say it aloud. Wren had been taken because of the people with me, and I'd trade them for her in a heartbeat.

I put my salt into the messenger bag slung across my body, along with the iron rod. Once we were all set, we made for the tree and crossed over onto Haven Crest land.

"You okay?" Ben asked me.

I nodded, but it was a lie. As soon as my feet hit hospital property I felt them—the teeming, impatient souls that tormented this place—or were tormented by it.

"We're not at the main buildings yet," Mace pointed out.

I looked at him. "I know." Didn't he get it? This place was bad news.

We only made it halfway across the field before I felt something coming for us. It wasn't the same thing that had come the other night—this was just a scout. These ghosts weren't the chaotic entities that I'd dealt with at Bell Hill. These ghosts knew what they were doing. They were organized. This thing coming at us had been sent.

They knew we were coming. They'd been expecting us. It *was* a trap.

And I was going to walk right into it. But I knew what I was getting into.

I stopped, watching the scout as it took form in front of me. It was a young boy—not much younger than me. He was dressed in old-fashioned clothing and the dark sockets of his eyes blazed with mockery. Jerk.

I drew back my arm and punched him in the face as hard as I could. The jolt—like punching a wall—drove up my arm like my bones were being shoved into my shoulder.

"Was that a ghost?" Gage asked.

I shot him a scowl. "No, I just thought now would be a good time to practice my kickboxing. Yeah, it was a ghost."

His dark eyes widened. "Wow. You are such a bitch when you're scared."

"That, too," I agreed, my shoulders sagging. How long would it take the scout to reappear at the hospital? To pull itself back together on this plane and report to Bent?

How long before a larger welcoming party was sent out?

"Listen," I said. They all turned to me. "This is a trap. Bent wanted us to come here, to his territory. I don't know if he's hoping to barter with Wren, or use her against us, but he's going to want me to back off so he can nibble on you. My sister is the most important thing in the world to me."

Mace nodded. "So, what you're saying is that you'd give us over for her?"

I met his gaze. "If I had to? In a second. I don't want to,

but if it comes down to it, yeah. I just want to be up front about it."

I didn't understand his expression, and I didn't need to. Ben, on the other hand, was as open as a book. "It's okay, Lark. We all want to help you get Wren back, but more important, I want to save my own ass. We all do."

The others nodded—hesitantly. I felt a little better about leading them into what might be their deaths—if it was possible to feel better about it. I knew why I had to do this. I knew why they had to do it. Out of all of them, though, Kevin's motivation was the most like mine. Wren.

I glanced at him. He was looking toward the buildings of the Haven Crest campus with a grim expression. He was thinking about her, I knew it.

"Positive energy," I reminded everyone. My sister was waiting. "Let's pick up the pace a bit."

We jogged toward the shadowy buildings not far away. Most were in total darkness—those still in ruins. Others were in the midst of being fixed up by the town. They were being reclaimed as some sort of community campus. I hoped they had a good exorcist or ten lined up.

"Where should we go?" Gage asked.

I pointed ahead and slightly to the right at one of the largest buildings on the site. "Patient residence." Might as well jump right in. "It's the epicenter."

"How can you tell?" Sarah asked. For someone who didn't like me, she talked to me a lot.

How could I tell? Right. Sometimes I forgot that norms didn't see things the way I did. "It's the brightest," I replied. That was the easiest way to put it. "I see spirit energy as a glow." More important, I knew that was where Wren was. I could feel her warning me away.

So, I was going to run right to her.

We kept low as we hurried toward the building. In addition to trying to avoid ghosts—and I was surprised we hadn't been jumped yet—we had to avoid security. There was only one car patrolling the area, and probably two guards in it. There might be more on foot, but I doubted it. There were signs all over the place to warn against trespassing, and locks and chains to keep people out, but there were too many broken windows, and anyone could get a pair of bolt cutters. When a place like Haven Crest stood empty too long and built up a reputation for being haunted, there was no keeping out the people who really wanted in.

Thank God ghosts didn't normally wander from where they were tethered; otherwise this town would have a real problem. I couldn't see them—they weren't gathered like a congregation, but I could feel them like a humming in my veins.

We were lucky—most of the lights were centered on the renovated buildings and main quad. This part of the property was pretty dim, a decrepit maze of overgrown shrubs and thick ivy growing up the sides of old brick buildings with broken panes and peeling paint. Tattered curtains fluttered in a window— No, that was a woman in a gown, watching us. She dipped her head to me and turned away. The ghosts didn't have to come to us—they were watching us come to them. I glanced around and saw she wasn't the only one. Pale, drawn faces with dark, glinting eyes watched from vantage points all around us—beyond what I could see in the dark.

The lack of lighting made it hard to see, but harder to be

seen. We waited for a moment, hidden behind some bushes as the security car drove by. Then I led the way around the red-brick building to a set of steps at the side. They were almost completely grown over with vines and weeds and would have been far too easy to miss if not for the sign that read Visitors with an arrow pointing down.

"I am not going down there," Sarah announced.

I ignored her. She was coming along. There was no turning back now. I pushed through the overgrowth and picked my way down the crumbling stone steps to the door. Its once white paint was grayish and peeling, revealing the aged wood beneath. One of the panes in the glass was broken, but not enough to slip my hand through. It was locked up tight.

"Now what?" Roxi asked.

I made eye contact with her, then the others. "Now's going to be one of those times I ask you guys not to freak out," I said. Then I raised my hand and knocked on the door.

"So what?" Gage asked. "Is someone just supposed to come along and—"

The locks clicked and the door creaked open.

"Fuhhhh," Gage began.

"Uuuccck," finished Roxi.

"Yeah," I said, crossing the threshold. I couldn't remember how old I'd been when I realized that ghosts would let me in if I just asked. Wren asked because it was just polite; most ghosts didn't trespass on each other's turf. I didn't know why it worked for me, but it did, and that was really all that mattered.

Once we were inside, the door slammed shut. Everyone jumped. Gage swore. I hadn't done either, but my heart thumped so hard against my ribs I thought something was going to break.

I heard locks clack back into place.

"Now they're just showing off," I said as I fished a small flashlight out of my bag. I switched it on, keeping it pointed down so it didn't flash in the windows. Behind me, two more clicked on, as well.

The inside of Haven Crest was exactly what I expected— chessboard floor, garbage strewn around. Old furniture, peeling paint. What I hadn't expected was the smell. It was a smell that struck something deep inside me and awakened a terror I thought I'd buried deep enough to never haunt me again. It wasn't the smell of insanity, or even death. It was the smell of hopelessness.

I'd smelled that same smell at Bell Hill, breathed it in until it coated my lungs like cigarette tar, compressing my chest like phantom tumors. It had held me tight until it had completely taken over. Only Wren had been able to pull me free.

"Oh, shit," I whispered. My heart was in full-on panic mode now. What had I been thinking? How could I have ever thought I could walk through that door and be okay? This place was never going to let me leave. Never going to let me go. The scars on my wrists began to itch, and the cuts on my hands—which had already healed—began to sting. The ghost that had inflicted them was nearby.

My gaze darted around the darkness, made all the more bleak by the flashlight beams. The floor beneath my feet hummed with barely restrained malevolence. Screams echoed down long-forgotten corridors. The sobs were worse.

God, this place was alive. No, it was *undead*.

Blood ran down the walls. Hands thrust from the shadows, black and strong, fingers clutching, longing to grab me and pull me in. One brushed my leg.

Someone grabbed my hand. I almost screamed.

It was Ben.

My first instinct was to pull away, shake it off and pretend to be a hard-ass. I wrapped my fingers tight around his. A crowbar couldn't have gotten our hands apart.

There was no blood. There were no hands. Maybe there had been, or maybe they'd just been in my head. There was just that smell, seeped into every molecule of this place that looked like it had only ever been half-left, because no one who had ever been in a place like this, as an employee or patient, ever really got away. If it weren't for the dust and decay, you might expect someone to walk behind that front desk and answer the ringing phone.

The phone was *ringing.*

Someone gasped. It sounded like Roxi. It might have been Gage. So they heard it, too. Okay, this one wasn't just for me. I took a deep breath. This wasn't in my head, this was ghosts. Ghosts I could handle. I walked over to the desk—Ben still attached. I handed him my flashlight and picked up the handset. It wasn't even connected to the phone base. The phone wasn't plugged into the wall…

"Yes?" I said, holding the receiver away from my ear.

The sound that came through was like the scream of ten thousand tortured souls wrapped in static and buried in a well. It wasn't loud, but I knew every one of us felt it in our heads and in our bones.

"Who is this?" I asked.

"You're mine," growled a voice.

I hung up. "I don't know if that was Bent or not."

I heard a sob and looked up. Roxi was crying, and Gage had his arm around her.

"Don't," I told her. "That's what he wants." Just knowing it was a guy gave me courage to push on. "We're being messed with. Tested. It wants to scare you. You taste better when you're scared."

She nodded and wiped at her eyes. I had to give her credit for pulling herself together. I gestured down the hall, and Ben shone the light in that direction. "We need to find the stairs."

We moved quickly. None of us wanted to be there any longer than we needed to be. "Anyone feeling anything?" I asked. "Did something touch you?"

"I think so," Roxi whispered.

"That was me," Gage answered with a sheepish grin.

I laughed. I couldn't help it. Just a little release of anxiety.

That was when I heard the snarl—it came rushing at me like a hot gasp of decay, hitting me hard in the chest. It was angry and vicious—twisted. Visions of blood and gore danced behind my eyes. I saw those bodies again, strewn on the floor of this place, and Wren perched like a bizarre bird, a clutch of eyeballs in her sticky, crimson fingers.

And I felt pain—hot pokers deep behind my retinas.

"Stop laughing," I commanded. "It's making him angry."

I straightened, and took a look around in the dark. Our flashlights were the only break in the shadows before casting their own. "You know what I don't like?" I called out. "Cowards. Why don't you come on out, coward? Give me back my sister."

"Lark," Kevin warned. "Something's coming."

I kept going. "Come on, don't you want us? Don't you want us to see your big scary self? I've been told I taste really good. Don't you want a little taste of me? I'm fresh meat."

In a movie there would have been a loud noise, or maybe a ghost would appear. That didn't happen. Instead, Kevin turned to me, and I realized too late that he should have stayed behind.

Because he wasn't Kevin anymore.

chapter eleven

WREN

"Hello, child." His voice was like sandpaper.

I looked at the man who had grabbed and pulled me away from Lark, transporting me to his domain without much effort at all. He was medium height and lean. He had short hair and a handsome face. Ghosts usually looked in death as they had in life—unless they went the horrific route. Ghosts like this were more frightening, I thought. He looked perfectly normal, except that his eyes were black mirrors reflecting every horror he'd ever inflicted. He was the kind of thing mortals went insane after seeing.

I was impressed. Not afraid, but impressed.

"Where are we?" I asked.

He smiled at me—he had good teeth, too. I couldn't identify his time period from the way he was dressed. Lark probably could have, but she knew fashion better than I did. Not like it mattered—ghosts could dress however they wished.

"Now that would make it too easy for your little breather friends to find me, and I do so enjoy a good game."

I committed every inch of him to memory. "So long as you're the hunter, I think."

"Clever girl." He stepped close enough to touch my hair. "I do so love me a clever little girl."

"I'm not new-dead," I informed him. "Your practiced charm doesn't influence me." Because he wasn't charming, or sweet, or even nice, and I was insulted that he thought I'd be so easily fooled.

That sugary-sweet smile faded from his lips, leaving me staring into that soulless abyss that was his face. "That's better," I said. "Why hide your true nature?"

I thought he sniffed me then—something leftover from when he could actually breathe? We went through the motions of these things at times, but obviously they weren't necessary. I didn't understand how I was even able to conjure such experiences, when I hadn't been alive long enough to have any of them. When I felt like my heart was pounding, I knew my heart wasn't really pounding, though I was sure I had one.

Somewhere.

He smiled. "Dead Born. Yes, I realized it the first time I saw you."

Lark hated that title, but it held some prestige among the dead. Think of it as class snobbery. The higher your death-to-life ratio, the more pure you were. I was a rarity because most babies didn't linger between worlds, but moved on to whatever came next.

"Dead Born and naive as a new foal. Aren't you an interesting one? Why have you forsaken your kind, child? Why wallow with the breathers when you could be something truly special?"

I gave him a bored look, even though his words struck something inside me. I clung to Lark like she was some kind of safety net, watching her live her life while I had nothing. But I knew that wasn't really true. She was what kept me from becoming like the once-a-man standing before me—a creature that trembled with the effort it took to appear to me in an even remotely human guise. Did he think I'd be afraid of what he really looked like?

Show me yours and I'll show you mine.

"You're wasted on them," he continued. "You and your sister could be truly powerful in our world."

"My sister?"

He nodded. "Just think of what the two of you could achieve if she were to join you in the Shadow Lands. No more watching—the two of you could actually be together."

He spoke like he knew me, like he understood, but he didn't. He was just guessing, trying to sweeten me up. Trying to seduce me. "She'd never go for it. She *likes* breathing."

He made a face, as though the idea disgusted him. "The living." He made a spatting noise. "So afraid of dying, when they ought to embrace it." No, he didn't really know anything about me or about Lark if he thought she was afraid of death.

I humored him. "Foolish creatures."

"Exactly!" He had completely missed my sarcasm. "You should just join us and leave her to rot and wither."

"Us?"

I should have known better, but I was trying to uncover

his secrets. As soon as I asked, I regretted it. And when the ghosts started sifting through the walls, filling the hall where we stood, I knew I was in deep trouble. Their compulsion wrapped around me, drew me close. These were my people, my kind. They called to me—needed me. To be needed was a powerful thing in my world. They whispered to me, promises of knowledge and power, a gentle stroke of my ego, a compliment to my vanity. I didn't know how else to describe it, even though there were no words involved. It was as simple as the fact that they wanted me, and I wanted to be wanted. Maybe because I was Dead Born and they were drawn to that.

It felt amazing. Powerful. Terrible.

It had happened before, this test of my strength. In the asylum where Lark had been kept, the ghosts there had almost convinced me to join them. They had started to turn me into something I didn't want to be, a creature of fear and hate. Most ghosts are little more than whispers in the living world, and those ghosts tempted me with promises of screams.

We liked strong emotions—those were the ones we were actually able to feel. Passion. Loss. Anger. Fear. Love was lost to destruction, but I was lucky. I had Lark as my tether. She made it possible for me to feel. She kept some small part of me mortal.

I grabbed the man by the front of his shirt and hauled him close. I looked into those black, black eyes of his and saw the terrible things he'd done there. All those delicious moments of suffering he'd caused. I loved it and hated it, and I despised myself for being able to hold on as long as I did. I tore through his memories until I hit upon the thing I needed to see.

The place where he felt most powerful. The place he considered his own. It wasn't where we stood at this moment. This place was his as well, but the other place, that was where he'd lived while here, the place he still considered his.

The place where my sister could do him the most harm.

I shoved him backward, knocking him into several other ghosts. They kept calling to me. I needed to make them stop or I'd soon give in. I wanted to give in.

"Josiah Bent," I said with a triumphant grin. "Got you now."

His face twisted into something no one could ever mistake for human. This was Bent's real face. I saw it for a split second before he lunged at me.

Then I turned and ran.

LARK

Kevin swayed unsteadily on his feet. His eyes had rolled back into their sockets so that only white remained.

"That is so not right," Gage murmured behind me.

Suddenly, Kevin's head turned so that he stared right at me with those sightless eyes. "Third floor," he said in an old woman's voice. "Room 314. That's where you'll find him."

"Bent," I whispered. "You mean Josiah Bent?"

Kevin's shoulders slumped and his knees sagged. Ben stepped forward and grabbed him before he fell. Mace quickly took his other arm, and the two of them pulled their friend upright.

"You okay, man?" Mace asked.

Dark curls bobbed as Kevin shook his head. Then he lifted his gaze. This time I could see the bright blue of his eyes when he looked at me. "What the hell just happened?" he demanded.

"You were possessed," I replied. "Don't you remember?"

He glared at me. "Yes, I remember. I remember an old woman's voice telling me she was sorry and that it would only take a minute. That she would have gone right to you, but that you scared her."

I blinked at that. "I scared her?"

He just kept glaring at me like I was the villain. "Any idea why she would be afraid of you?"

Now I frowned. I shook my head. "No. And it's really not important right now. She told us where to find Bent, and hopefully Wren."

At the mention of my sister, Kevin's expression softened. "Let's go, then. Where is it?"

Weird that he didn't remember actually being possessed, but maybe that was normal. Whenever Wren or another spirit had hitched a ride with me I remembered all of it.

I turned on my heel and hurried in the direction of the stairwell. I hadn't felt Wren's absence so completely since Bell Hill. I couldn't sense her anywhere—it was as though she'd ceased to exist—something I refused to accept. I ran up the stairs to the second floor, then rounded the corner and sprinted to the third.

I was in pretty lousy shape.

There was a set of double doors at the top of the stairs— the kind they used to lock to keep the patients from getting out. They slammed shut the second I started for them—so hard the floor seemed to tremble beneath my feet. I grabbed the handles and pulled, but they wouldn't budge. I knocked like I had on the entrance door, then pounded with my fists when nothing happened.

"Let me in!" I shouted. "Open the damn door! Wren! Wren!"

The others stared at me like I'd lost it. They didn't know crazy. *I* knew crazy, and I wasn't even close. Not yet. I pressed my forehead against the cool, reinforced glass panel in the door. Out of the corner of my eye I saw the scar on my right wrist. I pressed it, and the one on my left wrist, against the wood.

"I'm one of you," I whispered. "I've cut myself, wanted to die. I've been drugged and told that I'm too wrong to be around normal people. I know that you're real and that you hurt, and you should know that I'm not leaving without my sister. Don't make me burn this place to the ground and salt the ashes. You know I'll do it. *Open. The. Door.*"

"We've got to get the hell out of here," Gage said. "She's losing it."

I gave the door a knock with my forehead. "We're not leaving her."

"Fuck that," Gage said. "Something already possessed Kevin, and you're sister's gone. We're next. I'm outta here."

I straightened and turned with the intention of punching him in the face. I even had my fists balled. Ben grabbed Gage by the arm, and Mace put himself between Gage and the stairs.

"We leave together," Mace said.

Gage shoved Ben, but the taller boy only moved back a step. "You're not leaving, G."

"Gonna stop me?" Gage demanded.

Ben just looked at him. "Yeah. Yeah, I am."

"Me, too," Mace added.

Roxi and Sarah joined them. They all stood by Mace, blocking the exit. Kevin came and stood by me, which was oddly touching. "We're in this together," he said.

Gage looked at his friends. I could see how scared he was, but their determination to see this through seemed to calm him. "Fine. So, what now?"

"We go back downstairs," I said. "There has to be another way to access this floor. Stick together, and if you see Wren, don't approach her."

"See her?" That was Sarah.

I so did not want to have this conversation, but it had to happen. "She might manifest. If she does, stay the hell away."

"What does she look like?" Sarah again. Really? Did she miss the part where Wren was my effing twin?

Kevin looked down at me. "Do you really think we'll be in danger if she manifests?"

My jaw tightened. "Yes." Sweet hell, yes. "Let me deal with her." And if she didn't tear me apart we might survive.

Mace jerked his head toward the stairs. "Let's go."

I took one step, that was it. Just one step before I heard the thunk of a heavy-duty lock slipping out of place, followed by an ominous creak. I glanced over my shoulder.

The doors swung open like arms waiting for a hug.

"Oh, hell."

I smiled. Poor Gage. He really wasn't cut out for this stuff.

I led the way across the threshold into the ward. "Don't touch the walls, don't open any doors, and for the love of

God, don't go into any rooms." When we found 314 I would be the one going inside.

The phone at the nurses' station started ringing—it echoed through the corridor. Its bell grew louder and longer each time, until it sounded like it was simultaneously gargling and screaming.

"Knock it off!" I shouted. "It's not scary, it's just fucking annoying!"

The ringing stopped.

"Did you hear that?" Sarah's eyes were as big as dinner plates. I could see her trembling.

"Yes," I said. "I did." After the phone stopped ringing someone had laughed.

"I want to go home," Roxi announced. "Just putting that out there."

"We all do," Ben agreed.

I was about to say that we weren't going anywhere without Wren, and then I saw her. Standing just outside one of the patient rooms, hair flowing around her shoulders as though lifted by a gentle breeze.

There was no wind in that corridor. Any energy came directly from her—not a good sign.

"*That's* your sister?" Gage asked. Again, not good. If they could see her…

"Lark!" she cried. "This is it! This is his room." She knew better than to say his name—that would summon him. As it was he was going to come for us soon.

As soon as we entered his room, I bet.

I didn't care about Bent at that moment. I ran to Wren and hugged her. "You're manifesting," I whispered.

She nodded. "I know, but it's all right. I'm in control. Um, Lark? You're squishing me."

I let go of her. "Sorry."

Behind us the doors slammed shut again. A warning, but was it friendly or hostile?

I beckoned for the others to join us, and then I turned to look into room 314. Wren was right behind me. It was like walking into a beehive, the buzzing was so loud.

Josiah Bent wasn't the only madman to have thought terrible things in this room, to have left part of himself behind. Every corner had someone hiding in it, smiling or wailing. A young man leered at me from beside the window.

"I'd like to taste your insides," he said.

Wren hissed at him, her hair flying out around her head like tentacles. I squeezed her hand when my own hair lifted. I could feel her pulling at my soul—feeding on it.

"Stop it," I said.

Luckily for me, she did. The young man grinned at her before flickering out of sight.

"Oh, my God," Sarah said, covering her mouth and nose with her hand. "What's that smell?"

"Rot," I replied. "Death and insanity. Pain and suffering. Take your pick."

"What are we looking for?" Kevin asked.

Wren turned her head to look at him. "His razor. Oh, and Adele says she's sorry for scaring you."

From the way his face tightened I guessed that Adele was the ghost that had possessed him. She had to be one of the many in this asylum under Bent's control.

"How could he have kept a razor in here?" Mace asked. "Don't they take those away?"

"They do now," I answered. "They may have then, I don't know. But it's here. Somewhere—and probably someplace hidden."

We began to scour the room. The ghosts zipped in and out, yelling at me, poking at me, pulling my hair. I swatted them away. I checked baseboards and in the closet, but found nothing.

"Here," Ben said. He was at the window—where the leering ghost had stood. Had the young ghost wanted to distract me rather than discuss the edibility of my inner organs?

Ben gave the windowsill a quick, hard kick. It crashed to the floor, revealing a hidden cache behind it. There were several items there, but only one I cared about.

A straight razor with a pearl handle.

"Don't touch it," I said, tone sharp. If Ben picked that thing up, Bent might possess him, and then we'd be in a lot of trouble. Worse, Bent might decide to take a ride in Kevin's head. Mediums were so open to spirits they were sometimes easily influenced. The last thing we needed was Kevin killing people.

I reached into the little cubby and curled my fingers around the razor. It ought to have been cool to the touch, but it wasn't. It was hot, as though it had been lying in the sun for hours.

Images strobed behind my eyes, slamming violently into my brain; Bent as a young man, holding that very razor to a girl's throat—a thin line of crimson. Using it on a man who had beat him at cards, on another woman who refused to have sex with him. On his own mother.

That was when he'd begun using the razor just for fun. He'd shave his face with it in the morning, then spend hours sharpening it so it could slice through flesh with almost painless efficiency. Bent's favorite part had been seeing the look of surprise on his victims' faces when they realized what he'd done.

Little nicks here and there—enough to sting. Enough to bleed, to incite panic. Slicing through flesh like it was butter, watching that sweet, red blood bubble to the surface. The smell of copper in his nostrils, the sobs in his ears. So. Damn. Good.

One girl, he'd licked the salt trail of her tears from her cheeks before following that same path with the razor.

"Ben," I rasped, because he was closest to me. "Reach into my bag and see if there's a plastic baggie in there."

He opened the flap of my messenger bag and rummaged inside. A second or two later, he pulled out a Ziploc bag. It had sandwich crumbs in it, but I'd be embarrassed about that later.

"Dump some salt in," I instructed. And once he'd filled a third of the bag, I tossed the razor into it. "Now add more and seal it."

A roar rose up around us as the salt mixture covered the weapon. It seemed to start in the basement and climb up the walls, shaking the floor beneath our feet. The windows rattled, panes cracking. The bars were on the outside and would not protect us if the glass blew.

Neither Kevin nor I should have that blade. Bent would go for one of us immediately. The only other person strong enough to handle it was Ben. He'd been raised with knowledge of how to protect himself, and he wasn't as afraid of ghosts—not like most people.

"Hide it," I told him. I didn't watch to see what he did. I turned to the others. "Get out."

The place was still trembling when we ran out into the corridor, but not with the same frenzy. I knew better than to be relieved.

"What the hell?" Mace muttered.

A wheelchair moved slowly toward us. There wasn't anyone in it. Cliche, but effective. Roxi yelped and grabbed Gage's hand. Wren glided over to it and stopped it from moving any farther. That wasn't good. The fact that she could interact with it meant that the spiritual energy in this place was strong. Too strong. Behind her I saw a flicker of light—like a glitch on a baby monitor. It was a man.

It was Bent.

"Wren!" I shouted, breaking into a run. Son of a bitch was not going to get her again. I pulled the canister of salt from my bag and wrenched it open, flinging it forward. "Duck!"

My sister dived out of the way just in time. Unfortunately, so did the man. The salt and iron scattered uselessly on the floor. That was okay—it bought us a few seconds.

I grabbed Wren's hand. "We have to get out of here. Now."

Her gaze locked with mine. "If he'll let us out."

"Oh, he'll let us out," I said. It wasn't all bravado. This wasn't my first bully of a ghost, and I still had a few tricks up my sleeve. And I had Wren.

Another flicker. I flung more salt, this time hitting a young girl in the chest. She screamed and fizzled out.

Sarah cried out. I whipped around to see several ghosts surrounding my friends. An old woman in a stained nightgown pulled at Sarah's hair. A small boy tried to bite at Gage's knee. Mace swung a heavy wrench and scattered a middle-aged woman in a nurse's uniform. Ben flung salt, taking out another ghost and the one on Sarah.

Josiah Bent materialized a few feet down the corridor. Lights flickered around him like camera flashes. He looked as solid and real as any of us, but he didn't have his razor—we did.

And from the look on his face, he wanted it back.

"Get to the door!" I shouted, putting myself between him and my friends as they ran for the stairs.

Wren put herself between me and Bent as I grabbed another salt can from my bag. Her hair spiraled like crimson tentacles as she drew herself up. She was taller—bigger than normal, her eyes bottomless black pits as she lashed out at him. Wicked claws slashed Bent's face and laid it open—black blood spraying.

He looked surprised. Then he grabbed her by the throat. I didn't hesitate. I emptied some of the can into my palm and threw a handful of the mixture—avoiding Wren—raining it down on him like hail. Bent shrieked and shattered.

I lifted my arm to shield myself from the spray of salt. When I lowered it, I blinked my stinging eyes. For a split second I saw a woman with white hair.

"You have to get out of here *now*," she said. And then she was gone.

"Let's go!" I shouted, reaching for my sister. She grabbed

my hand and started running after the others. Her touch gave me preternatural speed.

We caught up to our friends downstairs, where we'd come in.

"Get out!" I yelled at them. "If the door won't open, kick it down!"

"I'll kick it down," Wren promised. And she went and did just that. As it flew open, our companions ran toward it.

Mace fell to his knees, wrench clattering to the floor. He clutched his chest.

"No!" I shouted. I hit the floor hard beside him. The floor was so thick with dirt that I jerked to a stop rather than sliding. I caught Mace as he pitched forward. His eyes rolled back into his skull as he twitched in my arms. This was bad. So very bad.

Ben, Sarah, Gage and Roxi stopped just before the exit, each one staring at Mace in horror. Sarah must have been terrified or in shock, because she didn't move. She just stood there, staring as though she couldn't believe what was going on.

And all around us the building shook. Doors slammed. The telephone began to ring. I heard the shuffling footsteps of hundreds of lethargic and drugged inmates above my head. No longer just flickers. They had manifested. Goose bumps jumped up along my arms and neck. Bent was raising a damn army.

Wren heard it, too. "Lark? We have to go."

Ben—brave Ben—had started toward me, ready to help me with Mace. But he had Bent's razor, and if he didn't escape with it, we were all dead. "Run!" I shouted at him and the others. "Run now!"

And they did. Call them cowards; call them smart. It didn't matter. They did what I told them to do and that was all I cared about.

Wren grabbed at my arm. "Let's go."

I looked up at her. "I have to help him."

Shadows crept down the hall—a legion of darkness coming to claim us.

And then I heard the whisper, *"Child. Dead Born."* I froze. Bent wasn't coming for me, or for Mace. He was coming for Wren. No way was I going to let him have her.

"Get out of here," I told her.

"Not without you."

"Damn it, Wren! Get the fuck out of here!"

She just stared at me—scared. I swallowed. I couldn't help Mace and protect her, too. "I'm sorry," I whispered as I stuck my hand in my bag.

"For what?"

I lashed out, striking with the iron bar Ben had given me. Normally Wren was solid to me, but the iron cut through her like she was butter and it a hot knife. I heard her cry out as she exploded into sparkling confetti that rained down around me.

She was so going to kick my ass if I survived the night.

The shadows came closer. Apparently Bent had decided anything was better than nothing. I had to act quickly.

"Leave me," Mace rasped.

I made a face at him. "Don't be stupid. I owe you. I'm not leaving you."

He really didn't look good. His face, usually gorgeous, was contorted in pain. "You are so annoying."

"Shut up." And then I yanked up his shirt and took a look at that ugly, ugly gouge on his chest, weeping tar. It was so freaking awful. I slapped my hand on it, and prayed—yes prayed—that whatever mojo I'd worked on Sarah earlier worked again. It was my only chance of getting both of us out of there alive. I was not going to spend eternity in this place, and neither was Mace.

I felt a jolt up my arm—like sticking my finger in a light socket and then getting punched in the chest. Mace bolted upright, eyes wide. Apparently he'd felt it, too.

A tendril of shadow on the floor curled toward him. Another eased down the wall not far from my head. And down by the stairs, Josiah Bent began to flicker again. Any second he could manifest—and he was going to be so pissed.

"Let's go." I jumped to my feet—knees knocking—and held out my hand. Mace grabbed my fingers and pushed to his feet as I pulled. His arm went across my shoulders, mine around his waist. Together we ran toward the entrance, our fear giving us what felt like superhuman speed. I think I could have carried him if I'd had to.

The door was open, and we squeezed through a split second before Bent manifested enough to slam it shut.

Now we had to make it to the graveyard. There was no way we'd make it there before the ghost—or any ghost—came after us again. I just hoped I had enough salt and iron left to protect us. At least I still had the iron rod Ben had given me.

We ran for the street. I didn't care if security saw us. Two rent-a-cops were the least of my concerns at that moment.

My heart was in my throat and my lungs felt as though they were going to burst as we ran across the street, straight for the grass. Behind us a roar gathered; Bent and his minions weren't about to let us get away that easily. There was no way we'd get away at this pace, but if I could get Mace close to safety, I might be able to hold them off until he was with the others.

After that, I didn't know what would happen.

Suddenly, there was a flash of light—right in my eyes! I stopped short, almost falling to the grass. Mace slammed into me, pitching me forward. I blinked, and held up my free hand, shielding my eyes as I looked up at the source of the light.

Shit.

"Hey, kids," Officer Olgilvie said with malicious cheer. "Whatcha up to?"

chapter twelve

WREN

She expelled me. My own sister! Sent me to the Shadow Lands and made me have to pull myself together again. By the time I'd done it, everyone was out of the building, back to the graveyard, and Lark and Mace had been arrested by that terrible man. There was nothing I could do about it, either. If she hadn't expelled me I might have been able to frighten him enough that he let them go, but no—she had to be all overprotective of me. I understood it, but didn't like it.

At least getting arrested kept them safe. Got them off asylum grounds.

Josiah Bent was an awful creature. Even if I hadn't met him, or seen some of his deeds through Lark when she'd picked up that razor—it radiated off him like light from a bulb. I'd never felt anything like that maliciousness before, and to feel it coming through my sister... Well, I never wanted to experience it again, but I would have to. We couldn't allow him to kill more people, but how could we stop something so powerful that he commanded an army of ghosts?

"Ohmigodohmigodohmigod," Roxi bent down, head hanging by her knees.

Ben leaned against his car. He looked pale, but surprisingly stoic for what they'd all just experienced. I was a ghost and the whole thing had shaken *me*. "What do we do?"

Kevin threw his gear into the trunk of his vehicle and slammed it shut. "We find the bastard's grave and burn his remains."

"Not tonight," said Ben. "Not without a plan, and not without Lark and Mace."

"When?" Gage demanded. "Did you see what he did to Mace? For all we know Mace might be dead."

They all looked at each other.

"This thing wants to kill us," Gage went on, eyes wide, voice shaking. "It's going to kill us."

He was right, of course. Lark would have said something about not allowing that to happen—that they would kick Bent's ass. I didn't have anything like that to say. I was very scared at that moment that not only would Bent get my friends, but that he'd get me, too. He'd been coming for me, taunting me. The pull had been so strong, the urge to join him and let myself go so tempting.

Of the two of us, Lark had always thought that she was the "bad" one. My sister had no idea the things I sometimes thought—the things I sometimes wanted to do. If I could help it, she never would. The one thing keeping me from joining Bent—beyond Lark—was the fact that I was not going to be another ghost's servant. I was Dead Born. I might be fairly ignorant of my kind, young and still new, but I was aware that I was part of a special caste—one that I wasn't certain I wanted to embrace.

But I did know that I wasn't a follower.

"Mace isn't dead," I told Kevin. "But if any of you go back onto Haven Crest grounds tonight, you will be."

He repeated what I'd said.

Gage slumped against Ben's car. I thought for a moment that he might cry, but he didn't.

Ben folded his arms over his chest. "What about Lark and Mace? We just leave them?"

"They'll be fine," Sarah said. "Mace's father won't let them actually go to jail, not for trespassing. He wants Mace to go to an Ivy League so bad I think Mace could murder someone and his father would still try to cover it up."

I hoped she was right—not about Mace committing murder, of course. She didn't seem too worried about her boyfriend, but maybe she was just that confident that he'd be okay. Or maybe she was in shock after what she'd just experienced.

Or maybe she was just more concerned about herself, which was the conclusion I chose, because I didn't like her very much. I would have stuck my tongue out if I thought she might see it. I settled for tracing my finger along her spine just to watch her shudder.

"What do we do now?" Roxi asked. They were lost without Lark to take charge.

"We go home," Kevin said after a few seconds of silence. "Bent had to have a patient number. If we can find it, we can find his grave and burn the bastard."

"We've got his razor, too," Ben informed them. He pulled the plastic bag Lark had given him from his pocket. "Should we try to destroy it first?"

They all looked at Kevin. Kevin looked at me. "Yes," I said.

Kevin nodded. "Wren says we should burn it." He glanced around at the other cars parked nearby. "But not here."

Ben frowned at the baggie. "We should probably wait for Lark and Mace."

"We don't know when they'll be back," Sarah said. "Are you okay with holding on to...that thing while we wait?"

Ben shrugged. "I don't think Bent knows where it is."

"He's right," I said. "The salt, herbs and iron keep him from it. Ben will be safe as long as he doesn't take the razor from the bag."

Kevin repeated what I'd said. Ben tossed the baggie into his car.

"I need to check on Lark," I told him. To be honest, I was a little lost without her, too. I was more concerned about her than I was angry—although I was still really mad. Getting smacked with iron came as close to physical pain as anything in my world could. It was terrifying to be ripped apart like that, and my sister was going to hear just how much.

"I can come by later," I added. "Let you know what's going on."

Kevin nodded and looked at me. I could see that he was worried—his aura was wild with it. He was also frightened and angry. The only thing he could do about it was try to find Bent's patient number—I wasn't going to stand in the way of that. Going to Lark was the best thing I could do. She was my tether, and I'd regain my strength with her.

Kevin told the others that I'd update him later. It would be so much easier if I could just talk to them myself, but I didn't know how to make that happen. For someone who was supposed to be so strong, I felt pretty weak.

I was just about to go when Roxi cried out. I turned and saw Gage stumble out of Ben's car. I hadn't even noticed him get into it.

His hands were bloody.

"Oh, no," I whispered as he fell into Ben's arms.

"Wren!" Kevin cried.

I skipped forward, crossing the distance in a matter of blinks. Gage convulsed in Ben's arms. His eyes had rolled back into his head and his skin was covered in a fine sheen of sweat.

"What's wrong with him?" Sarah cried.

"Roll up his sleeves, please?" I asked. Kevin did. The spectral wounds on Gage's arms—invisible to all but me—were ragged, wet, red-and-black gouges in his flesh. But there were new wounds as well—self-inflicted.

Bent must have been whispering to him through his infection, like he had to Sarah at the coffee shop. Gage had gotten into the car and cut himself because Bent wanted us to know this wasn't over. He could still get us. I could see muscle and tendon, inflamed and infected. Tar-like pus ran down his hands, mixing with his blood, dripping from his fingers.

"He needs a hospital," I said. "Now. Pour salt on his arms."

"Put him in the backseat," Kevin commanded, opening his car. Ben put the twitching Gage inside. He grabbed a chip bag from the floor of the backseat and used it to pick up the bloody razor, which he closed before shoving it back into the bag of salt. He shook it so it was covered.

He was learning fast when it came to ghosts.

"Is he going to be coming for us?" Ben asked, glancing around as though there would be any warning. "He knows we have the razor."

"I don't feel him," I said.

Kevin didn't look up from the first-aid kit he'd pulled from the trunk. "Not yet," he replied. "I think he did this just to let us know he can."

Ben glanced down at the plastic bag in his hand. The inside was smeared with blood. His fingers tightened around it. "I'll keep the razor."

Kevin's head snapped up as he closed the trunk. "It's not safe."

"I'm the only one Bent hasn't come after. I can hide this— at least until we get Lark and Mace back and figure out what to do."

"Gage needs help!" Roxi reminded them, sharply. "Now!"

Roxi climbed in with Gage, cradling his head. Kevin gave her a bottle of saline solution. "Pour this on his arms."

I slipped into the front seat. I'd go see Lark after. Roxi didn't question Kevin. She simply opened the bottle and squeezed the liquid onto Gage's bare skin. I watched as the infection sizzled and blood ran pink. Salt had purification properties, and while I didn't like the idea that there might be something impure about me, I respected the mineral's power. I moved back to avoid being splattered.

Kevin drove fast to the hospital. It was the same one Mace had brought Lark to *that* day, her blood soaking into his clothes. I relived some of that fear as we pulled up in front of the emergency doors.

As we entered the hospital, Kevin glanced in my direction. "Wren, how bad is it?"

I wished I could lie to him and tell him I'd seen worse, but I hadn't. "Bad," I said. "Really bad."

LARK

"You two can just wait in here," Olgilvie said—rather gleefully, I thought—as he closed the door of the tiny room. Mace and I were sitting at a battered table on chairs with uneven legs. I waited until the door had shut before I raised my middle finger at it.

"There's a camera," Mace told me.

"I know," I replied, slowly lowering my finger. I turned to him. "What happens now?

He shrugged. "My father will show up eventually, and either decide to make examples of us or let us go."

"What are the chances of just letting us go?"

"I don't know. He hasn't been too impressed with me lately."

"And then there's the fact that you're with that crazy girl who tried to kill herself and dragged you into it."

"There's that." He slumped in his chair, stretching his long legs out beneath the table. "What did you do to me back there?"

I pushed my chair back, put my feet up on the table. "I'm not sure. It worked on Sarah earlier, so I figured it was worth a shot. How do you feel?"

"Better, so it must be good, right?"

"Unless my touch triggered something ghostly, and made it

worse, yeah. I guess." God, what if I'd made it easier somehow for Bent to do his thing? "Still new to this stuff, remember? Figuring it out as I go." Now I sounded guilty.

He held up his hands. "Hey, I didn't say anything. Thanks, though. I thought it was going to kill me."

"I think that was the intention." God, I was so tired I could go to sleep right there in that really uncomfortable chair. After Haven Crest, being arrested wasn't really all that scary. Though I wasn't looking forward to seeing the disappointment on my grandmother's face. Maybe she'd understand after I explained.

"So, I guess we're even now. You and me."

I stifled a yawn. "I guess so."

Silence. Was this the same guy I had blathered away to on the lake? Who had blathered away to me like we were actually friends?

"Are you okay?" he asked after a few seconds had passed, crossing his arms over his chest. "Did it hurt you?"

"Nah, I'm good. Wren's going to be pissed at me for whacking her with that iron bar, though." Olgilvie had taken that from me, along with my bag.

"Yeah, why'd you do that to her?"

"Bent was coming for her—calling for her. I had to get her out of there."

He looked at me for a moment, a slight twist to his lips. "You've got a real hero complex, you know that?"

I made a face. "That's hysterical coming from you." Then I saw a flicker out of the corner of my eye. "Oh, crap."

"What?"

I jerked my head to my right. I knew he couldn't see what was there, but maybe he'd figure it out.

Ghost? he mouthed. I nodded. This was *not* a good time.

"I know you can see me," the ghost said. He was a younger guy—maybe in his twenties—with long hair and a leather jacket. He looked like he should have been on tour with Bon Jovi in the '80s.

I rolled my eyes. "I know that you know. So what?"

"Hey, we've met before, yeah? Like, last night. Wait, that wasn't you, was it? I mean, it was you, but someone else was drivin'."

"Hardly makes us BFFs, does it?"

He held up his hands, palms out. "Touchy. Just relax, JB. I won't bite."

I raised a brow. "JB?"

He grinned—he had good teeth. He would have been kind of hot if not for all that hair. "Jail Bait."

And his personality. That definitely ruined his hotness more than the hair.

"You call me JB, so how about I call you DD?"

"Damn Dangerous?"

I smiled sweetly. "Dead Douche."

He winced. "You're cruel and heartless. If I was still alive we'd already be in the back of my van."

"If you were still alive you'd be pushing fifty, and we wouldn't even be breathing the same air."

"Who the hell are you talking to?" Mace demanded.

I shot the ghost a questioning look. "Care to introduce yourself? Or should I just tell my friend to call you DD?"

"Really? You don't know who I am?"

"Should I?"

The ghost came over and sat down across from Mace. He waved his hand in front of his face. "He can't see or hear me, can he?"

I shook my head. "No."

"Is he your boyfriend? Did you get picked up having sex at the graveyard? Man, I nailed a lot of chicks near the grave of some girl that died of a broken heart."

If stares could be iron he'd have been dusted right then. I knew that grave—it was sad.

He sighed. "Fine. I'm Joe Hard."

I laughed. "Joe Hard? You're freaking kidding."

Mace sat up. "Joe Hard? That's who you're talking to?"

Suddenly the ghost snapped to attention, too. "Nice to know not everyone's forgotten me."

"Skinny guy with big hair and eye liner?" I asked.

Mace nodded. "Tattoo of angel wings on his left arm."

Joe lowered the sleeve of his jacket. Beneath it he was wearing an electric-pink tank top. He did have angel wings on his biceps. "That's the one."

A huge grin took over Mace's face. He looked both goofy and gorgeous at the same time. "Dude, my mother had such a thing for you."

"Is your mother hot?" Joe asked, leaning on the table.

I opened my mouth to tell him off, but as luck would have it, that was the moment Wren arrived. She materialized right beside Joe, who turned and looked at her—then me—then her again. I swung my feet off the table and sat up.

"Twins." He said it with a sigh before giving Mace a dirty look. "You lucky bastard."

Wren looked at him. "I know you. And...bastard? I don't think it matters these days if Mace's parents are married."

Joe grinned. "You are so strange. Sit down, darlin'. You're way more my type than your sister."

Wren did sit down. "Oh, don't let the fact that she's alive stop you. We're tangible to her. See?" To prove her point she pinched me.

"Ow!" I rubbed my arm.

"You okay?" Mace asked with a frown.

I nodded.

Wren smiled the same smile I'd given Dead Douche. "That's for the iron."

"Tangible, huh?" Joe grinned. "Why don't the three of us get out of here, then? Come back for your boy later."

This was quickly spiraling into sitcom territory. To be honest, I was almost relieved when the door opened and Olgilvie walked in. What was interesting, though, was the way Joe's expression changed when he saw the cop. That was real hate on his face. Interesting. Finally, things were looking up.

"You've been chatting a lot in here, Miss Noble," Olgilvie remarked. "Who are you talking to?"

I pointed at Mace. "Uh, him?"

Mace nodded. "It's true. We talk."

Olgilvie wasn't fat, but he was big—burly. Nan would call him "solid." God, she was going to be so embarrassed that I got picked up by the cops. Reminding myself of that sucked some of the bitch out of me. I did not want to hurt her.

He pulled out the chair across from me—the one right beside Joe—and sat down. He set the can of salt and my iron rod on the table between us.

"Could I talk you into bashing his head in?" Joe asked. "Just a little?"

I didn't smile, but I wanted to.

"We found these things in your bag, Miss Noble."

"I had some tampons in there, too. Did you find them?"

Under the table, Mace nudged my foot with his.

Olgilvie didn't look impressed. "Please explain to me what these are for."

"Have you notified Lark's grandmother that she's here?" Mace asked. "She should have a guardian present."

I leaned my forearms on the table. I pointed at the can of salt. "That's where I hide my drugs. Open it up and take a snort."

"And this?" Olgilvie picked up the rod, and for a second, I saw that he wanted to hit me with it. Wow.

"Back scratcher." That was possibly the lamest thing to *ever* come out of my mouth, but it was all I could think of.

"Why were you trespassing at Haven Crest?"

"You don't have to answer him," Mace said. He kept his gaze on the older man. I had to hand it to him, Mace didn't intimidate easily. Then again, when your daddy was chief, you could be a little arrogant.

I shrugged. "Trespassing. Isn't that against the law?" I certainly wasn't going to admit to it. "Why were you there?"

"Security thought they heard screams. Did you see a ghost?" He grinned mockingly. Jerk.

The door to the room opened and an older man stuck his head in. I could tell from one look that he was Mace's father. They really looked alike. "Get your ass out here," he said to his son.

Mace got up. He glanced at me. "I'll take care of this."

I didn't need him taking "care" of anything for me. I'd just made things "even" between us, I didn't need to owe him another favor so freaking soon.

He and Olgilvie traded glares, but the cop looked more amused than anything else. He liked that Mace was in trouble—and he loved that Mace was in trouble along with me, which made me think that the chief didn't have much liking for me at all.

"Can I ask you a question?" I said to Olgilvie when Mace was gone.

He looked amused. "What?"

"How come you're being haunted by Joe Hard?"

The iron bar clattered to the table hard enough to leave a mark. Olgilvie's face went completely white. When he looked at me, his expression was a mix of fear and…hatred.

"Lark," my sister said. "What did you just do?"

I couldn't answer that, because I had no freaking idea. I regretted doing it, though—sort of. Olgilvie was afraid of me, and that was kind of cool, but I had a feeling that I'd just poked him about a secret he'd kill to keep. A secret that I didn't really know and wasn't worth me dying over.

"What do you know about Joe?" the officer rasped.

I looked at Joe, who was grinning at Olgilvie like a shark about to take a bite. "I'll do you a solid, JB. Tell him if he doesn't let you go I'm going to tell you where Laura is."

Oh, this was all kinds of stupid. "Joe says if you don't let me go he'll tell me where Laura is."

For a second, I thought Olgilvie was going to have a stroke. He went from white to crimson in seconds, and a vein on his forehead bulged. If looks could kill, there'd be nothing left of me but a pile of smoldering bone.

"You *idiot*," my sister said. Then to Joe, "If he tries to hurt her, I'm going to come for you."

For a second, Joe didn't look all that impressed, but then Wren…changed. She felt and looked ominous—like a thundercloud ready to spit lightning, only one hundred times more dangerous. Her eyes turned into mirrors, reflecting the darkness I'd only glimpsed once before and never wanted to see again, but I couldn't look away. She was my sister, and I refused to be scared of her.

Joe swallowed, his eyes wide. "Riiiiiight."

I looked at Olgilvie. He was still flushed. He stank of desperation. "I don't know who Laura is," I told him. "And I don't really care. I just want to go home. Can I go home, sir?" I thought the "sir" was a nice touch—might make him feel a little more in control.

"Yeah," he said, his voice shaking. "Get the hell out of here."

I grabbed the iron rod and salt from the table and jumped up. Wren followed after me in silence. She was angry at me. I was angry at me, too. I'd blackmailed my way into going free, but I'd just made a huge enemy that I knew I was going to regret making.

"Be seeing you, JB!" Joe shouted.

I didn't acknowledge him. Our paths would cross again; I knew it. He'd better hope I wasn't dead when that happened.

chapter thirteen

LARK

It took me a few minutes to get my bag back. By the time Wren and I left the police department, she had filled me in on what had happened to Gage. It was hard to listen and not respond, but there were too many people around for me to even acknowledge her. I didn't say anything until we got out into the parking lot.

"I should have been there," I said as we walked. It was late—really late—and there wasn't anyone around to overhear.

"There was no way you could have known Bent would go after Gage like that."

"No," I agreed mockingly, "because what he did to Sarah wasn't a hint or anything."

Wren sighed—a long-suffering sound she'd used with me a lot. "You couldn't help Mace and help Gage, too. Suck it up."

I stopped and turned to look at her. "Suck it up?"

She shrugged and frowned at me. "Or get over it—whatever."

I shook my head. Slang and my sister just didn't mix.

"Mace seems to be all right," Wren commented as we started walking again. "What happened?"

I looked around to make sure no one was about—again. "Can you think of any reason why my touch would heal wraith wounds?"

She pretended to think about it. "We're not normal?"

Sarcasm and my sister, on the other hand, they mixed pretty damn well. "I touched him, Wren. Somehow I stopped the wound from hurting. It happened earlier with Sarah, too."

"I don't know. Lark, when you died and came back, everything got mixed up. We were odd before that, but now…"

"It's like all the rules got messed up," I finished.

She nodded. Her fingers brushed my hair. "How about, just this once, you just be glad you're weird instead of trying to figure out how and why?"

I was too tired to argue. "Sure."

"Wonderful. Now that that's settled—I can't believe you threatened that deputy. God, Lark! What if he decides you're his enemy? He's the law!"

"You're not saying anything I haven't thought of, Wren."

"Maybe you should have thought harder before opening your mouth."

"I said it because it got us out of there. I'm not going to think beyond that."

"Sometimes I think you don't think at all. If you hadn't ironed me I might have been able to scare him at the asylum and you wouldn't have been taken."

"How would that have been any better? He still would

have blamed me." I glanced at her. "Maybe you don't *think* as well as you think you do."

"You always have to be right. Well, if I'd scared him at the asylum we wouldn't be here right now."

So, she had a point. So did I. "But then I wouldn't have leverage against Officer Olgilvie, would I?" I checked my watch. It was well after midnight. "Think they'd let us into the hospital now?" It was just down the street. Maybe Ben would still be there and could give me a ride home.

"Let *you* in," Wren corrected. "I could just drift through the walls."

She could also just zap herself home if she wanted and leave my sorry ass to get back on its own. I didn't want to call Nan, but cabs were scarce around here, and I didn't have anyone else, damn it.

Screw it. I was going to walk.

"Want a ride?" came a voice from behind me. Mace.

I turned. "Thought you'd be long gone by now."

Hands in his pockets, he walked beneath the bright station lights toward us. "My father had some things he wanted to say to me first."

"I bet."

He pulled keys from his pocket. "But he had one of the guys go get my car, so I can drive you home if you want. Or you can come to the hospital with me to see Gage. I got a call from Kev. I assume Wren brought you up to speed?"

I nodded. "I figured they wouldn't let us in?"

"Nah, Kevin's aunt is on the ER desk tonight. You coming?"

"Yeah." I wanted to see Gage.

We turned and walked through the parking lot. Mace seemed to know where he was going, so I followed after him. Sure enough he led us right to his Jag. He opened the passenger door for me and I climbed in.

The interior smelled like Sarah's perfume, cloves and fennel. It was a weird combination.

"Sarah doesn't like me much," I said as I buckled my seat belt.

He checked for traffic before steering the car out onto the street. "That's random."

I shrugged.

"She likes you fine. She's just jealous."

That was a bit more direct than I had expected. I shouldn't be surprised. "Why?"

Mace glanced at me. "Because you and I have history."

I snorted. "Not the sexy kind."

He chuckled. "No. But we have a connection, and she feels threatened by it."

"I just can't imagine her feeling threatened by anyone. She's perfect."

I felt him look at me. "You think so?"

When I turned my head he was looking at the road again. "Yeah. Don't you?"

"No one's perfect." We turned into the hospital lot. After a few moments he asked, "Can you do that thing you did to me to Gage?"

"I can try."

"Good." And then, "What the hell was it anyway?"

I shook my head. "No freaking idea."

"Does it matter?" Wren asked from the backseat. She was

frowning at Mace. "How about a little gratitude there, pretty boy?"

I choked back laughter. Mace glanced at me. "You okay?"

"As well as can be expected."

"Yeah. Hey, what did Joe Hard tell you about Olgilvie?"

"Just what you heard."

He looked like he didn't believe me, and I was okay with that. Joe Hard had a horrible name, but I wasn't going to give away his secrets, not when I wanted to make them my own.

Mace fell quiet. We parked near the door and went inside. A pretty woman with dark skin and a gorgeously huge head of corkscrew curls was at the front desk. The security guard nodded at Mace, who nodded back.

"Hey, Ivy," he said to the woman. "Can we see Gage?"

She nodded. "Go on back. I'll let Kevin know you're here." Then she looked at me and smiled. "You must be Lark."

This gorgeous woman was Kevin's aunt? Had to be by marriage. No way they were related.

"Um, yeah. Hi." I didn't know how to feel about the fact that Kevin had obviously talked about me. I could only imagine what he might have said.

I followed Mace into the emergency ward. Wren stayed close to me. "I don't like this place," she whispered. "It's too sad."

I took her hand and held it close to my thigh so no one would notice. Hospitals always had a lot of spirit activity, but they retained a lot of energy, too. Wren responded to both. I guess I did, too, because I really didn't want to be there.

Just as we walked into the fairly open area with the curtained-off beds, Roxi's head popped out from behind a curtain down at the far end. She waved us down. As we walked, I heard a woman crying and someone else moaning in pain. Doctors and nurses scurried around, but no one seemed to pay much attention to us—not even the ghosts.

Mace parted the curtain and we walked into the small area around Gage's bed. Everyone was there. Ben grinned when he saw me. I smiled back like a demented idiot. I was just so glad that he was okay.

"Hey, jailbird," he teased.

Better than Jail Bait, I thought. "Hey. How is he?"

Ben shrugged. "Okay, I guess."

Gage was in the bed. He wasn't awake. His color didn't look too bad, but he was sweaty with dark circles under his eyes. His arms were bandaged from wrist to just above his elbow. What had Bent made him do to himself?

"Has he woken up?" Mace asked.

Roxi shook her head. She'd been crying, poor thing. "Once. After the seizures stopped. He's been asleep ever since." She looked at me. "Is he going to be okay?"

"I don't know," I said honestly. "I hope so."

"Lark's going to try to help him," Mace said, practically shoving me forward. Then to Ben he said, "Keep a look out for doctors."

"What are you going to do?" Sarah asked.

"Same thing I did for you," I told her. It was probably better if I didn't mention that I'd done it for Mace, too.

Her eyes brightened. "You think you can?"

"I can try." My hands were not terribly clean. "I need some sanitizer."

Of course there was some nearby. I cleaned my hands and

then peeled back the edge of the bandages on Gage's left arm.
Oh, hell.

"I know," Wren said at my side. "It's awful."

Awful wasn't a strong enough word. I did not want to touch
those things. They were terrible—as bad or worse than what
Bent had done to Mace. How had this happened? Poor Gage.
I'd never seen anything like this—not on someone alive. And
then there were the cuts he'd made himself with Bent's razor.
They were red and raw—and way too close to what I'd done
to myself for me to look at them for long.

I took a deep breath and set my hands over the worst part
of the wounds. Oh, God. They were sticky. And wet. And
warm. I had no idea how it worked, but I closed my eyes and
tried to focus whatever mojo I had into my hands, into getting rid of the infection. Slowly, my fingers began to tingle
and itch. I felt a strange sensation down my arms—like goose
bumps on the wrong side of my skin. I stayed like this until
my wrists began to feel numb and my knees trembled.

I opened my eyes and staggered backward. Wren stead-
ied me.

"Are you okay?" Ben asked with a frown. He reached for
me as well, but my sister kept me upright.

I nodded. I wasn't okay. I felt like I'd been hit with a sledge
hammer. "I need sugar."

Roxi—one hundred pounds soaking wet—pulled a candy
bar from her purse. "Here."

Heath. My favorite. My fingers shook as I tried to unwrap
it. Finally, Ben took it and peeled back the paper. "Thanks," I
said. I used more sanitizer and wiped my hands on my thighs

before taking it. God only knew what kind of ghost spooge I had on me.

He made me sit down on the side of Gage's bed and hovered a little while I ate. I kind of liked it. I mean, I was no damsel in distress or any of that crap, but most of the time people treated me like I didn't need anything. Sometimes I felt like I needed a lot, and there was no one there to give it.

"Did it work?" Kevin asked.

I glanced at Gage's arms. They were still pretty bad, but... "Yeah. I think so. Definitely." I could see now that the spectral gouges had closed up some and weren't so wet and black—which was good.

"Has his mother been here yet?" Mace asked.

Roxi made a face. "No. We called her, but she's in New York with her boyfriend. Didn't know when she could get back. His dad should be here soon, though."

"Seriously?" I asked. "His mother wasn't worried?"

Roxi shook her head. None of them looked terribly surprised. I felt a strange kinship for Gage at that moment. It seemed like so much more of a betrayal when it was your mother who didn't care. Your mother was supposed to be the one person you could always count on. The one person that would love you forever no matter what you did.

Your mother wasn't supposed to toss you over.

We all stayed for a little while longer—until Mr. Moreno, Gage's father, arrived. Then we decided to make ourselves scarce fast.

Ben offered me a ride home and I said yes. To be honest, I'd rather go with him than anyone else. Wren gave me a sheepish glance. "Do you mind if I hang out with Kevin for a bit?"

I shook my head. I was too tired to mind. That didn't stop me from shooting Kevin a dark look. If tonight had taught me anything it was that the living and the dead didn't mix. He caught my arm when I walked by him in the hall. Wren had gone ahead with the others and didn't seem to notice— which was weird.

"Problem?" he asked.

I looked at his hand on my sleeve, then up into his bright blue eyes. "You're going to hurt her. We both know it's going to happen. That's when you and I will have a problem." I pulled my arm free and glanced back into the ward. I stopped. Was that...? No, it couldn't be. There was no way Bent could be here.

Was there?

I walked away from Kevin, back toward where Gage was. There was no one there but him and his father. No ghosts at all, especially not Bent.

I needed to get some sleep. I could barely stand up, and now I was hallucinating.

"Do you mind if we take Roxi home?" Ben asked when I'd caught up with him outside.

I shook my head. "Of course not."

We all said good-night in the parking lot. We were a somber little bunch, everyone worried about Gage—and worried about what his condition might mean for them. I wished I knew enough to tell them if they ought to be worried or not. My instinct said they should be very worried. Then again, my instincts weren't always reliable.

Roxi sat in the backseat. We were pretty quiet during the drive, but when we pulled up to her house, she leaned between the seats and hugged me. "Thank you for helping him. For helping us."

I nodded. I would have spoken but my throat felt like there was something stuck in it. She hugged Ben, too, before getting out of the car. He promised to call her in the morning.

"I feel bad for her," he said as we drove away. He'd waited until she opened the door of the house to back out. "They just got together, but she's had a thing for Gage since freshman year."

"That's a long time to have a crush."

"You think so? I've had a crush on the same girl since I was twelve."

My head whipped around as disappointment flicked me in the chest. "Really? Does she know?"

He shook his head, a sad little smile curving his lips. "I used to think she was either blind or dumb, but now I think she just had more important things to think about than whether or not some chubby Twinkie kid liked her."

"Twinkie?" I asked.

"Yeah. You know, yellow on the outside, white in the middle."

I made a face. That was awful. "Don't call yourself that."

He shrugged. "Why not? I've never even been to Korea. Although, I have watched *Best of the Best*."

I glanced at him. "All I know about Korea I learned from M*A*S*H reruns."

Ben grinned. "That was filmed in California."

"Then I know nothing." We laughed. I leaned back in the seat. "I want to hear more about this crush of yours."

Sure, why not? I could compare myself to her or something equally stupid.

"What do you want to know?"

"I find it hard to believe she never noticed you. Have you ever tried to get her attention?"

"To be fair, I never really spoke to her until recently. I was shorter than her for a long time, and fat. I was pretty unattractive."

"The proverbial ugly duckling."

He grinned. "Are you calling me a swan?"

"You know what I think, Ben? I think if this girl isn't kicking her ass for not noticing you earlier, you should say fuck it and move on."

"How do I know if she's kicking her ass, though?"

"Ask her." I knew that was easier said than done, but wasn't it time to stop pining over some chick who didn't appreciate him? I mean, I could get seriously appreciative all over him.

"Okay. So, Lark, how's your ass? Left any footprints on it lately?"

My heart jumped so hard I felt it bounce off my ribs. "What?"

He laughed—there was a nervous edge to it. "You really didn't know, did you?"

I shook my head. This was what shock felt like. "How could I? No one's ever liked me. I was the crazy girl."

"Yeah, well I was taught to respect the dead, so I never thought you were crazy." He pulled the car into my drive. Nan must have parked her car in the garage. He cut the engine.

Silence.

Never thought I was crazy.

"Where did the ghost scratch you?" I asked, unbuckling the seat belt. "Can I see it?"

He looked confused. "My back. Sure." He unfastened his seat belt and turned in the seat, lifting his shirt.

I turned on the dome light, illuminating the inside of the little car. Ben had a really nice back—his skin was that smooth golden color that I envied so much, and I could actually see his muscles move beneath.

Running down the center of his back were three thin scratches. They were pink with a bit of dark around the edges, but nothing more substantial than what human fingernails might inflict if someone really tried. They were nowhere near as bad as Gage's, Mace's or even Sarah's or Roxi's.

He had been taught to respect the dead. He had looked at death and ghosts differently than the others. He wasn't afraid of them—and they weren't able to hurt him so much.

"Are they bad?" he asked.

I touched them, watched as one visibly faded beneath my fingers. I could have cried. Finally, something good. "No," I told him. "They're not."

He turned. "Really?"

I smiled. "Really."

He looked so relieved it almost broke my heart. I couldn't stop staring at him. He was really cute—sexy even. And he was smart, and nice. Really nice. Were nice guys supposed to have ripped abs? His shirt was still pulled up some and I could see them right there in front of me.

Ben's gaze dropped. "So, about my confession—"

I cut him off. "Yeah, about that. Ben, I'm sorry."

Oh, he looked like I punched him. "Right. You're not interested. I should have known." He started to draw back, but I reached out and grabbed his arm.

"No, I'm sorry I was such an idiot and never noticed you sooner. I was too busy protecting myself from people who wanted to hurt me to notice the people who wanted to be my friend."

Dark eyes locked with mine. *Oh, boy.* A girl could get used to being looked at like that. "I want to be more than your friend, Lark."

And there went my stomach—all fluttery and idiotic. "Okay."

His hands cupped my face—his fingers were warm. He looked at me for a second, and then his lips touched mine.

Yeah, so, *wow.* He was a really good kisser. Possibly extraordinary. When he pulled away I wanted to pull him back. As it was, I'd totally crumpled the front of his shirt with my hands.

"Can I call you tomorrow?" he asked.

"It is tomorrow," I replied. He had stolen all my intelligence with his pretty lips.

He chuckled. "Can I call you later?"

"Yes."

He brushed my hair back from my face. "Can I see you later?"

"Yes."

"Can I kiss you again later?"

Oh. My. Freaking. Gawd. "You'd better."

Ben smiled. "Good night, Lark."

"Good night." I really didn't want to get out of the car, but I was exhausted and needed sleep. Plus, Nan might be wondering where I was. I opened the door and stepped out into the cool night. I wasn't much of a romantic, but I was sure I grinned the whole way to the door. Ben started the car, waved and turned off the dome light before backing out of the drive.

I unlocked the door, stepped into the house and locked everything up again. Then I quietly crept upstairs to my room. It wasn't until I caught a flash of my reflection in the mirror—enough to give me a start—that I remembered the white-haired woman at Haven Crest who had spoken to me. There'd been something familiar about her, and Wren hadn't mentioned her at all.

Who the hell was she?

chapter fourteen

WREN

"I can't believe it." Kevin's shoulders slumped. He was at his computer—where he'd been for hours—looking for information on Josiah Bent's grave.

"What now?" I asked. He'd already found out that the original graveyard—and the one Bent was buried in—had been moved in the late 1970s, and that some of the inmates' remains hadn't been recovered. After another hour he'd managed to find out that Bent hadn't been one of those lost graves. Unfortunately, it had taken him a while to find Bent's patient number, only to discover that some of the grave markers had gotten mixed up in the move.

He sat back in his chair and shoved his hands through his hair. His curls were so thick they stood out like a halo around his head. It was too cute. "The records of the new graveyard layout were destroyed in a fire in 1979."

I felt his disappointment. "Are you saying the only way we

have to find Bent's grave is to physically search the cemetery for his marker?"

Kevin nodded. "And even then we won't be certain it's his."

"That's not true," I told him. "We'll know it's his when we find it."

His head whipped around. I was still trying to get used to the fact that he could see me sometimes. "How?"

"Because the closer we get, the harder he'll try to stop us."

His face fell. "That's not exactly comforting."

I wanted to comfort him, I really did, but I wasn't good at saying things people *wanted* to hear.

"There may be something in that book I brought back from the Shadow Lands. Possibly."

"That's the first good news I've heard in what feels like forever."

"Don't get too excited. I'll have to take a look through it."

"Still, it's something."

I shrugged. "Hopefully, because there's no way any of you—or even I—will make it through that graveyard to do a search. Bent and his minions won't allow us to linger that long. Even if we do discover which one is his we'd be lucky to get in there, dig it up and burn his remains."

He sighed. "What are we going to do?"

"We're going to destroy Bent." I said this as though it was obvious—not to be snarky, but because we had no choice. Lives depended on this.

"How?" he demanded. "You already said we won't be able to get near his grave."

"We'll figure it out!" I snapped back. His computer screen flickered. I really had to learn to get better control of my emotions. I couldn't go around wreaking havoc with electronics all the time.

Kevin sighed. "I'm sorry. I feel really helpless."

And guilty, I thought. I didn't say it, though. Kevin was in college, but he was the same age as Mace. He'd been born in the summer while Mace hadn't been born until that winter, throwing them into different school years. These people were his friends, and they were in danger. But Kevin hadn't been with them that night they were attacked, and hadn't been wounded. He felt like he'd let them down by not being in this with them. Silly boy.

"I feel it, too," I admitted.

"You?" His expression turned dubious. "Get out. You're powerful. You're the most capable person I know."

Person. No one—except Lark—had ever called me a person before. *Ghost. Spirit. Thing.* Never *person.*

"Are you okay?" Kevin asked.

"Do you really think of me as a person?" My voice quivered.

He looked confused. "Yeah. Shouldn't I?"

I burst into tears. Hands over my face, I sobbed into my palms. My shoulders heaved, breath hitched. Thank God I couldn't produce mucus, because I'd seen Lark make a mess of herself with less crying than I was in the middle of, and I had no tissues.

Then again, I didn't really produce tears in this realm, either. "Wren?"

I held up my hand. I just had to pull myself together. I couldn't talk to him when I was like this. How did mortal girls stand it? On some of the TV shows Lark watched it seemed like the girls cried all the time. It had to be exhausting.

Finally, the sobs subsided, and I was able to lift my head.

Kevin was watching me nervously. "Are you okay?"

I nodded. "Sorry about that."

"Did I upset you? I'm sorry if I did."

"I'm the opposite of upset. No one's ever called me a person before."

"Really?" The fact that he was truly surprised made me want to cry a little more.

"Kevin, you aren't a normal live person, you know that?"

He smiled. "I'm eighteen years old. It's the weekend, and my parents are out of town. What am I doing? Sitting in my room with a beautiful girl and we're talking about ghosts. I know I'm not normal, Wren."

"Would we be doing something different if I was alive?"

His smile faded. Had I said something wrong? "Yeah, we would."

"Like what?"

He sat back down at his computer. "I wonder if the grounds-keeper is familiar with the graves or has a plan of the cemetery? I think Roxi's uncle owns the company that looks after Haven Crest. I should get her to check with him."

I was confused. I must have said something. "Kevin...?"

"Don't," he said, not turning around. "Your sister was right."

"About what?" I was going to kill her.

At least he glanced over his shoulder this time. "She said I was going to hurt you—that it was inevitable, and she's right. I'm going to hurt myself, too."

"She is *not* right. You won't hurt me."

"No?" Finally he turned around. "You're dead, Wren. I'm alive. That's probably not going to change for a long time. Maybe it would be better if we stopped hanging out, just the two of us."

Pain blossomed deep inside me. "No. It wouldn't."

He removed his glasses and looked at me. His blue eyes were so sad. "I haven't had a girlfriend since you came to me and asked me to help you save Lark. I spend more time at your grave than I do with any girl I know. I'm infatuated with you, and it's no good for either one of us."

"But—"

"I think you should go. Please."

At that moment I understood the meaning of the term *heartbreak*. There was a pain inside me I couldn't locate or identify. It was as though my chest was being squeezed by giant hands, thumbs digging deep inside. It was like the time Lark tried to push me away, but sharper, because I'd known that Lark loved me, and wanted me to be real. I'd known that I would have my sister back one day. This felt...final.

I immediately left the house—flashing back to the Shadow Lands instead of returning to Lark. I needed a few minutes alone because I wanted to blame her for this, and I knew it wasn't her fault. She'd only said what Kevin and I both knew to be true. Our feelings had started to go beyond friendship, and there was no way that could ever work.

Maybe it was time for me to start spending more time with my own kind. As much as I loved my sister and wanted to be with her, the living brought me nothing but pain and aggravation.

I sat down on a park bench I'd never noticed before and wallowed in this new feeling. And then I tried very hard to let go of the blame, because it wasn't anyone's fault that I was dead, and it wasn't Lark's fault that I couldn't be with the boy I liked.

I would start spending more time here in the Shadow Lands. I would be more social with my own kind. I would stop pining over a stupid human boy.

But I would not forsake my sister. Lark and I were two puzzle pieces that were meant to fit together. Like it or not, we had a purpose. At least, I thought we did.

The white-haired woman had shown up at Haven Crest. Lark had seen her. Who was she, and why was she helping us? Why now? Had she been a patient there? Was that why she could show up at the hospital and in the Shadow Lands? Or was she something else? And could she help us destroy Bent?

One thing was for certain, I wasn't going to find any of these answers sitting on a bench in the dark.

Besides, in the end, my sister was the only person—living or dead—that I could rely on. In the end, all either of us had was the other.

LARK

There was something wrong with Wren, but she didn't want to talk about it. I didn't have to be a freaking genius to figure out it had something to do with Kevin. Did it make me an awful sister that I hoped he let her know it couldn't work between them? I didn't like to see her upset, but I really didn't want to see her get her heart broken.

Because let's just think about how Wren might take that. Strong emotions in ghosts were what led to hauntings and other generally bad things. I had no idea what my sister was capable of—and neither did she.

She hovered over my shoulder as I flipped through the book she'd brought back from the Shadow Lands. There was some interesting information in there—stuff on patients and staff alike. I paused to look at a black-and-white photo of a kid from the '90s.

Olgilvie? He'd been a patient at Haven Crest just a few years before it closed down. Maybe Wren was right to worry about me antagonizing him after all.

"I told you not to antagonize him," she reminded me.

"Yeah, yeah. We'll look at that later." Sometimes when she said what I was thinking I didn't know whether to punch her or laugh. I did neither, but I did keep flipping.

I found the records about the graves being moved around—and the new plans that Kevin had said were lost in a fire. I also found a few mentions of the mixed up graves—Bent's number was mentioned.

Mentioned twice. As in Bent had *two* freaking graves. What had they done, sawed him in half? Obviously, it was a mistake, but why did it have to be Bent they got messed up?

Okay, so I was tempted at this point to set the whole cemetery ablaze and cleanse the whole damn place in one fell swoop. That wouldn't do it, though, and I knew better. You had to get right down to the corpse—get the bones. If there wasn't a corpse then you had to find whatever tethered the ghost to this world.

"Oh, hell," Wren said with a scowl.

"Well," I said with fake bubbliness, "at least we have it narrowed down to two spots. That's better than the entire graveyard."

"These spots are at opposite ends of the graveyard," she pointed out. "The breathers will never make it from one to the other before Bent kills them."

"Breathers?" I echoed. Wow, that wasn't like her to be derogatory. "Hey, I'm one of them."

She shot me a dirty look. "Please. You're not."

"Do I need to kick Kevin's ass?" I asked. "Because you are not you right now, and if he is responsible I need to hit him."

Her shoulders sagged. "No, don't hit him. Well…" She smiled slyly. "You could maybe give him a sharp pinch next time you see him. And no, I don't want to talk about it. Not right now. He was right— I just don't like it."

I might not have been a genius, but I wasn't completely brainless. Kevin had taken what I'd said to him to heart and ended things with Wren.

I hugged her—hard. I'd wait to tell her about Ben. It would be cruel not to, and I needed some time to accept that it was real. There was a part of me—a paranoid, suspicious part— that expected to go to school on Monday and find out it had all been a joke.

"Sorry about whacking you with that bar," I said. "I was terrified Bent was going to grab you again."

"It's okay," she replied. "I'm sorry about giving you a hard time about that police officer."

"No, you were right." I opened the book and looked at his photo again. He'd been hospitalized for "delusional" behavior, whatever that meant. Ghosts didn't keep the same kinds of records that the living did, I guess. "That's going to come back to bite me on the ass someday, but I can live with it for now."

"I was thinking…"

She wasn't looking at me, but out the window. That was never a good sign when Wren couldn't make eye contact. "Yeah?"

"Maybe after we get rid of Bent I should start spending more time in the Shadow Lands. There's so much I don't know about what I am."

It was like a punch. I wanted to protest. I wanted to order her to stay here with me. "You really want to do that?"

She turned her head. "I need to have some friends of my own—ghost friends. Young ghosts, not just Iloana."

Fucking Kevin. Well, this was my fault, too. I might not like it, but it felt like the right thing for Wren to do. She had to have a life—or death—of her own, and so did I.

"Can I meet them?" I asked.

She looked alarmed. "Of course! Lark, you're my *best* friend."

I blinked back tears. "Okay, then. Just so we're clear on that. It probably would be good for you to spend more time there. Besides, you cramp my style."

She frowned. "What does that even mean?"

I shrugged. "I think it's a polite way of calling someone a cock-blocker."

Her frown deepened. "I'm not sure I understand that, either."

I laughed. "I love you."

My sister grinned. "I love you, too."

Were all sisters this way? Could you go from anger to annoyance, then sadness and betrayal, then to acceptance and happiness in the span of seconds? Or was it just us? Every once in a while I wondered if maybe we weren't two halves of the same whole. That somehow, we shared a soul.

She crawled into bed with me a little while later. It was so late, and I was exhausted.

"Hey," I said, half-asleep. "Who was that white-haired woman at Haven Crest?"

"I don't know. She's the one who helped me find the book in the Shadow Lands." I sensed, rather than saw her frown. "She said her name was Emily."

"So, she just popped up?"

"Yes. She said she was from here. Maybe she's one of Bent's victims?"

"Hmm." Maybe, but why not say so? I was too tired to think about it. "Maybe she's our ghostly godmother."

"That would be nice," Wren said. "Now go to sleep."

So I did.

My cell rang at ten. I picked it up but didn't recognize the number. "Hello?"

"It's Ben."

Honestly, I hadn't expected him to call, and he made me grin like a stupid idiot—a fact not lost on my sister, who suddenly sat up straight and took great interest in my conversation. "Hi."

"I didn't wake you up, did I?"

"No, I'm up." God, it was still the weekend. Twenty-four hours hadn't even passed since the séance.

"So you're not in bed?"

Okay, I didn't embarrass easy, but my cheeks burned. Wren raised her eyebrows in silent question—one I was going to have to answer later. "No." I cleared my throat. "Just got out of the shower."

A low chuckle vibrated in my ear and raced all the way down my spine. "So, if I came over in about fifteen minutes you could be ready to go?"

Hells yeah. "Go where?"

"Hospital. We're all going to go see Gage."

Not quite what I'd hoped for, but still a good thing. I wanted to see how Gage was doing, too. "Make it twenty. I need to grab breakfast."

He agreed and we hung up. Wren was still watching me as I stuck my damp hair up into a messy bun and rushed to my closet. "Who was that?"

"Ben."

"Ben? Not Mace?"

I stuck my head out of the closet. "Mace has a girlfriend, and I think I already told you that he doesn't like me like that."

She looked genuinely confused—and put out. "I could have sworn he did. Still, Ben's cute."

"He is." I hid my smile by searching for a shirt. "He's nice, too."

I could have sworn I heard her mutter, "And on the right side of death."

I pulled on jeans and a light shirt. September was still a warm month in Connecticut, and today was bright and sunny. "We haven't really talked about it, and this might not be the best time, but are you okay with the fact that Ben seems to like me?"

Wren shot me an annoyed look. "Of course I am. I saw how he looked at you at 'Nother Cup the night we met them. It was obvious he thought you were awesome."

"It was?" I slipped my feet into a pair of flats. "Why didn't you say anything?"

She shrugged. "You wouldn't have believed me anyway."

There was that. I put on mascara and lip gloss—the two things I would never be seen without—grabbed my bag and ran downstairs. Wren was already in the kitchen when I walked in. Cheater. Nan was at the table sipping what was probably her third coffee and reading a book on her tablet.

"I hope you're going to eat something before you run out," she said.

"Yes, ma'am." I grabbed a mug for coffee, a banana and a bagel—which I shoved in the toaster. I ate the banana while I waited. Then I sat down at the table with a coffee and a hot bagel with melting peanut butter dripping off it. I was starving.

"I heard a bunch of kids broke into Haven Crest last night," my grandmother remarked without looking up. "You wouldn't know anything about that, would you?"

I chewed and swallowed. The peanut butter caught at my throat. "Should I?"

"I would think not." She took a sip of her coffee. "I'm sure if you ever got caught doing something like that you'd call your grandmother to come get you rather than take on that jerk Olgilvie on your own." *Now* she looked at me. Pointedly, I might add.

"Of course," I agreed, a little stunned. She knew, right? I mean, she wasn't dumb, and from the way she looked at me…

"Good." She went back to her reading. That was it. She didn't yell or tell me how disappointed she was, but I knew where I stood. I reached over and squeezed her hand. She squeezed back.

Ben actually came to the door when he arrived. Of course Nan knew him. I think she knew everyone in town. She gave me twenty bucks in case I needed anything and told me to be careful.

As soon as we got into the car, Ben turned toward me as though he was going to kiss me. "Wren's with us," I blurted.

He froze halfway to me, startled. "Are you just saying that so I won't kiss you?"

"No!"

"Good. Hi, Wren."

"I can leave," she offered. Poor thing looked really uncomfortable. Fucking Kevin.

"She offered to leave," I repeated.

Ben shook his head with a grin. "Don't be foolish. A little anticipation's good for the soul."

I grinned, too. All that anticipation went right to my stomach and fluttered away. In the backseat I think my sister actually swore. She really wasn't herself. I didn't like it.

We didn't talk about anything serious during the drive. Mostly we listened to the radio and I felt that stupid rush of happiness every time we liked the same song. I think Ben might have been as nervous as I was, and it was hard to be flirty when you had company. I had to give him props for not being weirded out by the fact that my sister was invisible to him.

At the hospital we found out that Gage had been moved out of emergency into the IC unit. Was that a good thing or bad? It sounded bad. We took the elevator up to that floor and ran into Kevin at the nurses' station. He looked scared. Behind him a handful of people were in a small, glass-front room, fussing over the person in the bed. Gage's father was in that room with his arm around Roxi's shoulders.

"What's going on?" Ben asked. "What happened to Gage?"

Kevin looked at me—normally he would have looked at Wren, the jerk. "He's gotten worse."

chapter fifteen

LARK

Had I done this? Had I hurt Gage when I touched him? Was Mace worse now, too? Sarah?

I looked at the girl standing beside Mace. The marks on her face looked better, or no worse than they had after I'd touched her. Mace had told me he was fine, and he didn't look sick. Obviously I couldn't haul up his shirt in the middle of the hospital, so I had to believe him.

So what had happened to Gage?

I caught a nurse looking at me. "Are you all right, dear? You look a little pale."

"I'm fine thanks." Just a little warm. Just a little dizzy. Something tugged at my hair. I turned my head and almost screamed. I caught myself just in time, so it came out like a hiccup.

Freaking hell.

There was a girl playing with my hair. Her face was completely caved in—a bloody hole of flesh and bone. Only one eye remained perfect. It blinked at me.

"Go away," I whispered.

She did—thank God.

I turned around, the corridor spinning a little around me. I braced my hand against the wall for support. Standing a few feet away was a man in a hospital gown , his blood-splattered legs white and bare. He even had blood on his toes. I didn't know where the blood was coming from, but he was clean from the waist up. He tilted his head to look at me, his milky eyes blank.

"Why?" he asked.

I whirled around once more, only to find a toddler sitting on the floor a few feet away from me. My stomach rolled at the blood on its overalls. And when it turned toward me and spoke in gibberish, I looked at its face...

I turned to the wall and pressed my forehead against it. I wouldn't scream. I would *not* scream.

Warm hands came down on my shoulders. I jumped—made some sort of pathetic noise. It was just Ben.

"Come on," he said. He put his arm around me and guided me down the hall. "Guys."

The next thing I knew, I was sitting in a chair in the family room, and someone was pressing a paper cup of water into my hands. I took a sip, washing the sick taste out of my mouth. Ben crouched in front of me. Mace stood behind him, a concerned look on his face.

"What happened?" Ben asked.

I took another drink. "There are a lot of ghosts here."

"You didn't have this sort of reaction last night."

I looked into his dark eyes and felt the world shift back into place. "Something's not right. They sought me out."

Suddenly, Wren was there beside me. Where had she been while I'd been bombarded with images I was never, ever going to unsee? That kid... I swallowed. That poor little kid.

"Bent's here," she whispered.

My head snapped up and turned toward her. "What?"

"It still freaks me out when she does that," Sarah said. "I know someone's there, but it doesn't look like it."

Wren looked worried—scared even. "Bent's here. I don't know how, but he's here, and he's been draining Gage."

"What's going on?" Mace demanded.

I glanced at him. "Bent's here." Someone gasped.

So I *had* seen Bent last night. God, why hadn't I said something? Done something? Just because I hadn't known it was possible for him to travel like that didn't mean I shouldn't have doubted my own eyes.

But then, he'd been gone when I looked again. And Wren hadn't seen or felt him, either. We'd been too distracted. Too confident that we were safe.

"What do we do?" Ben asked.

I shook my head. "I don't know."

"What do you mean you don't know?" Sarah cried. "You have to know! Can he follow all of us?"

I opened my mouth—

"No," Kevin said as he entered the room. I hadn't noticed he wasn't with us before. "He can't follow us. Ghosts can't at-tach themselves to the living like that—not to do harm any-way. They can possess and influence those they've infected, but

they're bound by their surroundings unless something or someone strong enough for them to hitch a ride with shows up."

I closed my eyes. "Me. He followed me. This is my fault."
I had taken the razor. I was strongly connected to the spirit
world through Wren and my own time there. Of course it
had been me he grabbed on to. I was ashamed that I hadn't
even noticed, but then it wasn't as though he would have to
shadow me the entire night—just when he sensed that I was
around the others. My being with them gave him the extra
juice to leave the asylum and come for Gage. He wouldn't
have been able to stay for long, but then he hadn't needed to.

"Yes," Kevin said. "It is."

I lifted my chin and looked him in the eyes. He wasn't
wearing his glasses, which made it easier. "Asshole."

"None of this would have happened if we hadn't gone to
Haven Crest in the first place," Ben reminded him. "None
of this is Lark's fault."

"How do we get rid of him?" Roxi asked.

"We don't," Kevin replied. He was Mr. Know-It-All. "He
will leave when he's ready." He looked at Wren. "Or when
you agree to join him. Actually, come to think of it, this is
all *your* fault."

"Dude," Mace said, "What the hell is wrong with you?"

I looked up. "He's just saying the truth. We don't know
how to get rid of Bent." But we knew how to make things
difficult for the bastard. I finished off the cup of water. "Hey,
Ben, could you get me another drink?"

He gave me a questioning glance. I nodded my head very
slowly at him, hoping he got my meaning. Ben stood up.

"Sure. Be right back." When he reached the corridor, he stuck his head back in. "Hey, Gage's father is outside his room."

Everyone started to file out to check on our friend. I stood up, too. Ben watched me from outside the room as one by one, everyone else filed out. Kevin was behind me, so when I stopped and shut the door, it was just me and him left inside.

"What are you doing?" he asked.

I turned around.

And punched him in the face.

WREN

"Lark, what are you doing?" I cried.

My sister shook her fist. It had to hurt—she'd hit Kevin very hard. "Wren, inside me. Now."

Kevin started laughing. He pressed a hand to his jaw as he turned his head toward Lark. That was when I saw what my sister had already realized.

Josiah Bent had possessed Kevin. It didn't matter that Kevin hadn't been marked. He was a medium—fair game.

"What gave me away?" he asked.

Lark glared at him. "Kevin's an idiot, but he'd never blame Wren, or suggest she join you." She glanced over her shoulder at me. "I said *now*."

I leaped into her, settling my limbs into hers, letting my energy fill her, letting her envelop me. I wished I'd been as certain that Kevin wouldn't be mean to me as she had been.

Bent straightened. It was so unsettling to see Kevin's face wearing Bent's hateful expression. It made me angry.

"Get out of him, Bent," we said. My voice echoed inside Lark's. "Get out of him, and leave Gage alone."

He smiled. "But I like this body. It's very young and fit. He practically invited me in."

Oh, no. *Kevin, why would you do that?* He knew about these things, he wouldn't just let Bent in—not without a reason.

"I don't care. Get out or I'll beat you out."

He laughed. "Do you really think two little girls can defeat me? This boy is stronger than you, breather."

My sister's response was to punch him again. He staggered backward, lip split. I winced. I didn't want her to hurt Kevin, but Bent couldn't be allowed to maintain control of him.

"Six years of kickboxing, a year in a mental hospital, a lifetime of having to defend myself and ghostly possession," Lark said. "I think I'm strong enough."

This time Bent didn't mock her. He lifted the back of Kevin's hand to his mouth, wiping at the blood there. "You've meddled in my plans long enough, witch. The children are mine."

Lark threw another punch, but he moved out of the way. This time he punched back. Oh, that hurt! Lark's pain tore through me. Still, she came back with a kick to his ribs. She was tougher than she looked, my sister. Bent hit her hard, sending us flying backward into a table. It smashed into our side as our head hit the wall.

"Anytime you want to get pissed off, feel free," Lark growled.

Oh, I was pissed off, and an invitation to let that out was just what I needed. We spun around and cracked our foot against the side of Kevin's head, then delivered a punch to his chest. Bent was older than me—stronger in many ways, just as Kevin was stronger than Lark. What Bent didn't have was the connection my sister and I shared. Her body might be heavy, but it was familiar, and I'd worn it so many times it felt natural. We were attuned to one another. He struck out and we dodged to the side, coming up to punch him in the kidneys. We swept our leg behind him and knocked his feet out from underneath him. We pinned his arms with our knees and straddled him. We reached into Lark's bag and found the iron bar Ben had given her. We shoved this under Bent's chin.

"Get out or I'll beat your ass and salt you like a freaking ham," we snarled—both of our voices coming out of one mouth.

Bent didn't need to be told twice. He pulled free of Kevin— a scab peeled from a wound—and stood over us. We lunged to our feet, iron in hand.

Josiah Bent's gaunt face twisted into a sneer. "I'll leave for now, but I'll be back. There's only one way to stop this, Dead Born. Join me and I'll leave these children alone. Deny me and I'll drain them all. And I'll save this one—" his foot passed through Kevin "—for last."

And Lark said, "What, not me? I thought I was your favorite, princess."

Bent roared at her, and then spun himself into a black whirlwind that tore past us and through the wall. A print of a barn in a field fell to the floor.

On the floor, Kevin stirred. I slipped out of Lark just as she offered her hand to help him up.

"Why did you beat me up if you had the bar all along?" he asked.

My sister smiled at him as she wrapped one arm around her front. She had to be sore after that. "I think you know why."

I loved her so much at that moment.

He looked in my direction, but I concentrated very hard on not letting him see me. "Is she here?"

"You can't see her?"

He shook his head.

Lark let out a breath. "You must have been a real douche, Sixth Sense."

Kevin's expression turned sullen. It would have been cute if he wasn't all battered and bloody. "You know, deciding we shouldn't see each other hurt me, too."

"Yeah," Lark said. She glanced at me before patting his shoulder. "I know. Come on, we need to check on Gage before they kick us out."

She opened the door and left the room. Kevin followed after her, but he paused at the threshold and looked over his shoulder. He might not see me, but he still *felt* me. "You have no idea how much it hurt me, too."

His words hit me harder than Bent ever could have. I stayed there a moment after he left, taking a moment of quiet just for myself.

When I left the room a man with bloody legs was in the hall. He'd been a ghost for maybe a year or so. He looked at me. "Thank you for getting rid of that awful man. He made us all uncomfortable."

"I'm afraid it was my fault he came here in the first place. We'll try to make sure he doesn't come back."

He nodded and turned away. He really should have been wearing something underneath that open-back gown.

I joined the others. They were gathered at the door of Gage's room. Lark was inside talking to his father, so I drifted closer so I could hear them talk. Mr. Moreno had a lovely Colombian accent.

"They tell me you can help protect my son against the evil spirits," he said to Lark.

She nodded and shoved her hand into that huge bag of hers. She pulled out two of those iron rings that strange man Chuck had delivered to the coffee shop. She gave one to Mr. Moreno and slipped the other on Gage's finger. I supposed the hospital staff had removed the one he'd been wearing when he'd come in. Then Lark took a small, polished piece of moss agate from the bag and slipped it beneath Gage's pillow. Ben taped one of his grandmother's *pujok* to the wall behind the bed.

"Tell the nurses not to move it," Lark instructed. Then she gave the older man her cell phone number and told him to call her if he needed anything. She also told him to use any items from his faith that guarded against spirits, or to have a priest come in if he wanted. I was proud of her as she made Gage's father feel better. It was so much easier for her when she could deal with people who believed in ghosts, regardless of their religion.

"It wasn't your touch that hurt him," I told her. "It was Bent."

She nodded.

"You could always try to heal him again." I knew it took a lot out of her, and I knew she couldn't completely heal him, but maybe she could undo some of the damage that awful lunatic had done.

She set her hand on Gage's left forearm. Poor thing was a

mess. Why had Bent done that to his victims? Why flay and infect them? It seemed unnecessarily cruel. But then, Bent had been cruel in life, as well.

We left the hospital shortly after. In the parking lot everyone wanted to ask Kevin—and Lark—what had happened. That was when Kevin admitted why he had let Bent in.

"I thought I could get a sense of him," he said. "He's been in my head. I know him now."

Lark shook her head. "You freaking idiot. He could have used you to kill somebody. Besides, Wren and I found out where his grave is. Sort of."

He frowned. "You found out about the Japanese chestnut tree? How? She didn't go to the cemetery, did she?"

Did he think I was stupid? The Japanese chestnut tree?

My sister scowled. "She's not *that* stupid." She didn't explain that we hadn't known the exact location, though. We did now, and that was all that mattered, I supposed. I really didn't like that his dangerous experiment had managed to uncover what we couldn't.

Mace nodded. "I know that tree—it's the great big one in the lower corner."

"Great." Kevin licked at his cut lip and winced. "So, we'll burn his remains tonight."

"Whoa." Lark held up her hand. "No. We need to plan this. We can't just walk in there. That cemetery isn't on consecrated ground." When they all looked at her blankly, she sighed. "Bent and his army will tear us apart. We have to find a way to protect the grave and ourselves, and dig it up. A backhoe is too conspicuous, so we have to try to do it by hand."

"Security doesn't patrol there," Mace said. "That's how we got into this mess in the first place."

"That's a bit of a help," Lark allowed. "Ben, can you get some more iron from your mom? Just some to borrow?"

He looked like he'd do anything my sister wanted. "Sure."

"Great. We'll do it Monday night."

"Why Monday?" Kevin asked.

"I heard one of the officers at the chief's office say Olgilvie was off duty Monday night. If we get caught, I don't want it to be him that catches us."

Mace nodded. "Agreed. No one would expect us to be there on a week night, either."

"Bent surprised us last night," Lark said, making eye contact with each of them. "I don't want that to happen when we go for him. We have to be prepared and protected."

Kevin didn't like it, but he was outnumbered. I understood that he wanted immediate payback against Bent, but he was in no shape to go after him again. He looked exhausted, and the group needed him to be strong. If he went in there weak Bent might take him again. I'd tear the bastard apart if that happened.

"What about Gage?" Roxi asked. Her eyes were red but dry.

"He's got protection now," Lark said. "His father will do everything I told him. Plus, I don't think Bent will come back so soon, if he can at all."

"How do you know?"

Lark smiled at her. "Because he's saving all his energy for me."

"And me," I whispered. My sister glanced at me, but she didn't speak.

Finally, everyone went their separate ways. Ben drove Lark home and I followed after Kevin. I didn't intend to stalk him, I just wanted to make sure he was all right, and that we hadn't hurt him too badly.

He went to the graveyard. I followed him down a familiar path to my grave. A deep ache flared to life inside me as he knelt on the dry grass and began pulling weeds from around the stone. There was a wilted rose there that I knew he'd left days earlier. He put it with the pile of weeds before lying down, using his arm for a pillow.

He was lying on the spot where my tiny mortal remains were buried six feet below, in a tiny little box. I watched him as he closed his eyes. A tear trickled into his hair. "I'm sorry," he said.

I didn't say anything. I just left him there.

chapter sixteen

LARK

"Kevin looked pretty beat up," Ben remarked casually as we drove back to Nan's. "You do that?"

"Yep."

"Did he give you that bruise?"

"Josiah Bent did that. Kevin was just his meat suit."

"I know. I've been friends with Kev a long time. He'd never hit a girl."

I snorted. "I've known plenty of girls who needed to be hit."

"Did you hit them?"

"Some." I glanced out the window. "Does that bother you? That I fight?"

"Are you kidding? It's hot."

I laughed. "If I'd known that, I would have started punching people a lot earlier."

"We can spar if you like."

"So, unlike Kevin you will hit girls?"

He shrugged. Thankfully he seemed to realize that I was joking. "I'll let you hit me."

"Let?"

"Oh, sorry. I'll let you *try* to hit me."

Smack talk—I loved it. "You're on, Jackie Chan."

Ben laughed. "You know he's Chinese, right?"

"Yeah, but he's the only martial artist I know other than Bruce Lee, and I think you're sweeter than him."

"You knew him personally, did you?"

"I might. You don't know who I'm hanging out with beyond the veil." Unfortunately, Joe Hard was the closest-to-famous ghost I'd ever met. Why couldn't I meet cool ghosts? Most of them just seemed to want to rip my face off. I bet Kurt Cobain wouldn't be so violent.

"Wren wants to start spending more time in the Shadow Lands," I said suddenly.

Ben didn't miss a beat. "Is that her ghosty place?"

That was as good a description as any. "Yeah. She thinks she needs to meet more people like her."

"That's probably a good idea, right?"

"Yeah."

He glanced at me. I guess I hadn't sounded all that convincing. "It's not like she's going to meet anyone she'll like better than you."

"I know." What the hell, I might as well be completely honest. "I just feel like this is going to change everything."

"That doesn't mean it'll be a bad change."

"I guess not." Still not so convincing. I couldn't even convince myself.

Suddenly, Ben pulled the car into a gas station, turned it around, and pulled back out onto the road—headed back the way we'd come. "What are you doing?" I asked.

"I don't feel like going home," he said. "Want to do something?"

Yeah, I did. "Okay."

We went to Marle Lake, where I had gone kayaking.

"Want to go for a walk?" he asked.

"Sure." Walking with him was definitely better than going home and thinking about ghosts.

There was a wooded path not far from where we parked, and that was where we went. It was late afternoon now and it was getting a little cool, but the breeze felt so good on my face. Ben had loaned me a sweater that he'd had in the car, so I was nice and warm.

"This is weird," I said after a few minutes.

"What?"

"I've never just spent time with a guy who didn't want to argue or make out."

"Which did Mace want to do?"

I laughed. "Why does everyone want to know about me and Mace? We're friends. At least, I think we are. Sometimes I'm not sure."

Ben shrugged. "The two of you seem to have a connection."

"He found me lying in a pool of my own blood, Ben. He saved my life. Yeah, we have a connection. We'll always have that connection. That doesn't mean I'd rather be with him than you." That was true. Mace was gorgeous. Mace seemed to get me more than most people, but he also pissed me off and sometimes made me very self-conscious.

He squinted at me with a self-deprecating smile. "Yeah?"

"Yeah."

"All right, then. No more about Mace."

"Good."

"Except that he's mean and unattractive. Right?"

I laughed. "Very. An ogre, really."

We walked a little farther, talking about movies and books. And then, on the path near the edge of park where it met a field, I saw a man—or rather, what used to be a man. He was a ghost now. Covered in mud and grass and…mushrooms. Gross.

I stopped. So did Ben. "What is it?" he asked.

"Dead guy."

He glanced in the direction I was looking. "So?"

"I'm just so sick of dead guys." Really. If I never saw another ghost—other than Wren—I'd be freaking happy.

"Ignore him."

"Easy for you to say."

"Lark, if you were like me and couldn't see ghosts, would there be anything keeping you from walking around that trail?"

"No."

"Then pretend just for now that you don't see ghosts and let's keep walking." He offered me his hand. Taking it would mean we kept going, and I would have to walk past that ghost like it didn't matter. I would pretend that I was just a normal person.

I took his hand.

And dropped hard to the ground. My knee struck a tree root as my vision went black. Suddenly, I was in a building at Haven Crest, kneeling on the floor. Blood, thick and clotted like canned cherries, crept down the walls. The lights above my head flickered off then on with a menacing hum.

Ben was on the floor in front of me, on his back, limbs splayed. One of his eyes had been gouged from his skull, leaving a gory, gaping hole. The other eye was open wide—staring at me. Beyond him lay the bodies of our other friends, broken and battered, eyes torn from their sockets. Drops of blood covered their faces, dripped across the dirty floor. I followed the trail with my gaze. The carnage rendered me mute, unable to even sob.

The blood led to an eyeball, alone on the floor—a tiny, octopus-like thing with its trailing tentacles. A dirty, bare foot dangled just above it. I looked up. Sitting on the reception desk was Wren. Her bloodred hair was a matted tangle around her head. Her eyes were huge and black—no whites at all. Around her mouth, her face was crusted with dried blood. In her hand was a morbid limp-balloon bouquet of hazels, browns and blues.

She was chewing. I didn't want to know what.

"Lark," she said. Her voice was a horrible groan—like a screen door with rusted hinges. She hopped off the desk, landing in a squat. Her gore-caked fingers dug into the tiles, still clutching her trophies. She crouch-crawled toward me. It was then that I noticed she was wearing a hospital gown—stained and foul. She was gaunt and feral, and smelled of death. Her nails clicked on the floor.

"Wren. What happened to you?"

Her head cocked to one side—at more of an angle than anything living could ever achieve. "Nothing. I'm just as I ought to be."

I shook my head. "No. This isn't you. You're not a monster. You would never kill anybody."

She laughed. "Silly Lark! I didn't kill them—you did. You brought them here. You made it possible for Bent to get them, and to get me. I just took some treats." She shook the eyeballs at me.

I glanced at my friends—all dead and defiled. How could I have done this? I was doing everything I could to protect them, to keep Bent from getting them.

When I turned back to my sister she was right there in front of me—so close I jumped back. She grinned—baring teeth that were stained with red, and had stringy bits caught between them.

"You know, Lark," she began in a singsong voice, inching closer. "I've always thought you had the prettiest eyes."

Then she jumped, and I screamed.

WREN

Lark's scream summoned me immediately to her side. One second I was in the Shadow Lands after leaving the graveyard, and the next I was being ripped through space and time like a piece of lint being sucked up by a vacuum cleaner.

When I appeared beside Lark—who was sitting on the ground in a place I didn't recognize—she was with Ben. She was pale, and there was the ghost of a man not far away, watching us with interest.

"Did you do something to my sister?" I demanded of him, letting the wind catch me up.

He actually shrank back from me. His face had been partially eaten by animals, but I could see enough to know I frightened him. "No. I've never hurt anyone."

He had that disconcerted look of someone who had died suddenly and traumatically, but was foggy on the details. "Most people don't end up left to rot in densely wooded areas unless someone brought them there for a reason." And he didn't look like anyone's innocent victim.

The ghost's response was to fade away.

I turned back to my sister. Ben sat beside her, his hand on her leg. He was asking her if she was okay. Had I corporeal form I might have kicked him then, I was jealous of them being able to touch. Then again, if I had form I would be with Kevin right now. Or someone. Probably.

What if I'd been the one born alive? What if we both had been?

"What happened?" I asked, taking her hand. No point thinking about what never was and could never be.

Lark's gaze met mine. "What are you doing here?"

Ben glanced in my direction.

"You summoned me." My anger began to dissipate the longer I looked at her shocked face. "Are you all right?"

She shook her head. "I had another vision."

"I think I can see her," Ben said, his tone full of wonder. "Just a little."

My sister patted his hand. "That's my fault. You're both touching me, and I'm upset. It won't last."

"Too bad." He waved at me. "Hey, Wren. It's cool to see her, even for a little bit. She looks pissed."

I waved back, and tried to look more pleasant.

"I pulled her here," Lark explained. "She didn't have a choice."

"Huh." He seemed to find that fascinating. Let it happen to him and see how much he liked it then. He gestured down the path with his thumb. "Do you want me to leave you alone?"

"No!"

I drew back. Lark was afraid of me. Oh, I didn't like this feeling—like I was trapped in a vise that wanted to slowly crush me into nothingness.

Ben looked surprised, too. "Are you sure?"

Lark shook her head, wisps of white hair lifting in the breeze. "Maybe just for a minute. If you don't mind."

"I'll meet you back at the car." He kissed her cheek, then rose to his feet and set off down the trail.

I sat down opposite Lark, just enough off the trail so I wouldn't end up with a bicycle or jogger bounding through my skull. "How bad was it?"

"Bad." It had to be—she couldn't even look me in the eye.

"Tell me." I didn't want to hear it, but I had to.

"We were at Haven Crest. Everyone was dead—you helped kill them."

I shook my head. "I'd never do that." Would I? Could I? "It had to be Bent."

She lifted her chin and finally met my gaze. "Their eyes were gone."

Oh. Now it made sense, why she was so afraid. I remembered that night at Bell Hill when I'd gone into Lark's room.

She had been there awhile, and I'd finally managed to get past the drugs and her defenses to visit her. It was one of the first times I'd seen her since she'd shut me out, and I was so worried about her. So anxious.

I was surprised to find someone else in her room—a young nurse. He was in his twenties, maybe. One of those kinds of people who base their career choices on how many people they'll be able to bully and abuse.

Lark was groggy, wearing only her pajamas. The nurse kissed her, pressed her back on the bed, his hand underneath her shirt.

"Stop," she said. "Please. Stop."

He laughed. *Laughed.* "You just be quiet, sweet-meat. I'll make you like it."

"No!" She couldn't even scream—the lethargy kept her voice a hoarse whisper. She struggled, but he held her arms above her head with one hand as the other crept toward her waist.

"You know you want it," he snarled.

I'd been shocked into stillness, but not anymore. At that moment I felt a rage that I'd never—ever—felt before. I manifested with little warning. One second I was nothing and the next I was a full-on screaming banshee. The nurse had cried out and sat down hard on the tile floor. He'd looked at me. All of the color had drained from his face. His eyes were so wide I could see the whites around his irises.

"Jesus Christ!"

"No," I whispered, my voice a growling, terrible vortex. "Not quite."

I didn't remember much after that. No, that was a lie. I remembered all of it, but I didn't like to, and most of the time I refused to remember at all. I'd leaped on him, and when Lark had reached out and touched me, tried to stop me, she'd given me form—for just a second.

It was all I'd needed. I popped my thumb through his eyeball.

Sometimes I still heard his screams. What Lark didn't know was that I smiled every time I thought of it. That was why I didn't like to remember.

The doctors thought it was some kind of bizarre accident. The nurse never blamed Lark. How could he? There was no way she could have hurt him like that in the condition she'd been in, and he'd left marks on her. If anyone had examined her they would have seen that she'd been assaulted.

But they didn't look. The people at Bell Hill didn't see half of what they ought to have. The nurse had left on medical leave and had never come back—at least not to Lark's floor.

"You're afraid I'll hurt them," I said, then felt foolish. Of course that was what she was afraid of.

"I'm more afraid for you." She picked at a twig—snapped it. "I don't want to lose you."

That was not the moment to reassure her that she wouldn't lose me, because if I went bad I'd probably take her with me. "Why don't you ask me what you really want to know?"

Her head lifted. She looked at me finally. "What?"

Did she think she was that good of a liar? Did she really think she could hide from me? "If I ever want to devour the living, and if I've ever thought about killing you."

Lark swallowed, but she didn't look away. That made me extremely happy given the circumstances. "Do you?"

"No. Not when I'm just me."

"You've lost your temper a lot lately."

I smiled. "Well, we've been dealing with people who make that very easy."

She laughed—thankfully. "That's true. I've lost mine a lot, too."

"That's what you do."

She didn't argue. "I guess what I'm trying to say is that you don't have to do this if you don't want to. I want you with me, but it's okay for you to bail if you feel threatened."

"All right." Silence fell between us. "Ben's really cute," I said, because I didn't know what else to say.

Lark actually turned pink. "Yeah. He was...unexpected." She brushed her hands against her thighs. "I'm sorry about Kevin."

It was like a knife to the heart, but I could take it. "At least I know he liked me. That's something."

She patted my leg. "We just have to find you a nice dead boy."

"Maybe Bent can set me up."

"Don't even joke," Lark warned, rising to her feet. "Although, you know, if Kevin means that much to you I could always toss him in front of a train. The thought has occurred to me."

"Don't you joke," I shot back, because honestly, it was tempting. Wrong, but tempting.

We walked to the parking lot and found Ben waiting inside his car. He was reading a book with his feet out the window. His face lit up when he saw Lark. It made me both like and hate him at the same time. Jealousy was not a pleasant emotion, and not one I wanted to feel toward my sister.

"I'll see you at home," I told her. I might have been dead, but that didn't mean I wanted to be a third wheel.

She squeezed my hand and then I drifted away, slipping into the Shadow Lands as I made the distance between the park and Nan's disappear. How would I go about meeting a "nice dead boy," as Lark had put it? Surely there had to be at least a handful of boys I'd find interesting lurking about. I mean, the definition of *unfinished business* had to be teenager. Right?

Nan was making dinner when I entered the house. She actually lifted her head when I came into the kitchen. "Hello, Wren, dear."

I smiled and breezed out into the hall. As I moved toward the stairs to our room, something flashed in my peripheral—a shadow flitting across the wall. I turned my head—there was nothing there.

But there had been.

Frowning, I moved in the direction the shadow had gone. It wasn't the first time I'd thought I'd seen something in the house, though I hadn't picked up on any other ghosts here. That didn't mean anything, though. We could hide from each other just as well as humans could.

I ended up in the sunporch, where Nan did most of her crafty things. There were lots of plants out here, and comfy old furniture that was a little too shabby to be in the main part of the house.

"Hello?" I said. Stupid, really. Humans did it all the time, as though they actually expected a ghost to jump out and say, "Hey ya!"

No answer, but I felt like I was being watched. It wasn't Bent—this was my sanctuary. I'd never felt another ghost in that house, and it would be difficult for any ghost who wasn't bound to the house or family to come in. Private homes were even harder to enter than public places—almost impossible for most ghosts. So, was I simply paranoid, or was there someone actually there?

Was I being haunted?

chapter seventeen

LARK

School on Monday was different for me than it had been before. Ben picked me up and drove me—even though I could have walked the short distance. We attracted a bit of attention arriving together. It was a small high school and I was still big news. I hoped being seen with me didn't cause trouble for Ben, but beyond that I didn't care what anyone thought.

Roxi was waiting for me at my locker. Ben had gone on to his, so it was just me and her. She had circles under her eyes and she looked tired.

"Hi," she said.

"Hi. What's up?" I frowned a little. "Are you okay? You're not starting to feel sick, are you?"

She hugged her books to her chest and shook her dark head. "No more than I was. I just wanted to say thank you."

"For what?" As far as I could tell I hadn't done much more than piss Bent off.

"For helping Gage. I saw him before school this morning. He's doing better."

That was a relief. "The agate worked?"

"Yes." She sounded so relieved. She looked as though she might cry. "Mr. Moreno said he slept all night, and he was hungry this morning."

"That's the best news I've heard since I moved back here," I told her, opening my locker. She still looked a little shaky. "Bent can't have him, Rox. He can't have any of you."

She grabbed me and hugged me so hard I couldn't breathe. I patted her back, and hoped she'd let me go before I passed out. Thankfully, she did. And then she left me alone.

And I really was alone. Wren wasn't with me. She would be later, but she decided that she really didn't want to sit through my first-period history class—the teacher was boring, she said—and that maybe she'd take that time to poke about the Shadow Lands.

I wished I could just not come to school. God, that would be so freaking awesome.

Being at school without Wren left me feeling vulnerable, open to attack. I kept waiting for someone to accost me, or call me names. It didn't happen, but that didn't mean that it wouldn't someday. Wren always said how brave she thought I was, but she was the one who made me that way. Hard not to be brave when you had a paranormal force at your back.

I gathered the books I needed and closed my locker. As I walked down the corridor, I spied Andrew walking toward me. Oh, great. I squared my shoulders, bracing myself for whatever he might say or do.

He took one look at me, gasped and immediately turned

into the nearest classroom. He almost knocked a girl over doing it.

Huh. Whatever Wren had said to him had obviously done the job. Although, that thought didn't make me feel as smug as it would have before that vision of her smacking her lips while holding our friends' eyeballs.

I knew Wren could be dangerous, but she was my sister. I just couldn't think of her as a monster—as something like Bent. If she ever turned into something like that, would I be able to do what needed to be done?

At least I knew where her remains were.

The thought made my chest tight. Blinking back tears— I was not going to cry over something that *might* happen— I made my way to class and tried to focus on the here and now, and not some future I couldn't control. It worked—for the most part.

At lunch I met up with the others. Wren came by to check in, as well. I wouldn't admit to anyone but myself how much more relaxed I was once I saw my twin. I didn't want her to see how dependent I was. I didn't want her to feel like she had to stick to me, especially now that I knew how much she needed a life of her own.

Sarah didn't look so great. The wound on her jaw was raw, but that wasn't it. She was exhausted.

"Nightmares," she said. "I didn't sleep at all last night. I dreamed that Bent came and tried to possess me again. He kept telling me that if I cared about you all that I'd help you ascend, whatever that means."

The others closed in to comfort her, as well. I didn't hug her. I just looked at her and said, "It will all be over tonight."

Her wide gaze locked with mine. "Promise?"

I nodded. "Yeah." Of course I couldn't promise that, but I'd do everything I could to make it happen.

"Lark, in my dream Bent said that he was going to come for Gage, and that not even your little trinkets could stop him."

"Bravado," I replied, but I wasn't so sure. Bent might very well have figured out a way to get to Gage. It was a hospital—lots of people in weakened states just primed for possession. Gage might get out of bed to go to the bathroom and Bent could attack. He might possess a nurse, or a doctor. Killing Gage wouldn't mean anything to him—it would be his revenge. He was going to fight us, and if we tried to take him out, he'd take Gage with him. He could do that easily in the amount of time it was going to take us to dig up his bones. There was no quick way to do that—at least not a quiet one that wouldn't get us arrested.

"I'll stay with him," Wren said. "I can protect him, and if you need me, you can just summon me."

It was a sound plan—and it would keep her off Haven Crest grounds, away from the violent ghosts there. At least the ones at the hospital had been somewhat friendly.

I would not think of that little kid...

"What about Kevin?" Sarah asked. "Is he coming? Or is there too much of a chance that Bent might possess him again?"

Wren looked away, but it wasn't as though anyone but me could notice.

"He's coming," Mace replied. "He wouldn't sit this out."

"Why?" Roxi piped up. "He wasn't with us that night. This isn't his problem."

"It's not Lark's, either," Ben said. "Or Wren's, but they're helping us."

"Because we asked," Roxi reminded him.

I jumped in. "Kevin's your friend. That's why. Now, let's talk about how this is going to go down."

We had shovels and salt. Sarah had lighter fluid that her dad used on the charcoal grill he insisted on using instead of buying a gas barbecue. Everyone had their iron rings and weapons, and Ben had managed to grab parts of an old iron fence from his mother's workshop that we could lay out around Bent's grave to protect us from attack while we dug.

"But how are we going to get all of this stuff into the cemetery?" Sarah asked. "We can't carry it up that tree and across the field. It's too much."

"I've got that taken care of," Mace said.

His girlfriend looked surprised. This was obviously the first she'd heard of this. "How?"

"I've got it." From the expression on his face that was all he was going to say.

Sarah turned to me. "Do you know anything about this?"

I scowled. "Why the hell would I know what he's up to?" Then to Mace. "Where do you want to meet?"

He mentioned a side road not far from the asylum.

"Can you take us all?" Ben asked.

Mace nodded, but he still didn't give his plan away.

"Could what you're doing get us into big trouble?" I asked.

He merely smiled.

Oh, crap.

★ ★ ★

"Is that a cop van?" Ben asked that night, slowing his car as we approached the meeting spot.

"It's a freaking paddy wagon," I growled. And Mace was standing next to it on the shoulder of a dark, deserted secondary road.

Ben laughed and pulled over just ahead of the van. "If we get caught, we are so screwed."

He had that right. Screwed didn't even begin to describe what we'd be. My God, I didn't know whether to tear a strip off Mace for dragging us all into his theft, or hug him for being so damned ballsy. Regardless, no one was going to bat an eye at a police presence around Haven Crest. Our only problem would be if security came by to check it out, and according to Mace, security rarely patrolled the cemetery.

Ballsy and smart. I was almost jealous for not having thought of it myself.

Mace grinned at me when I got out of the car. "Not bad, huh?"

I shook my head, but I couldn't help but grin back. "You're insane."

He patted the side of the van. "No one will even miss it. They keep it in an old garage near the back lot of the station. They only use it when there's a festival or concert going on."

Ben opened the trunk of his car. "You've got balls, man."

Mace shook his head. "Nah. I'm just willing to do whatever it takes to end this." He unlocked the back doors of the van and came to help Ben load the iron fencing into it. I took care of the shovels and cardboard box full of salt cans and other supplies. As we were loading everything up, the rest of our group arrived. Roxi was with Wren and Gage at the hospital—mostly because I figured she'd be too worried about her boyfriend to concentrate here. And, call me a romantic, but whatever happened tonight, they deserved to be together for it.

Sarah stared at the van. Her face was pale. "Mace, what did you do?" I hadn't even noticed that she and Kevin had arrived.

Ben and I exchanged glances, and then with Kevin. If this was going to turn into a thing, none of us wanted to be there.

"What I had to," he replied.

She shook her head. "If we get caught we can kiss college goodbye."

"Getting caught is the least of our worries," I reminded her, ending the argument before it could escalate. "Does everyone have their rings and weapons?"

They did.

"Fabulous," I continued. "When we get to the grave, Ben and I will set up the barricade while the rest of you start digging."

"Why do you get to do that when we have to dig?" Sarah asked.

Yeah, she wasn't even trying to hide how she felt about me now. "You want to be the first thing Bent and his minions hit when they show up, be my guest." That shut her down pretty damn quick. Honestly, when this was over, I was going to go out of my way to avoid this chick. If I didn't, one of us was going to end up sorry.

And it wouldn't be me.

Before we left for the cemetery, I dabbed clove essential oil I'd picked up at the local health store on each of their wrists.

"Aren't you wearing any?" Ben asked when I put the bottle away.

I shook my head. "I can't use any wards." I held up my hands. "No iron, either."

That seemed to alarm everyone—especially Ben. "Why not?"

Wasn't it obvious? "Wren. I can't do anything that might block her from me. Occupational hazard." It was a lame joke, but I felt like the mood of the group dropped ten points with my announcement. "Look, guys, I'll be okay."

"What if you're not?" Sarah demanded. "You're the only one of us who knows how to stop this thing."

I smirked. At least she was honest. "So you're not worried about my safety, just what happens to you if I get taken out. That's sweet, really."

She looked embarrassed. "I don't want to see you get hurt, but I *really* don't want to die tonight."

That was fair. "Dig him up, open the box, soak him in salt and then lighter fluid, and light him up. Then get the hell out of here."

"How will we know if it worked?" Mace asked.

"You'll know." I nodded at Kevin. "He'll know. He'll hear the screams."

Kevin might have paled a little—it was hard to tell in the moonlight. "Thanks for the warning."

I glanced at my watch. It was after eleven and I had a history test in the morning. "Let's go."

"There's a service road the police use," Mace informed us. "It runs right by the cemetery. We should be able to avoid security altogether, but if they do see us, it won't look weird."

He held the back door of the van so we could climb inside. At least there were places to sit. He shut us in, and then climbed in the front. Sarah was in the passenger seat. *Cow.*

Ben held my hand on the drive. No awful vision this time, thankfully. I'd never really held hands with anyone—other than Wren, and sisters didn't count. It was nice—comforting. And a little distracting when he stroked my thumb with his.

We were all quiet on the drive. Nervous. Afraid.

"Do you think Roxi and Gage will be all right?" Sarah asked. I thought she was talking to all of us, not just me.

"Yeah," I said, but I wasn't convinced. Roxi and Gage would be fine, provided Bent didn't come after them, and provided we could toast his skeleton ass first. I couldn't guarantee that any of us were going to get out of this alive. Bent was powerful—really powerful. He had enough juice to kill without trying too hard. Most ghosts were minor-league and had to infect and work on a victim over time. Bent's infection of Gage had worked incredibly fast. Plus, he'd managed to infect the entire group at one time. If we hadn't already seen how strong he was, that would have been a big hint. He was old and powerful. The spirits in this place made him stronger, as did his own malevolent nature. And then there was the energy he'd syphoned off my friends—and Sarah. If he came after us tonight, I didn't know if I could fight him without Wren.

And I didn't know if Wren could fight him without me.

The van turned onto a dirt road. We jostled from side to side over every rut and bump. It was going to be too funny if tomorrow came and the worst bruises I had were on my butt.

"Sorry," Mace called back through the screen that separated the two sections of the van. "The road's really bad."

I clenched my jaw. "No shit." My head bounced off the wall as the van jerked sideways. If it was ghosts, I could do something about it, but I wasn't about to jump out and start filling potholes.

Finally, we slowed and stopped. I waited until Mace killed the engine to get up. By the time he opened the door, I already had iron ready for him to take.

"How close are we to the tree?" I asked him as I jumped out.

"Few hundred feet," he answered.

I swore. "Okay, you guys go ahead. I'll catch up."

"Second thoughts?" Sarah asked.

"Hey!" Mace admonished.

I held up my hand. "I'm a ghost magnet. I don't have any protection to keep me out of their notice, remember? I'm giving you all a chance to get to the grave before company comes calling. Now get moving."

Her lips tightened, but she didn't say anything. She walked away.

"I hate girls," I muttered under my breath as I watched her back.

One by one, hauling gear, they set off across the dark cemetery. The moon provided enough light to see by so we wouldn't need to use the flashlights until we got to the tree. I stood alone by the van, the breeze lifting my hair. I didn't feel any buzzing yet—they hadn't noticed me. Or maybe they were just waiting for the right moment to come out and play.

I waited until the others were a little over halfway to the tree before setting out to follow them. The moment I swung my leg over the dilapidated fence and let my foot hit asylum ground I felt a jolt up my leg. This place had gotten a taste of me the other night, and this second taste was only going to increase its appetite.

The ground wasn't consecrated. How could they not consecrate a freaking cemetery? Consecration wasn't a guarantee that ghosts couldn't get in, but it made it really difficult for them. The fact that this land hadn't been blessed meant that it was just another part of the asylum—and Bent had free domain.

I had two shovels over my shoulder as I broke into a jog. I wanted to yell at them to find the grave, but I didn't dare make that much noise. Up ahead I could see the flashlights come on, beams moving across the ground. I thought I heard Ben call out that he'd found it. A few seconds later they all gathered around one spot, and Ben began placing iron on the ground.

I ran faster. When I reached them, I dropped the shovels and immediately went to work on the iron rods. "Start digging!" I ordered.

No one argued. Shovels struck the grass—clumps went flying.

And a buzzing like a thousand bees grew louder in my head. They were coming, and we didn't have iron around three quarters of the grave yet. We were laying the rods lengthwise on the ground, end to end around the perimeter, leaving enough room for the diggers inside. I tossed Kevin a can of salt.

"Pour it inside the iron," I instructed. The air went still—too still. My heart hammered in my chest, slamming my ribs. So many of them coming. I could feel them in my head, under my skin. They whispered to me in incoherent dark-tongues, trying to heighten my fear with their voices.

I drew a deep breath. I was not afraid. Okay, I was very afraid, but I would not allow my fear to rule me. I grabbed for the little flags I'd put in the supply box and began shoving their pointed ends into the ground inside the iron rectangle. On them, Ben had drawn *pujok* like the one in Gage's hospital room.

A screech pierced my mind. I glanced up and saw what looked like a giant bat flying toward me. Only it wasn't a bat. It was ghosts. And they were manifesting.

Shit. I hoped no one else looked up. Frantically, I kept slapping rods onto the grass, shoving flags in every few feet. There was just one corner left to cover. The others had a couple of feet dug down already—there hadn't been any rain in a while and the ground was dry and light. But they still had a lot of grave to uncover.

The bat broke up, bits of black dropping to the ground. They were maybe five or ten feet away. At least ten of them— the rest circled above. Reinforcements. If just one of them attacked right now we'd be screwed.

I shoved the remaining flags into the ground and stood up. I took the iron bar Ben had given me out of the box. It was cool against my hot, damp palms.

"Lark?" Ben asked. I could hear a little tremor in his deep voice. "What are you doing?"

I glanced over at my shoulder at him. "Get that perimeter down."

And then I stepped out to confront the ghosts. I smiled as I looked at their decrepit faces. "Which one of you bitches wants to go first?"

chapter eighteen

WREN

Roxi and Gage were nervous, I could tell. If I could communicate with them I could calm their minds. Bent wasn't going to come for either one of them.

Bent was going to come for me.

I wasn't sure if Lark knew it, though some part of her must. It was the only reason she'd have allowed me to be somewhere other than her side. My sister was overly protective, and paranoid, but she wasn't stupid. Not usually. With me somewhere else, it forced Bent to chase me. That meant he couldn't attack them.

That was the theory. I'd never met a ghost who could be in more than one place at once. Of course, there was always the chance that Bent would completely destroy me and then my sister, or start with Lark and then come for me. I tried not to think about that. Instead, I reminded myself that Bent thought himself incredibly powerful—and he was. But so was

I. I might not know how to best use my power, but I was well aware of possessing it.

So, I lurked as Roxi and Gage watched some awful reality show on the hospital television, and waited. I'd have left here altogether if I hadn't been worried there was some small chance that Bent would attack the two of them just for fun. He didn't seem to have an agenda beyond increasing his forces.

"You're here again" came a voice from the door of Gage's room.

I turned—it was the man with the bloody legs and hospital gown. "Hello."

"If you're here, does that mean *he'll* be here, as well?"

"I think so."

He frowned. "Why would you do that?"

"Because I want to stop him, but I need to protect my friends."

He peered past me at Gage and Roxi. "They don't even know you're here."

"That doesn't matter. I'm still going to protect them."

"Who's going to protect us?"

He had been a grown man when he'd died—at least in his early forties. I assumed he'd been a fully functional mortal. "You are."

Johnny Shirt shook his head. "He's too strong."

"There's one of him, and a whole bunch of you just wandering these halls. If you stand against him he can't hurt you. That's just simple math."

"That's easy for you to say, you're Dead Born."

Could they smell it on me or something? Did I glow an odd color? "And I know next to nothing about what that means."

It was embarrassing to admit that. "Yet here I am. I'm going to stand up to him. I'm going to fight him."

"You're going to lose."

I scowled. "Go find some underwear."

And then he was gone—just blinked away. I guessed I'd hurt his feelings, but he annoyed me. Maybe it was wrong of me to lure Bent here when so many of the hospital's ghosts were vulnerable to his power, but surely they'd faced bullies before? Either in life or in death. I was surprised a hospital this old didn't have its own version of Bent. At least some sort of hierarchy. Other than Johnny Shirt I hadn't really spoken to anyone else. There was that poor little toddler who had upset Lark, and that strange girl with no face, and that was it.

Why hadn't anyone come to inspect me? They had to be curious. I was still wondering about that when I felt a jolt up my spine. Lark was in danger. The ghosts at Haven Crest had found them. I shouldn't have to wait much longer...

"Hello, child."

I closed my eyes—just for a second. I had to gather all my courage just to turn around. Bent scared me. There was only one thing that scared me more.

"Don't call me that," I said. "It's condescending."

Bent put his hands in his pockets as he entered the room. "What should I call you, then? Miss Wren?"

I lifted my chin—tried to look imperious. "That would do."

He chuckled. "I think I'll just call you Girl."

"And I'll call you Douchebag." Oh, wouldn't Lark have a laugh?

Bent's brow furrowed. "What sort of name is that?"

"An appropriate one," I replied.

"It sounds like it might very well be an insult."

I crossed my arms over my chest. "That's because it is."

A smile curved his thin lips. "Then perhaps I should simply call you Wren and you may call me Josiah."

"I'll call you Bent."

"Even better. Wren." He glanced around the room. He looked so out of place in his old-fashioned clothes. "You've given the boy some protection from me. The girl, too."

"Did you think we would leave them vulnerable to attack?"

He shrugged. "I suppose I'd hoped that you might be ignorant enough to do just that." He leaned his shoulder against the wall. "You know I would have been content just to toy with them a bit if you and your sister hadn't come along."

"I may be ignorant, but I'm not naive," I informed him. "You would have slowly infected and killed them all."

"Perhaps. You'll never know, will you? Because now my focus has shifted to something much, much more dear."

Why did he bother trying to be cryptic about it? "Me."

"And that delectable sister of yours. Where is she, by the by?"

As if he didn't know. "Right now she's probably putting an iron bar through some friends of yours."

"They'll eat her alive."

I shook my head, even as fear kicked up in my stomach. "You don't know my sister."

"I know she's not nearly as strong without you—or you without her."

"You have no idea how strong we are." Of course, neither did I.

Bent moved away from the wall. "I'm older than you are, sweetheart. I've been doing this a long damn time. You think I'm going to let two little bitches come between me and what I want?"

I made a tsking sound. "Such ungentlemanly language."

His face changed—became harder and sharper. "I'm done playing nice with you. It's time you learned your place, and I intend to put you in it."

On the bed, Gage turned to Roxi. "Does it feel cold in here to you?"

She gave him a worried look. "Yeah."

He took the moss agate from beneath his pillow and held it in his fist. Then he pulled his girlfriend close. "Kick his ass, Wren."

I smiled. It was the most perfect thing for Gage to say at the most perfect time. I turned to Bent. "So, what now, Douchebag?"

A lot of people thought that ghosts fought by flinging things around, but that wasn't really it. We were as physical as humans, but it was also about exerting one's will over another ghost. It was like dominance. I expected Bent to stalk me, like a cat on a mouse.

He charged me, coming at me in a streak of malevolence. He caught me up in the force of his attack, whipped me around and threw me through the wall out into the corridor. The force of it made the cupboards in Gage's room clatter.

I spun myself right and landed on my feet in front of the nurses' station. The faceless girl sat on the counter, watching. She had the toddler in her arms, and it was playing with her hair.

Bent stepped through the wall. It was grandstanding, because he could have just come out the door.

"You could make this easy on yourself," he told me as he approached. "Just join me and spare yourself a world of hurt."

"Or you could just go away, stop picking on teenagers and end all of this now."

"Why on earth would I want to do that?" He seemed genuinely perplexed. "Their fear feeds me. Their torment strengthens me. Why should I give that up?"

"Because mortals aren't here to provide you with a buffet." It was how ghosts drew energy, though. "You used to be one, a long time ago."

Bent's face contorted into a twisted mask. "You think you're superior to me because you never lived."

That wasn't what I'd meant at all, but I'd take it. "I'm superior to you because I don't need to make others afraid to feel important."

"Important." He spat a gob of ectoplasm on the floor. *Disgusting.* "No one but your sister and that puny medium can even communicate with you."

That struck a nerve. "Did killing all those girls when you were alive make you feel important, Josiah Bent? Could you only be a man when you had someone's throat under your blade?"

Apparently that struck a nerve as well, because he charged me again. This time I was ready. I caught him up in my arms, engulfed him in my darkness—the power all ghosts have, that boils deep within us, black and tempting—and then threw him to the floor. He could either go through it, or take the blow. He took the fall, skidding across the tiled floor until he hit the wall.

Slowly, he rose to his feet. He hadn't expected that from me. "I'll feel like a man when I rip your sister apart," he said. "I'm going to enjoy her."

It was a cheap trick, but effective. Anger bloomed deep inside me and spread like a wildfire. I went at him like a freight train, only to be caught up in his energy—that swirling choking mass. He didn't let me go right away, either, but held me tight.

"That's it," he crooned in my ear. "Get furious. I want you to lose control. Give in to your true nature and join me. No one will be able to stop the two of us together."

He was right. We'd be so powerful, he and I. We'd take whatever we wanted. Even the ghosts watching our struggle were afraid. The fear of other ghosts was even more potent than the fear of humans. I felt it tickle my spine, fill me with anticipation. I wanted that fear. I wanted the power he promised me.

Bent released me. We were back in Gage's room. He and Roxi were still on the bed. They watched their show, but their eyes darted about the room and they clung to each other like vines.

As if one was really any protection for the other. Foolish little mortals.

"Do it," Bent whispered. "They're yours for the taking. Don't let a little piece of rock stop you. Imagine how afraid they'd be of you."

I didn't have to imagine—I knew. I could kill them so easily, slip my thumbs into their eye sockets… I would like it, and it would all be because of Josiah Bent.

I turned on him with a smile. He was smiling, too.

"You have really pretty eyes," I said.

LARK

Three ghosts down, and I was exhausted. I wasn't going to last much longer.

As I swung the iron bar through another ghost, I could feel Wren like a whisper inside my head. She was fighting Bent. I couldn't stop long enough to be afraid for her.

"Lark!" Ben shouted. "Get back in here, now!"

I glanced over my shoulder. They'd finished placing the iron and flags. I started walking backward, keeping my attention on the ghosts closing in on me. It was like something out of a horror movie—a whole line of corpses pressing down upon me. Some looked good, as they had in life, while others looked like twisted, monstrous things. I believed that what a person was in life manifested when they were dead—it showed on them in ways they'd managed to hide when living.

My steps were careful. I glanced behind me again as I neared the iron bars. If I knocked them with my foot I could create an opening. A fraction of an inch would be enough to let a ghost in. I wanted to reach out my hand to Ben, let him pull me in, but that might mess up the line, as well. Sarah's thick barrier of salt was only going to hold out as long as the breeze.

"How far are you?" I asked.

"I just hit something," Mace answered. "They didn't bury him six feet down."

"Awesome." And I meant it. It was about freaking time something worked in our favor. If all we could have was lazy grave diggers then I'd take it.

I was maybe a foot from the edge of the perimeter when a new ghost appeared before me. She was tall and sturdy—what they would have called "handsome" in her day. She had really strong, striking features. She was dressed in capri pants and a snug blouse—very rockabilly without the tattoos. I could feel power rolling off her.

And then I felt it in an entirely new way when she back-handed me.

I fell to the side, landing hard on my hip. Thankfully, I missed the bars.

Ben shouted my name.

"Keep digging!" I yelled back. "Get that son of a bitch un-covered!" It was the quickest way to end this and ensure my safety. As it was, I was a little skeptical on that last part at that moment. I reached for the bar I had dropped, but before my fingers could wrap around it, I was picked up, and held up in the air so that I looked down at the ghost. She smiled—like a shark—and then tossed me like a rag doll.

I flew through the air and came down hard on a grave marker. They were flat and not very large, but they were still stone. I felt one of my ribs crack under the force as all the air rushed from my lungs.

Oh, crap. Oh, hell. That *hurt*. Slowly, I struggled to get to my feet, holding my hand against my ribs. I'd barely made it to my knees when she grabbed me again. This time she hauled me to my feet and slammed her forehead into my face. Blood spurted from my nose. Had she broken it? Great. I liked my nose, and now it was going to be all messed up.

I should have been more frightened—I realized that. I didn't know why I wasn't. Adrenaline, maybe. Stupidity. Whatever the cause, it made me focus enough to land a good solid punch to her throat. She staggered backward—surprised that I'd managed to strike her—and I used that hesitation to come at her with a spinning round kick to the head. She retaliated with a hard left. Then she picked me up and slammed me to the ground.

Something else snapped inside me. I tasted blood in my mouth.

She was going to kill me. I knew that.

Having died once already, I wasn't afraid of repeating the process, but I'd be damned if it would be at the hands of a ghost. I was more afraid of what would happen to the others with me gone. With any luck I'd end up with Wren, but more than likely I'd end up a prisoner of this place—and that was what really terrified me. I didn't want to be one of Bent's puppets.

I would *not* be one of Bent's puppets.

I kicked her hard in the knee, and she went down. Then I landed a kick to her face, crushing her nose. Ha! Then suddenly she was on me—moving with the speed of the dead. I was aware of her fists slamming into my face, but I couldn't tell you which one or how many times—it was all a blur. A painful, bloody blur.

Behind the red film seeping over my eyes, I saw the white-haired woman. Was she there or in my mind? Looking at her filled me with a sense of peace.

"My dear girl," she said in a low, melodic voice as she reached out and touched my face. "This is not how you end. Now get up and fight."

It was like she had flicked a switch inside me. Awoke something. One moment I was a battered meat-sack on the verge of death and the next… Well, I didn't know what the hell I was.

The white-haired woman was gone, and so was the blood in my eyes. I reached up and grabbed my attacker's wrists. I threw her to the side and leaped to my feet. My ribs hurt, but it didn't matter. In fact, none of the pain or blood mattered. I felt strong—so strong.

"What are you?" the Bettie Page wannabe asked, her eyes wide.

I smiled. "I'm Lark."

When I lunged for her I moved faster than I'd ever moved before. I hit her hard and sent her scattering. My fist was more effective than an iron bar.

What the hell?

I couldn't even wonder at what I'd just done because another ghost took her place. This one was a kid from the '70s. I might have had some sympathy for him if he hadn't called me a disgusting name before he attacked. I kicked him in his ghostly nads before shoving my fist under his chin and up into his skull. Poof! He was gone.

This time two more came. They managed to get a couple of punches in before I nailed them both. A third sneaked up behind me and kicked me hard between the shoulder blades. I staggered forward, right into the path of another ghost, but

I dived out of the way before he could strike. I lashed out, scattering both of them.

I was surrounded. At least six or seven dead had formed a circle around me. My mysterious savior had made me incredibly strong and fast, but there was no way I could take on this many at once. I bent my legs into a crouch, then pushed up hard. I jumped high into the air and did a backflip over the heads of the ghosts that had been behind me.

I'd never done a backflip in my life. Never. I scooped my iron bar off the ground where I had dropped it and threw it at the circle. It took out three of them before embedding itself in the ground. The remaining three came at me. One hit me hard about the head, but I shoved my fist through her chest. Another went for my stomach and doubled me over, but I managed to punch him in the groin. The last one I kicked and then struck as he fell.

They were just going to keep coming. The ones I scattered would eventually regroup and return. I couldn't win this fight. It didn't matter how good I was. Eventually they would wear me down and finish me.

"Got him!" Mace yelled.

I ran for the grave and jumped over the barrier. The ghosts charged after me, smashing hard into the barricade we'd built.

Sarah stared at them. Her face was pale and streaked with dirt. "Oh, my God."

They meant business if they were manifesting. That meant our crude defenses didn't have much time before they fell. Against one ghost we'd do great, but not against an army. The ghosts might not be able to touch the iron or the salt, but they could disrupt the energy around them enough to break through.

I looked down. Several feet below me, in a roughly dug hole was an old wooden coffin. The lid had been busted open by Mace's boot. I gave him a hand up out of the grave. He dumped the can of salt all over the coffin and through the hole in the lid and followed that with lighter fluid. Then he handed me a box of matches.

"You want the honors?" he asked.

I shook my head. "You do it."

"You sure?"

"One of you just fucking do it!" Sarah shouted. "They're getting through!"

Mace struck a match and dropped it. It fell into the hole in the coffin, flickered and then—just when I thought it had gone out—burst into beautiful blue-and-orange flames.

The ghosts screamed—a thunderous screech that froze my soul. For a second I thought they were going to charge, but they didn't. Some of them disappeared. Others took to the sky. A few turned and walked away. And a few...a few smiled before fading from sight.

They were free.

"Is that it?" Sarah asked, wide-eyed. "Is it over?"

"Not yet," I told her as I caught a glimpse of headlights coming toward us. "We've got to get out of here. Now."

We raced to the paddy wagon and tore out of there like the hounds of hell were snapping at our heels. We were a mile away before I realized I was all alone on one side of the van. I looked up to find the others watching me.

And I knew they were afraid. Of me.

chapter nineteen

WREN

I was sitting on Bent's chest, the fingers of my right hand buried in his right eye socket when he burst into flames. I barely managed to jump off him and avoid being engulfed.

"Do you smell something?" Roxi asked Gage. She wrinkled her nose. "Smells like burned hamburger."

He frowned. "Yeah, I do." Then he looked down at his arms. He ran his hands over his bandaged forearms. "I feel better."

She put her hand to her neck. "Me, too. Do you think this means they did it?"

He didn't say anything. He just took her face in his hands and kissed her. That was my cue to leave.

I went to the Shadow Lands before going to Lark, to the little space I'd made for myself and called my home in that realm. There I found the ornate box in which I kept my treasures and opened it. I put Bent's eyeball on the red velvet—

right next to the other trophies I'd collected. Then I closed the lid and cleaned myself up before going to look for my sister.

I found her sitting on Nan's front step. I supposed it was our front step, too. She was bloody and wild-looking. Fierce. There was something different about her...

"So, you did it." I sat down beside her.

She nodded. "*We* did."

"Where is everyone?"

She laughed, but there wasn't any humor in it. "As far away from me as they can get, I imagine."

"What happened?"

"I'm not sure." She turned her face toward me. Despite all the blood, she looked fine. "I had the crap pounded out of me tonight, and then that white-haired chick showed up and told me it wasn't my time. I believed her. I've never fought like that before, Wren."

"You think they're afraid of you because of how you fought?"

"I guess so," she said with a shrug. "They didn't really say much about it. No one spoke to me at all, really. Not even Ben." Her voice cracked.

I put my arm around her shoulders and pulled her close. Her arm went around my waist. Tonight had been terrifying. A test of my will. I'd both failed and triumphed. We both had. We'd defeated Bent, but there was a price to be paid.

I was beginning to think there was always a price. And then I thought about my trophy. I smiled.

"You look creepy," Lark murmured.

I adjusted my expression. "Who is this white-haired woman?" I wondered out loud. "And why is she helping us?"

"I don't know, but we should find out."

We sat in quiet for a few minutes. Then I asked. "When you burned Bent, did the wounds he inflicted heal?"

"They started to, yeah. By the time Mace dropped me off, Sarah's wounds looked like old scars."

"It's really over then."

"Yeah," she said softly. "I think it is."

I wasn't the smartest when it came to understanding the living, but even I understood what my sister didn't say. For a few days she'd had friends, a boy who liked her. Now she was certain it was all gone. Lark liked to talk tough, and pretend she didn't care, but she cared too much. It was her one big flaw, and I loved her for it.

Her obvious hurt made me want to hunt down everyone responsible and turn them inside out. "Bent tried to control me tonight," I confessed. "He tried to make me do dark things."

"And?"

I smiled, remembering the shock on his face when I went for his eye. "I kicked his ass."

Lark laughed. "I bet that felt good."

"Oh, it did. Come on, let's go inside. You look exhausted, and you have a test tomorrow."

We stood up. Lark unlocked the door and went inside. I followed after her rather than phase through the wall, Nan was in bed, of course, but she'd left a note on the kitchen table saying that our father had called. Lark crumpled it in her fist and tossed it in the garbage.

"You have to talk to them sometime," I said to her.

"No," she replied tightly. "I really don't."

I didn't push it. Our parents were a touchy subject.

Upstairs, Lark washed the blood off her face and hands. As I suspected she looked perfectly fine underneath. Something very strange had happened to her tonight, because she didn't have a mark on her, and she felt different to me. She was still my Lark, but she had changed. She was…more. That was the only way I could explain it. I wondered if I felt changed to her.

There was a box on the desk in our room, with a note on top. As Lark picked up the paper, I recognized Nan's handwriting.

"'Dear, girls, I finally found the box of my grandmother's belongings in the attic. Hopefully something in here will be of use to you. Love, Nan.'"

Lark opened the box. Inside it smelled of powder and age. There were journals, photo albums, a pair of gloves, a powder box, a small jewelry box and a few other personal items, along with a birth certificate for Emily and a death certificate for her twin, Alys.

"Twins," I whispered. Nan had mentioned it before, but seeing *stillborn* on that piece of paper really drove it home. Dead Born, like me.

"Like us," Lark added.

At the bottom of the box was a spirit-board—an old one. It looked to have been carved and painted by hand. It was beautiful and a little scary at the same time, because it also had twins on it—one on either side of the board. One had red hair and one had white.

My sister and I exchanged glances. This was getting stranger and stranger.

Lark set the board aside and picked up one of the photo

albums. There were only two—the old-fashioned kind that had paper pages that pictures had to be pasted onto. The first one had a red leather cover embossed with the name *Emily Murray* in gold foil.

"Open it," I said, anxious for a glimpse of our ancestor. But part of me dreaded it, as well.

Lark opened the book and there she was. We both gasped, even though I think we both had our suspicions. I was surprised, but then…I wasn't.

Emily Murray had been very pretty. The photograph showed her in an old-fashioned gown, like from that movie about the huge boat that had sunk. And though the picture was black-and-white, there were two things we didn't need color to know: Emily Murray had white hair just like Lark's, and she was the woman who had appeared to both of us when we'd needed help.

"It's her," Lark said.

"I know."

We looked at each other, and I saw my own confusion in my sister's eyes.

"Why are we just seeing her now?" Lark asked, her voice raw. "Why didn't she come to us before this?"

I knew what she meant—why hadn't Emily helped us when Lark was in Bell Hill? "I don't know." My jaw tightened. "But I'm going to find out."

My sister closed the book. "I'm too tired for this crap. I'm going to sleep."

Lark changed into some pajamas and got ready for bed. We talked about what had happened that night as she went through her nightly ritual. She told me about fighting the ghosts and how strong she'd felt. And I didn't tell her how good it had felt to take Josiah Bent's eyeball out of his skull. I wanted to, but I knew she wouldn't understand.

After she finished brushing her teeth, I tucked her in. Ever since we were children I had the ability to put her to sleep simply by whispering to her. I hadn't done it for a while, but tonight called for it. I wanted her to rest, and she wouldn't if I didn't help. She'd lie there all night and think about how she could have done things differently so the people she'd started to care for wouldn't look at her like she was a freak.

What she failed to realize was that we were all freaks— every last one of us, living or dead. It didn't matter.

Once I was sure she was asleep, I slipped away. Lark would tell me I was a fool, but I couldn't help it. I had to go check on Kevin. I'd done well not to ask her about him. But I couldn't pretend I didn't care about him.

I found him in his car outside Sarah's house. Sarah was in the car with him.

"Thanks for the drive," she said. "The neighbors would freak if they saw the paddy wagon pull up. Not like Mace could have driven me home in it anyway."

Kevin chuckled. "I can imagine. Anyway, it was no problem."

She didn't get out of the car. "That was crazy tonight, huh?"

"Yeah, it was."

They stared at each other. I knew I should leave, but I couldn't. I wouldn't. I needed to see what came next.

They kissed. It was messy and desperate, and it broke my heart. I could sit there and tell myself it was because of what they'd just gone through, that it didn't mean anything, but that didn't change the fact that he was kissing someone else.

That she was his best friend's girlfriend.

I started to leave, but before I left the car I leaned close to his ear so that he'd be sure to hear me and whispered, "Don't you ever visit my grave again."

And I knew he heard me because his eyes flew open. He jerked back.

"What?" Sarah asked.

I didn't wait to hear his reply. I returned to the house to find Lark still asleep and a girl sitting on her bed.

"Who are you?" I demanded.

The girl's head whipped around. Her hair was an impossible shade of red. She took one startled look at me and disappeared. I stood there like an idiot and stared at the spot where she'd been.

"Alys?"

This night just kept getting stranger and stranger, and I for one couldn't wait for it to be over. If only I slept. I could shut myself down for a bit—just let this world go, drift back to the Shadow Lands where things at least made sense to me. But first, I curled up with my sister and wrapped my arms around her as she slept. She was important. She was what mattered—not the dead, or the living, or whether or not either of us were freaks.

In the end, all we had was each other.

LARK

I seriously contemplated pretending to be sick the next morning so I didn't have to go to school. It was only the fact that I didn't want anyone calling me a coward that made me get out of bed. I chose a fabulous outfit—and a fantastic pair of secondhand Prada pumps I'd gotten off eBay—to wear as armor. I was putting on eyeliner when Wren appeared behind me.

"You look nice," she said.

"Thanks."

"So, something weird happened last night."

"Yeah," I said, moving on to the other eye. "I was there."

"No, not that." Suddenly, she appeared in the mirror, taking over my reflection. God, I hated when she did that. It was so freaking creepy. "I went out for a bit. When I came back, I swear there was a girl sitting on your bed. She had hair like me. I think it was Alys, Emily's twin. She looked just like her."

I frowned at the mirror. "That's impossible."

"Why? Because there's only room for one ghost in this house?"

"No, because it was a long time ago, and she... Don't you think she would have moved on?"

Wren shrugged in the glass. "Maybe she can't. She disappeared the moment I spoke to her."

I shook my head. My reflection didn't. "Why would she do that? It doesn't make sense."

"I don't know," Wren replied a little sharply. "I'm just telling you what I saw."

"You should try to find Emily in the Shadow Lands. Maybe she knows something." It had to be a mistake, right? Residual energy, maybe? But this house had been in the family for a long, long time. Maybe Alys was bound to it in some way. Maybe she had shitty timing just like her sister.

I managed to eat a little breakfast and downed a quick coffee. Wren walked with me, even though I couldn't really talk to her—people might see or hear. She talked to me, though. Mostly she sang silly songs, or talked about something she'd read in a magazine. It was an obvious distraction tactic and I didn't care—hearing her talk about sex articles was hilarious. I had to bite the inside of my mouth to keep from laughing.

I made it through first period, and second. Third period I normally had with Roxi but it was the one I had a test in, so I didn't have to even look at her. I just concentrated on my paper until the end of class.

By lunchtime I felt better—a little more confident in my ability to navigate high school with some degree of success. No one called me a freak or mocked me to my face. No one talked to me at all. Whatever. It didn't matter. I was okay. I would always be okay. I didn't have a choice.

I found a seat by myself in the cafeteria and sat down. I had a reading assignment for English that I'd decided to get started on and was deep into the book when Wren said, "You've got company."

I looked up. Mace, Sarah, Roxi, Gage and Ben all sat down at my table. I didn't know they'd even let Gage out of the hospital. Sarah was the only one who didn't meet my gaze. She was staring at the wall.

"Can we talk to you?" Mace asked, already sitting down. The rest followed him. Ben came and sat next to me.

I marked my place and set the book aside. "Sure." I sounded

so calm and composed. Like I couldn't care less, but I was very aware of Ben beside me, and how every muscle in my body was stiff as a board.

Mace leaned his forearms on the table. "So, first of all, we want to thank you for what you did for us."

"And Wren," Roxi interjected. "For what she did for us, too."

"You're welcome," Wren chirped, even though they couldn't hear her.

My gaze locked with Mace's. I couldn't quite make myself look at Ben. "But?"

He frowned. "No but. Thank you. You saved our lives and we appreciate it."

"Yeah," Gage added. "Like, more than you'll ever know."

"And we're sorry for bringing you into this—and for being weird afterward." That came from Sarah, which surprised me most of all.

"Not so freaked out that you couldn't suck face, you over-sexed witch."

I blinked and glanced at my sister. What the hell was that all about? If looks could kill Sarah would be a ghost now, too. Sucking face? Oversexed? Oh, no. Had something happened between Sarah and Kevin? Was that where Wren had gone when she'd "slipped out" the night before? No. Sarah was with Mace. She wouldn't... Would she?

"Don't worry about it," I told her. I didn't tell her that what she needed to worry about was a jealous teenage ghost.

"No," Ben said. "Let us explain."

I looked at him. It hurt. "You don't have to explain. I

wigged you out. I get it. You saw what a freak I am and it scared you."

They all stared at me—even Sarah.

"Scared us?" Roxi echoed.

"Yeah, it was a little scary," Ben allowed, "but you were hot." He blushed when Gage laughed and nudged him in the ribs.

"You were amazing," Mace informed me. "You moved so fast. Kevin said you moved like them—like the ghosts. We could only see them sometimes."

Wren sat up straight, suddenly interested. She gave me a strange look. "That *is* fast."

"It was pretty cool," Sarah added, making my eyebrows jump. A compliment? Really?

"Anyway," Roxi said, "we just wanted to say thanks." She handed me an envelope.

Gage grinned. He was so adorable. "It's from all of us."

I took the envelope, watching them warily as I opened it. Inside was a card with a picture of a tabby dressed as Wonder Woman. I opened it up. Inside it simply said, "Thank you!" and everyone had signed it. There was also a Fluevog gift certificate inside. It was enough for a pair of shoes from the new fall line.

"You guys…" I was speechless. I was touched. I had never been so glad to be so wrong in all my life. "I thought you didn't want anything to do with me."

"Why?" Gage asked. "Because you're a ghost-fightin' freak?"

Ben smiled at me. "You're our ghost-fightin' freak."

"We'd like to be your freaky friends," Roxi informed me. "Your Scooby Gang."

"Oh, God," Wren groaned. The magic of Scooby-Doo was lost on her.

I laughed. "Let's think of something else—I'd rather keep you all away from creepy old amusement parks and haunted mansions."

"Speaking of creepy amusement parks," Gage enthused, "there's that old one up 84 that shut down a few years ago."

Roxi perked up even more—if that was possible. "And there's an old abandoned house across town that everyone says is haunted."

"Tell me you're joking," I demanded, gaping at them. "You're *not* serious?"

They all started laughing, and I let out the breath I'd been holding. For once, I didn't mind being the butt of the joke.

Underneath the table Ben took my hand in his. Around us the others were tossing out different haunted locations all over the state and talking about which ones we should visit first. Their laughter made me smile. Even Wren was laughing.

"You know," Ben said, his voice low, "my house isn't haunted at all. I know for a fact that my room is a ghost-free zone. Maybe you'd like to come over later?"

My stomach fluttered. "I'd like that, yeah."

His fingers tightened around mine.

"Oh, there's that old boys' school near Bridgeport," Roxi said. "We should go there."

"What's so special about it?" Gage asked. "People have seen ghosts, but I've never heard of anything bad happening there."

"Exactly," she said. "There might be a nice boy there for Wren."

I looked at my sister. She was staring at Roxi, and looking as though she might cry.

"Yeah," I said, smiling as Wren met my gaze. "The boys' school sounds good."

Then we all started making plans for the trip, and for the first time that I could remember, I didn't mind being a freak.

I didn't mind at all.

★ ★ ★ ★ ★